The Stranger at the Door

A J WILLS

Cherry Tree Publishing

The Stranger at the Door

Copyright © A J Wills 2024

This book is a work of fiction. Any resemblance to actual persons, living or dead is purely coincidental.

In loving memory of my stepfather, John, who sadly passed away while I was writing this book. Thank you for everything.

1941 – 2024

Prologue

After seven days she must be dead.

No one can survive that long without food or water, but his heart still canters in his chest as he hauls open the door.

The smell is overwhelming, the air rank with the stench of death. He buries his face in the crook of his arm, fighting the urge to gag, his instinct to turn and run.

But he can't. Time is ticking. He needs to clean up the mess and it's going to require a lot of bleach and scrubbing.

He squeezes his eyes shut and steels himself.

When he opens them again, he sees her coiled up like a baby, her hands under her head and her knees pulled towards her chest. He calls her name. Softly at first and then louder.

He searches for the rise and fall of her chest and takes a step closer, wary of a hand shooting out to grab his ankle.

He drops a roll of tape and a handful of black plastic sacks on the concrete floor and lowers himself to his haunches, whispering her name for a third time as he sweeps a shock of platinum blonde hair off her brow. Her eyes are not quite closed. Not quite open. Two cat-eye slits which turn his blood to ice.

The smell is so much worse inside the confines of the room. He worries it will stay with him forever, seeping into his clothes and his nightmares. It's not his fault she's dead. It's not as if he attacked her with a knife or put a bullet through her skull. He didn't loop a noose around her neck or lace her cereal with arsenic. She came down here willingly. All he did was lock the door. He hadn't planned to kill her. He's not a savage. But she wouldn't do as she was told.

Gingerly, he takes her arm and pulls out a hand. Her skin is cold and waxy. Her body stiff. When he pushes back her sleeve and feels for a pulse, he notices two of her fingernails are missing and the ends of her fingers bloody stumps. He glances over his shoulder at the inside of the door. It's smeared with blood. An abstract work of art of desperate, rust-brown streaks like a child's finger painting. Long lines and swooping swirls. Blotches and blobs. He can only imagine her hopelessness. Her fear. Her misery. And he smiles to himself.

He's already dug her grave, but no one's going to mourn for her or report her missing. It's a shame really, but no one cares. She has no family to speak of and he doubts she has any friends. There won't even be a headstone. It'll be as if she never existed.

4

He struggles to his feet, letting her hand slip from his and hit the floor with a dull thump. He flaps open a plastic sack and gets to work.

Time is not on his side.

He's expecting his wife home soon.

Chapter 1

Harvey's in the barn sifting through boxes of old books and clothes belonging to his wife's husband when the police arrive.

The vehicle speeds up the drive with crude haste, grinding over the gravel and coming to a stop with an aggressive short skid. He thinks it's probably another delivery for Gwyneth, who's forever buying things online. Mostly jewellery and ceramics these days. Sometimes figurines and paintings and occasionally glassware and pottery, to stock in her little antiques shop in the village.

Curious, Harvey pokes his head outside, wiping his hands on his trousers. He expects to see a white van and a harried courier, but is greeted with the concerning sight of two uniformed officers stepping out of a marked police patrol car.

Harvey strides across the drive to meet them, carefully pulling the barn doors closed behind him.

'Can I help?' A quiver of excitable butterflies soars in his stomach.

'Mr Harvey Kerrison?' a short, slim woman, who looks too diminutive to be a police officer, asks.

'What's this about?'

The officers are both wearing serious faces. Lips pressed together and eyebrows pulled tight. Expressions that come with bad news.

'Can we talk inside?'

Harvey's stomach lurches. 'What's going on? What's happened?'

'Perhaps we could sit down?'

Harvey doesn't want to sit down and talk. He just wants to know what they're doing here, interrupting him when he's up to his eyes shifting boxes that should have seen the inside of a skip years ago.

It's all Lionel's threadbare suits, shirts and ties. All his shoes, cufflinks and wristwatches. Old books. Journals and ledgers. Photographs and yellowing letters bundled up with elastic bands. Things that shouldn't still be in the house five years after his death.

Harvey was making room for his new ride-on mower, but even stacking the boxes high around Lionel's old Range Rover, which Gwyneth's also refusing to sell, it's still a squeeze.

He's been through it with her a million times, but she refuses to throw any of it away or even donate it to charity. He's explained that it's natural to have an emotional attachment to her dead husband's belongings, but he's worried keeping it all is impacting her mental well-being. She needs to move on, but won't. And so, like a ghost that refuses to pass into the spirit world, Gwyneth's first husband remains a constant presence in their marriage.

Harvey has suggested keeping a few select items in a memory box. A watch. His fountain pen. Maybe even one of his favourite shirts. All the rest could be donated to a cancer charity. She won't hear of it, of course, maybe because the shock of his sudden death still resonates after all this time.

Lionel was only fifty-eight when he died. Eight years older than his wife, which is far too young to become a widow. From diagnosis to grave, there were just four miserable months. A month in denial, and three watching his slow, cruel, steady decline.

'Is it Gwyneth? Has something happened to her?' Harvey's voice cracks.

The male officer hangs back by the car with his thumbs hooked in his trouser pockets and his feet planted squarely on the ground.

'I'm afraid we have some bad news. There's been an accident,' his female colleague says, unable to hold Harvey's gaze.

He stares at her blankly. 'Accident? What accident?'

'Your wife has been involved in a serious road traffic collision. I'm so sorry.'

'Is she hurt?'

'She was knocked down and I'm afraid she's sustained some serious injuries. She's currently on her way to hospital for emergency treatment.'

Harvey shakes his head. 'B- but she was at work.' He glances at his watch. 'She should be home any minute.'

'The details are still unclear at the moment but —'

'Where was this?'

'On the road out of the village,' she says.

'I thought I heard sirens, but I didn't think anything of it. Gwyneth always walks home. She never takes the car, not unless it's raining. I've warned her so many times it isn't safe. I knew something like this was going to happen. She wouldn't listen to me though, would she?'

'I understand this is upsetting, but —'

'Is she - is she going to...?'

The officer breathes heavily through her nose. 'I don't know, I'm sorry.'

He wishes she'd stop saying she's bloody sorry.

'I need to see her.'

'She's currently on her way to Kingstown General. They'll be able to give you an update on her condition.'

Harvey pats his pockets. 'I'll go now. I just need to find my car keys.'

'We can take you,' the female officer offers. 'Hop in.' She turns back towards the patrol car with a determined stride. Harvey blindly follows, his mind whirring.

The male officer dutifully opens the rear door and Harvey is about to climb in when it occurs to him he's not locked up.

'Hang on a minute.' He hurries to the house. Gwyneth would kill him if he left the doors open and the house unsecured. All those antiques she and Lionel collected over the years must be worth thousands. Tens of thousands, probably.

Harvey grabs his house keys from the bowl next to the hideous George III clock on the table in the hall and locks the front door.

Sitting in the back of a police vehicle is a surreal experience. There's an unpleasant hint of body odour and vomit, only partially masked by the sickly sweet scent of a citrus air freshener, while the doors lock automatically and the windows won't open.

'We'll get you there as quickly as we can, sir,' the male officer assures him, feeding the wheel as he turns the car around. 'Don't you worry.'

'I begged her not to walk along that road,' Harvey says. 'I told her it was dangerous, that all it would take was one careless driver. Someone on his phone. Someone checking their satnav.'

At the bottom of the drive, they turn right. Harvey is about to point out it's a longer route to the hospital, before it occurs to him it's patently a deliberate decision. If they'd turned left, they would have to pass the spot where Gwyneth was injured, where there's probably police tape and half a dozen emergency vehicles. Maybe even blood on the road.

The female officer turns to face Harvey. 'It's best not to speculate until we can ascertain the facts.'

'What about the driver? Have they arrested him?'

'I'm afraid the driver didn't stop. The alarm was raised by another motorist who found your wife lying injured in the road.'

'They didn't stop? You mean they hit her and drove off?'

'That appears to be the case, yes.'

Harvey slumps back in his seat, his eyes fixed on the tarmac ahead. 'How could this have happened?' he mumbles. The walk from the shop is only two miles, but the way the road dips and curves, following the contours of the land, makes it a perilous route.

Gwyneth has always insisted on walking to the shop when she covers for Ruby on Wednesdays, although he has no idea why she would want to walk anywhere when she has a perfectly decent car sitting on the drive.

Nor does he understand why she hasn't sold the shop already and retired. He's been going on about it to her for months. For a start, it's in entirely the wrong location. The only time it's ever busy is at weekends when the village attracts a few tourists. But it's another gift from Lionel, and even though he suspects it's been running at a loss for the last two years, she won't give it up. But that's Gwyneth for you. She won't do anything he tells her.

When they arrive at the hospital, the female officer speaks to the receptionist in the accident and emergency department on Harvey's behalf, and to his amazement they're whisked into a deserted waiting room and told that a doctor will be out to talk to them soon.

Harvey sits with his head in his hands, staring at the tiled floor.

'Is there anything I can get you?' The officer puts a kindly hand on his back. 'Coffee? Tea?'

'I just want to see my wife.'

'I know. But she's in safe hands. They'll be doing everything they can for her.'

'But what if that's not enough? What if Gwyneth dies?' Harvey sobs.

The officer doesn't have an answer for that.

It's a long, agonising wait, but eventually, when Harvey's virtually climbing the walls for news, a doctor with a squashed nose and a rugby player's cauliflower ears, walks in running a hand through his thinning hair.

He conjures up a smile. 'Mr Kerrison? I'm Doctor Peshko, one of the team treating your wife.'

Harvey lifts himself out of his seat. 'How is she? Is she badly hurt?'

The doctor pokes his tongue into his cheek. He has dark rings around his eyes and a heavy five o'clock shadow. 'She's stable.'

'Stable? What the hell does that mean?'

'She's been seriously injured, Mr Kerrison, but we've made her comfortable for now. She has a number of broken bones, including a fracture to her right arm and some damage to her hip.'

'Okay,' Harvey nods, encouraged. 'That doesn't sound too bad.'

'We're more concerned about a cranial injury she's sustained. She's suffered a serious blow to the back of the head.'

Harvey swallows. 'How serious is it?' he asks, a sliver of fear snaking down his spine.

'We're about to transfer her to intensive care.'

Harvey gives a slight shake of his head.

'It's the best place for her,' the doctor adds. 'We're still trying to establish the extent of the injury, but unfortunately we can't be sure until the swelling on her brain subsides.'

Swelling on the brain?

'Is she going to die?'

The doctor puts a hand on Harvey's upper arm and gives him a grim smile. 'We're doing everything we can. At the moment, there's a lot of pressure under her skull and we have to wait for that to go down before we can be sure of anything.'

'How long will that take?'

The doctor shrugs. 'It's impossible to know for sure. It could be a few days. It could be a few weeks. Mr Kerrison, I have to tell you, I think your wife's lucky to be alive.'

'I want to see her,' Harvey demands, the shock still sinking in.

'Yes, we can arrange that, but there's one more thing.'

'What?'

'I ought to warn you that your wife is currently unconscious and unresponsive,' the doctor explains.

'Yes, but she'll come round soon, won't she?'

'No, I don't think you understand. I'm sorry, there's no easy way to break this to you, but your wife is in a coma, and until the swelling in her brain reduces, there's no way to tell if or when she'll recover.'

Chapter 2

A serious-looking consultant stands with his arms folded, rattling off information with the enthusiasm of an air steward giving a safety briefing on the tenth flight of the day. Bored and uninterested.

'She'll be unresponsive to any stimulus and her eyes will remain closed,' he says. 'She's unlikely to respond to sound or pain, she won't be able to communicate or move on her own, and even basic reflexes like coughing or swallowing will be greatly reduced. I'm afraid we've also had to put her on a ventilator to help her breathe, so you'll see a big tube going into her mouth.'

Harvey struggles to take it all in. There's so much to remember. Maybe he should write it down.

The consultant's face softens into a smile. 'Don't worry, it'll all become clear when you see her. I just want to prepare you - your wife is going to look very different.'

Harvey takes a deep breath and nods. Gwyneth is usually so immaculately turned out, never a hair out of place or a misplaced crease in her clothes. The thought that they might have dressed her in one of those awful hospital gowns would be mortifying for her.

How can anyone prepare for something like this?

'There will be a lot of machines and noise in the room, but it's nothing to be alarmed about. They're all doing their bit to keep her alive and make her as comfortable as possible.'

Harvey nods again, still uncertain. He has no reference point, other than what he's seen in the movies, and they're probably nothing like reality.

'If you're ready, I'll take you in to see her now.'

It's been over three hours since Harvey arrived at the hospital with the two police officers, and he's probably sunk his own body weight in tea. The officers were called away and Harvey has been sitting on his own in a second waiting room in the intensive care unit on the third floor for the last thirty minutes, until the consultant, who introduced himself coldly as Idris Usman, arrived.

'I'm ready,' he says. 'I just want to see her.'

He follows Usman into a stark white room that Gwyneth has to herself. Even though he's been warned what to expect, the sight of his wife lying in a hospital bed in the middle of the room, with all sorts of tubes, wires and electrodes attached to her body, and surrounded by noisy machines bleeping, whirring and clicking, stuns him into silence.

He stands at the door staring, overwhelmed, trying to make sense of it. Gwyneth's head is swathed in bandages and the swell of a bruise across the bridge of her nose looks like a raccoon's mask.

He snatches a breath, blinking under the bright lights.

'Gwyneth?' he whispers. 'Can she hear me?' he asks the consultant.

'Probably. It's important to talk to her. Let her know you're here. She's going to need all your support to get better,' Usman says.

She looks far worse than he imagined. Her skin is grey but worst of all, she has a thick tube in her mouth helping her to breathe. Her right arm is in a cast and is resting on her stomach over the covers. At least with her eyes tightly shut, she looks at peace, almost as if she's sleeping.

Everything in the room is so sterile. The walls and skirting boards are white. The floor has been laid with white Lino. Even the lights in the ceiling shine a bright, dazzling white. The only colours that catch Harvey's eye are the red flashing numbers and buttons on the machines, glowing amber, green and blue, and a scarlet blanket draped over the sheets on Gwyneth's bed.

At least she has a view, although she's in no state to appreciate it. A huge picture window looks out over the car park and probably beyond to the green hills in the distance, although it's too dark to be certain. On the other side of the room, another window overlooks a nurses' station. Or more accurately, the nurses' station looks into Gwyneth's room so they can monitor her around the clock.

'Is she going to make it?' Harvey asks.

Usman scratches the back of his neck and screws up his face. 'It's hard to give any guarantees, but I believe in a positive mental outlook. Let's stay focused on getting your wife well, shall we, and not worry too much about the ifs and buts? Now, if you'll excuse me, I need to be somewhere. If you have any further questions, I'll be back later. In the meantime, I'll leave you in Leanne's capable hands.'

Harvey spins around as a nurse with a beautiful smile and kindly eyes walks into the room carrying a tray of syringes and vials, her trainers squeaking on the Lino.

'I'll be looking after Gwyneth day to day,' she says with a child-like, innocent voice. 'Don't worry, we're going to get through this together.'

Harvey appreciates her optimism. She seems like the kind of shining soul that's probably the heartbeat of a unit like this where they must encounter so much tragedy. So much desperation. So much fear.

'Anything you need, just shout,' she says, her face lighting up with a smile so broad it immediately gives him confidence that Gwyneth's in good hands. It's a rare, natural skill.

'It's been a bit of a shock.' Harvey's too afraid to approach the bed, not sure what he's supposed to do or say. Is he allowed to touch his wife? Hold her hand? He has no idea of the right or wrong things to do. It's all so unfamiliar.

'Of course it has,' Leanne coos, 'but we're all here to make Gwyneth as comfortable as possible while she's recovering.'

'Is she - is she in any pain?'

'No, not at all.'

'Are you sure?'

'Trust me, Harvey. Is it okay to call you Harvey? She's not in any discomfort.'

'Okay. I'd hate to think she's suffering.'

Leanne drags a vinyl-covered armchair closer to the bed and pats the cushion. 'Why don't you come and sit and talk to her?'

Harvey shuffles across the room, his gaze fixed on Gwyneth. Watching her. Half expecting, half hoping that at any moment her eyes will spring open and a smile will creep across her lips when she sees him. And then everything can go back to normal.

But it's as if she's been cryogenically frozen, suspended in a weird catatonic state between life and death.

Harvey lets out an involuntary groan as he eases himself into the chair and sinks into the soft foam.

'Try holding her hand,' Leanne suggests.

Hesitatingly, he reaches across the bed and lays his hand on top of Gwyneth's. He's surprised her skin is warm and soft. He thought she'd be cold. He squeezes her fingers, tightening his grip, resting his arm on the edge of the bed.

'Oh, Gwyneth, what's happened to you?' he sighs. Close-up, her two black eyes look even worse. Purple and swollen, still to fully develop.

'She was hit by a car, wasn't she?' Leanne asks.

'A hit-and-run driver who left her for dead.' Harvey's voice quivers. 'I told her she shouldn't walk along that road, but that's typical of my wife. Gwyneth always knows best. She never listens to me.'

Leanne chuckles. 'Sounds like a woman who knows her own mind.'

'You could say that.' Harvey allows the faintest smile to surface, his shoulders slumping.

Gwyneth's always been strong-willed. Along with her self-confidence, it's part of the attraction. Only he sees the insecurity and self-doubt behind the mask, something he discovered as her therapist, when he peered behind the curtain of her mind. He found that hidden vulnerability utterly irresistible. It's no wonder he fell so hard for her when he really should have been maintaining a professional distance.

'Try talking to her as you would do normally. Tell her about your day. What you've been doing. Who you've spoken to,' Leanne says, hovering behind him.

'What I've been doing is wondering what the hell happened,' he says. 'You gave me quite a shock. I didn't know if you were alive or dead, especially when the police turned up at the house.'

'Try talking to her about what you were doing before that. Mundane things. Things you might chat about over dinner. Reassure her. You don't want her worrying.'

Harvey shrugs. If she can't move, can't breathe for herself and her eyes are closed, what makes them so certain she can hear him?

'I made a start on tidying up the barn,' he says. 'Moving all Lionel's crap you insisted on keeping. Don't worry, I've not thrown any of it out. At least not yet.' He chortles to himself. If Gwyneth's in a good mood, he'll occasionally threaten to throw Lionel's things out, but he'd never go through with it. It all means too much to her. She'd be heartbroken.

He draws circles on the back of her hand with his finger, wondering what happens next.

'Do you really think she can hear me?' he asks.

'Absolutely. Research has shown it's vital to keep talking to coma patients, and sometimes it can even help the patient recover. Just be aware that she can probably hear everything, so be careful what you say. Let's keep things positive and upbeat.'

'Right.' Harvey nods. 'And is there anything else I can do that might help?'

He has a vague notion that playing patients in comas their favourite pieces of music can help them recover, but he's not sure if that's something he's only seen in movies or whether it works in real life.

'Being here, talking to her, is the most important thing...'

'What about music?'

'That's a good idea. You could bring some head-phones for her and a playlist of her favourite songs. Or even spray her with her favourite perfume. Anything stimulating like that.'

He'd not considered that smell might help, but it makes sense. Perhaps he should pick up a bunch of those roses she likes. What are they called? It's like the book, Jekyll and Hyde, but named after a famous garden designer he'd never heard of. Gertrude Jekyll roses, isn't it? She's always talking about how she adores their scent.

'You look tired,' Leanne says. 'You should get some rest.'

Harvey shakes his head. It's gone midnight, but he can't leave Gwyneth, even if it has been an emotionally draining day.

'Why don't you head home and get some sleep? Come back in the morning when you're feeling fresher.'

'No, I can't.'

'At least grab a tea or a coffee.'

Harvey rolls his neck. Knots in his muscles creak and click. Maybe a short break isn't such a bad idea.

'Take ten minutes for yourself. It's been a lot for you to process.'

Maybe Leanne's right. Now he's seen Gwyneth is comfortable, he might grab some fresh air to clear his head. It's suffocating being surrounded by all this medical equipment and noise, and so much to get his head around, wondering whether Gwyneth is going to live or die.

He hauls himself out of the chair with a grunt and hitches up his trousers.

'I'll only be ten minutes.'

'Take as long as you like. I'll be here.'

With legs as heavy as lead, Harvey trudges into the corridor and follows the signs for the exit. Even though it's late, the unit is alive with doctors, nurses, porters and cleaners. A low hum of activity and serious chatter hangs in the air.

He buzzes himself out, shouldering open a heavy wooden door and almost colliding with a couple coming the other way.

They're dressed in smart clothes, although the guy's suit is crumpled, the top button of his shirt undone and his tie hanging loose around his neck. The woman, who is almost painfully thin, with a scraggy neck and hardly any waist, is wearing a trouser suit. She reminds him of one of those long-distance endurance runners, all bone and sinew.

'Sorry,' Harvey mutters, stepping out of their way.

The man's eyes narrow. 'Mr Kerrison?'

Harvey's head jolts with surprise.

The man reaches into his jacket and pulls out a small wallet that he flips open. 'DS Murray Chalk,' he says, 'and this is my colleague, DC Alison Enright.'

The woman nods, her face drawn. Her angular, pointy features give her a permanent sneer.

'We were wondering if we could have a word? We're investigating what happened to your wife. How is she?'

Harvey feels himself frowning, totally thrown off balance. 'She's in a coma,' he says bluntly.

'I'm sorry to hear that.'

'I suppose it could have been worse.'

'You're aware that Mrs Kerrison was struck by a car?' Chalk looks Harvey up and down, as if he's judging him. 'And that the driver didn't stop?'

'That's what I've been told. I wasn't there.'

'No, of course.'

'So I'm not really sure how I can help.' There's something about Chalk's manner that raises his hackles. Maybe he's just tired. 'I was getting some fresh air. Can this wait?'

'The problem is your wife appears to be the only witness to the crime,' Chalk continues.

'Unfortunately, she's not in any state to talk to you or anyone at the moment.'

Chalk bows his head. 'I understand, but we still need to investigate. It's a serious crime. Your wife could have been killed.'

As if Harvey needs reminding.

'I'm not sure how I can help. I didn't see anything.'

The female detective, Enright, smiles smugly, as if she thinks Harvey is being obtuse. 'We need to establish the circumstances.'

'What circumstances? It was an accident, wasn't it? Some idiot not paying attention to the road, driving too fast.'

'Possibly,' Chalk says. 'But until we establish exactly what happened, we can't rule out this might have been something more serious.'

Harvey shakes his head. 'What could be more serious than a hit-and-run?'

'Let's find somewhere quiet to talk,' Chalk suggests.

Chapter 3

GWYNETH

I can't feel my hands or my feet. I can't wiggle my fingers or my toes. Or turn my head. Or lift an arm. In fact, everything is numb.

All around, I'm surrounded by dazzling white, as if I've been dropped into the middle of a giant marshmallow light bulb.

Have I died? Is this what the afterlife looks like?

I've never particularly believed in heaven or hell, but maybe I was wrong. At least it appears I've ended up on the right side, the side of good and light. Although if this is all I have to look forward to for eternity, it's less like heaven and more like hell. An eternal damnation of nothingness.

I close my eyes and cast my mind back, hunting for memories to explain how I ended up here.

I recall a deafening noise. The roar of a car, its engine screaming. Being frozen in horror, blinded by sunlight. A heavy, thumping impact. Flying through the air, head over heels, my limbs tossed around like they were attached to my body with string. How the landing knocked the air from my lungs and the pain was so sharp I wanted to scream.

But then darkness falls, and it's all I can remember.

A nightmare? Or a bad memory?

I can't be sure.

I'm not sure of anything anymore.

Chapter 4

'We're not jumping to any conclusions, but it would be useful to know if there's anybody who might want to do your wife harm,' Chalk says.

'Not that I can think of. Why would they?' Harvey shrugs.

The office that the female detective, Enright, has found where they can talk in private, is so small they have to stand in a circle staring at each other.

'The spot where your wife was knocked down is pretty remote. There are no CCTV cameras in the area and so far we've been unable to locate any drivers who witnessed what happened. Hopefully, we'll find someone who caught the incident on their dashcam.' Chalk leans against a wall with his hands hanging loosely at his sides. 'But if there are no witnesses, we'll need to be a little more inventive in our investigation.'

Enright is standing with her back to the door. 'We have teams searching the scene for any physical evidence, but in the meantime, is there anyone who might have a grudge against your wife? Anyone who might have a reason to want to hurt her?'

Harvey blinks rapidly, his mind in turmoil. How can they possibly think this is anything more sinister than a terrible accident, even if the driver didn't stop? 'She's not the sort of person who makes enemies.'

'I know it's all been a bit of a shock, but have a think. Is there anyone at all who might have wanted her dead?'

'No,' Harvey says. Why would they? She's funny and intelligent. Sharp-witted and unassuming. She'd do anything for anyone if they were in a bind. He can't imagine anyone in their right mind wanting to hurt - or kill - Gwyneth. It's inconceivable.

'Have a think about ex-partners. Work colleagues. Business associates.' Enright runs the tip of her tongue along her bottom lip.

'No, there's no one. Isn't it more likely it was someone who just took their eyes off the road for a minute?'

Chalk lifts his chin a fraction, studying Harvey down the length of his nose. 'How long have you been married?'

It's none of his business, but Harvey doesn't want to appear obstructive. 'Three years. We're both on our second marriages.'

Chalk's eyebrows shoot up. 'And Gwyneth's first husband? Where's he?'

'Dead.'

'I'm sorry.'

'Cancer,' Harvey adds.

29

'No other ex-boyfriends we should know about?' Enright has taken a notebook and pen from a shoulder bag and is writing it all down.

'No.'

'Gwyneth has a shop in the village, doesn't she?' Chalk asks.

'An antiques shop. A gift from Lionel, her first husband. She was there today.'

'She goes in most days, does she?'

Harvey shakes his head. 'Only on Wednesdays when Ruby has her day off.'

'Ruby?'

'Ruby Pettifer. She runs the shop day to day on Gwyneth's behalf.'

Enright scribbles furiously. 'Apart from Wednesdays?' she checks, glancing up.

'Apart from Wednesdays.'

'And how's business?' Chalk asks.

Harvey sticks out his bottom lip. 'As far as I'm concerned, she should sell up and retire. She doesn't need the money, but she has this idea that it would be dishonouring Lionel's memory. She's losing money hand over fist, I'm sure of it.'

'She doesn't discuss the finances with you?'

'It's Gwyneth's shop. It doesn't have anything to do with me.'

'But it's a source of income you rely on?'

Harvey snorts. 'Hardly. Gwyneth hasn't needed to work since Lionel's death. He left her more than comfortable.'

'And what about you, Mr Kerrison? What do you do for a living?'

'I'm a therapist. I specialise in grief counselling. It's how I met my wife,' Harvey explains, 'although I don't see how that's relevant to anything.'

'She was a client?' Chalk sounds surprised, like most people when they find out how he and Gwyneth met. It's all perfectly ethical. It's not as if he was her doctor. There are no rules against it.

'You can't help who you fall in love with, detective.'

'So you didn't know her before she was widowed?'

'No.'

Chalk glances out of the window into the darkness beyond and rubs his nose, thinking. 'So, Gwyneth would have been on her way home when she was hit?'

'I assume so, yes.'

'Does she always walk home from the shop? It must be a good mile or so to your house.'

'Two miles exactly. She likes the exercise,' Harvey says.

'It's a dangerous road. The traffic's fast along that section.'

'That's what I told her, but she wouldn't pay any attention to me.'

'Where were you this afternoon?'

'Me?' Harvey's hand flies to his chest.

Chalk's brow furrows.

'I was at home all afternoon, sorting out the barn.'

'Any witnesses who can vouch for your movements?'

Harvey sighs wearily. 'No, I was home alone. I didn't see anyone all day.' Enright makes another note. 'Come on, this had nothing to do with me before you even think it.'

Chalk shrugs. 'Your words, Mr Kerrison, not mine. We think our best hope of catching the driver is to find an eyewitness, which is why we intend to put details of the incident out to the press as soon as possible. We can use it as an opportunity to appeal for witnesses.'

'Right, great.' Harvey nods. It seems like an obvious thing to do.

'But to get maximum exposure, we'd like to humanise the story. With your permission, we'd like to name your wife and let the press have a recent photograph of her. I think the idea of a businesswoman walking home alone and being left for dead on the side of the road will resonant with people. They'll want to help.'

'Okay.' Harvey pulls his phone from his pocket. He has hundreds of photos of Gwyneth on his camera roll, but he'll have to find one she'd approve of. She'd never forgive him if he handed over a picture with her eyes half-closed or her hair a mess or one in which she thinks her forehead looked too big. Her chin too jowly. Her ears too sticky-outy.

'But to really give it impact,' Chalk says, shuffling from one foot to the other, 'we wondered if you'd do an interview.'

Harvey stops scrolling through his phone and glances up, not sure if he's heard correctly. 'An interview?'

'Just a few words about how upset you are and how you'd like anyone with information to come forward. The thing is, the driver is almost certain to have some damage to their car. Someone will have noticed. A wife. A girlfriend. A body repair shop. And if we can get the word out, the more likely it is someone will come forward with a name.'

In other words, they want Harvey to do their jobs for them.

'I don't know,' Harvey mumbles. Does he really want to talk to the press? He's never done anything like it in his life. He's not sure he would know what to do or say. It's completely out of his comfort zone.

But if he refuses, how's that going to look?

Panic floods his body like a virus.

'You want to find whoever did this to Gwyneth, don't you? You want them brought to justice?' Chalk asks.

'Of course, it's just that —'

'One quick interview, that's all. And we'll both be there to hold your hand. You won't have to answer any questions you don't want to and we'll practise what to say beforehand.'

They've backed him into a corner. Ambushed him when he's at his most vulnerable. He really doesn't want his face plastered all over the press. But what choice does he have? If he says no, they'll think he has something to hide.

'Can I at least think about it?' he asks, hopeful they might forget all about it.

Chalk and Enright exchange a glance. 'Sure, but don't take too long. The clock's ticking. We want to catch the coward who did this to your wife and get them off the road before they destroy any more lives.'

Chapter 5

Harvey sits on a bench outside the hospital, alongside the desperate smokers grabbing their nicotine fix, some in wheelchairs, others attached to portable IV drips. The thought of doing an interview, talking about Gwyneth and laying his soul bare, makes his insides curl, but his hand's been forced. How can he refuse?

What's he even supposed to say? The facts are black and white. Gwyneth was walking home from work along the road and was knocked down and left in a coma by an unknown motorist. What more can he possibly add? Do they expect him to break down in tears?

He's never been someone who wears his heart on his sleeve. Just ask Debbie. It was one reason his ex-wife left him. She accused him of being, in her words, a cold fish. Too detached from his emotions. Never willing to discuss how he was feeling or how *his* behaviour made *her* feel. He's never been into all that touchy-feely New Age mumbo jumbo. And he's not about to start now just because two detectives are applying pressure.

An overweight nurse joins him, puffing on a vape, the sickly sweet smell of vanilla and strawberry wafting over him in a vaporous cloud as he stares at the sky.

'You look like you have the weight of the world on your shoulders. Is everything okay?' she asks, frowning.

He turns his head and forces a smile. 'I'm fine. Thanks.'

'Are you visiting someone?'

'My wife. She's in a coma.' He's not sure why he feels the need to tell her, but it spills out like a secret he can't keep.

'I'm sorry.'

'She's in the ICU. Lucky to be alive, they reckon.'

'She's in good hands then.'

'What about you? What do you do?'

'On one of the surgical wards. It's been hellish this evening. I thought I'd grab five minutes while I could. What happened to your wife?'

'She was knocked down by a hit-and-run driver. I'm still trying to get my head around it,' Harvey says.

'I can't understand how anyone could hit someone in their car and just drive off.' She shakes her head. 'It's inhuman.'

Harvey nods. 'To be fair, the police are treating it seriously. They've put two detectives on the case.'

Harvey glances at the time on his phone. It's been nearly an hour since he left Gwyneth. 'I ought to be getting back,' he says, standing.

'I hope it works out for you and your wife. Try to stay positive.'

When he returns to intensive care, Leanne is rubbing moisturising cream into Gwyneth's hands and chatting to her as if she's an old friend.

Harvey watches for a moment from the door until Leanne spots him and beckons him in.

'It's important to keep her skin moisturised,' she explains. 'We don't want it drying out and cracking. That's how she can pick up an infection. It's a job you can do when you come to see her.'

At least he'd be doing something useful, rather than just sitting around having a one-sided conversation.

'What time do you clock off?' Harvey asks as he watches Leanne massage Gwyneth's fingers one by one.

'I'm on the night shift.'

She says it so cheerily, but Harvey can't imagine anything worse. He'd be wandering around in a constant fog of exhaustion if he had to work nights.

'Don't you have family or a boyfriend at home?'

'It's just me. I share a house with a couple of other nurses, but we're always on different shift patterns, so we don't see much of each other.'

'I don't know how you do it.'

'You get used to it. It's rewarding.'

Harvey studies his wife's face, looking for any sign of life behind the immobile shell of her body. A flicker of her eyes. A shuffle. A groan. But she just lies there.

'You know, she'd hate the thought of being in here,' he says. 'She hates hospitals.'

'Nobody likes hospitals, especially when they're ill.'

'No, I mean, she's terrified of them. She spent some time in hospital when she was a child and I think it's haunted her ever since.'

Although Gwyneth would never admit it, he's fairly sure it has something to do with all those scars over her stomach. Little pockmarks dotted randomly across her abdomen from her sternum to her belly button that she's normally so conscious of keeping covered, like a rash of ragged, pale moles that pucker her skin.

He noticed them when they made love for the first time and made the mistake of asking about them, running his finger over them one by one as they lay in a post-coital glow. She rolled away from him, covering herself with the duvet, embarrassed, and refusing to say.

'She wouldn't even put her husband in a hospice when he had cancer,' Harvey adds.

'How did you meet?' Leanne asks.

'She came to me for counselling after her husband died,' he says.

'She was your patient? Is that ethical?'

38

'We didn't get together at the time,' he says, 'and as long as there isn't an ongoing professional relationship, there's nothing wrong with a client and her therapist getting together.'

'So you helped her with her loss? That's so lovely.'

'Not everyone sees it like that. But we were lucky. We found a connection, you know?'

Leanne shakes her head. 'Not really. I caught my last boyfriend texting and sending pictures to my best mate behind my back.'

'Oh, I'm sorry.'

Leanne shrugs. 'It's alright. He was an asshole anyway. I'm best off without him. How long have you been married?'

'Three years. It was Gwyneth's idea. She was worried what people would think if we moved in together and we weren't married. She wanted to do it properly.'

'You obviously care about her deeply.'

'I do.' A sudden surge of emotion catches Harvey by surprise. Tears spring to his eyes and a lump swells uncomfortably in his throat. 'I don't know what I'd do if she... if she...'

Leanne puts an arm across his shoulders. 'She's going to be fine. Don't worry. We're taking good care of her.'

'I'm sorry. I don't know where that came from.'

'No need to apologise. You cry as much as you like. It's a safe space. Are there any other family members who can help? Anyone who can pop in and share the load?'

'It's just me. Gwyneth never had any children, and she's an only child. She lost her father when she was younger, and for whatever reason, she's not seen her mother in years.'

'I phone my mum every day. She panics that something's happened if I don't speak to her.'

Harvey smiles. 'It must be nice being so close.'

'Sometimes.'

A yawn creeps up on Harvey from nowhere.

'You're tired,' Leanne says. 'Go home. Get some rest.'

'I can't leave Gwyneth.'

'You're no use to her sleep-deprived. I'm here. I'll look after her. Come back tomorrow. Go on, go home.'

It's tempting. A rush of adrenaline has kept him going for the last few hours, but now his body is heavy and his eyes sore.

'Is there somewhere in the hospital I could sleep?' he asks. 'So I can be near if anything happens.'

'Nothing's going to happen.'

'What if she wakes up?'

'Harvey, go home, will you? If anything changes, we'll call you.'

'Are you sure?'

'Absolutely. I'll see you in the morning.'

Harvey wearily pulls himself to his feet and pushes the chair back. He leans over the bed and places a delicate kiss on Gwyneth's forehead. 'Goodnight, my love. Leanne's going to look after you, but I'll be back in the morning. And don't worry, we're going to find out who did this to you, and we're going to make sure they pay.'

Chapter 6

GWYNETH

Voices.

I can definitely hear them, but I don't know where they're coming from or what they're saying.

They're muffled and indistinct, like I'm listening to a conversation between two people on a bus with cotton wool in my ears.

I lie perfectly still and close my eyes, concentrating. Focusing on the cadence, the rise and fall of their sentences, trying to pick out the odd word.

But it's hopeless.

I open my mouth to scream, but I can't make a noise. I can't even lift my head.

At least I'm getting sensation back in my body. A throbbing in my wrist. A deep-seated ache in my hip. I suppose it's better than not feeling anything at all.

There's another sound I hadn't been aware of before.

A mixture of mechanical and electronic. Clicking and whooshing with a regular, uninterrupted beat. And the occasional bleep which reminds me of the sound our smoke alarms make when the batteries are running low.

I don't know what it can be. There's nothing visible in my bright white globe.

Whatever I'm hearing, it's coming from beyond my confined world.

The voices pick up again, louder.

It's almost certainly a man and a woman, I think. One with a deep, bass tone. The other sounds lighter and girlish.

I sense that they're close by, so why can't I see them?

It must be another dream. My brain filling the void.

And yet, there's something familiar about the male voice. I'm sure I recognise it.

It almost sounds as if it could be my husband.

Harvey, is it you?

Chapter 7

Harvey returns to the hospital early the next morning to find Gwyneth lying in exactly the same position, although they've tilted the bed slightly so she's more upright.

He's brought a few things he thought she might need but wasn't sure. Two pairs of pyjamas, some clean underwear and a set of headphones he found in a drawer in the kitchen so he can play her some music. He's even downloaded one of her favourite pieces on his phone, Mahler's Fifth Symphony. He thought she'd like that. All those rousing strings.

'I didn't know what else to bring,' he says as Leanne welcomes him with a wide smile. 'It's not as if she can read or eat fruit, is it?'

Leanne nods her approval. She looks amazingly bright for someone who's worked through the night. 'No, but the music is a great idea.'

'I'm surprised to see you. I thought you would have clocked off by now.'

'I'm staying on a few extra hours to help,' she says. 'There's been some staff sickness. But it's fine. I enjoy being here looking after Gwyneth.'

'But you've not slept.'

'I'll sleep later.'

Harvey's stomach rumbles noisily. He jumped straight in his car and didn't stop for breakfast.

'Sorry,' he says, smoothing his hand over his burgeoning paunch. Gwyneth's been nagging him about his weight in recent months, but there's no way he's going on a diet. Or exercising. He's certainly not taking up jogging, or, god forbid, going to the gym.

'Haven't you eaten?'

He shakes his head. 'I was going to get something later.'

'You need to keep your strength up. For Gwyneth's sake. Why don't you grab something in the canteen?'

'Are you sure? Do you want anything?' He'd kill for a bacon bap and a coffee.

'I'm fine. Don't rush. Take your time.'

'I won't be long,' he says.

But there's a long queue for food in the canteen on the ground floor. He's caught the morning rush and has no choice other than to take his place in a line that's patiently shuffling forwards. While he waits, Harvey's assaulted by the smell of fried food. Sausages, bacon, mushrooms and egg. Never mind a bacon bap, he decides he deserves a full English breakfast. He's not sure when he'll get the chance to eat again so he might as well fuel up, and besides, Gwyneth frowns on him having a cooked breakfast at home. She says it's not good for his health or his waistline.

A middle-aged woman serving behind the counter piles his plate high and shoots him a conspiratorial wink. It's a good start to the day after yesterday's drama.

He takes his tray to an empty table and dives in, savouring the saltiness of the bacon and the sweetness of the cooked tomatoes, which he washes down with a mug of strong, black coffee sweetened with three sachets of sugar.

'Mind if we join you?'

Harvey looks up as a shadow crosses the table.

The detectives, Chalk and Enright, stand waiting for his permission to sit. Harvey sighs. Just when he was enjoying the peace and solitude.

'Sure,' he says, nodding to two empty chairs on the other side of the table.

'How's your wife this morning?' DS Enright, her face pinched and waspish like she's just swallowed a tumbler of vinegar, sits with her hands resting in her lap, her slim legs crossed.

Harvey doesn't like the way she looks at him, like she doesn't trust him.

'The same.' He shovels a forkful of beans into his mouth and pushes what's left of his breakfast to one side. He's suddenly lost his appetite. 'Have you found the driver yet?'

'We're working on it,' Chalk assures him. 'A tyre mark we found at the scene appears to be quite distinctive. We're hopeful it will lead us to the vehicle that was used. The tyre hasn't been in production for the last ten years, so the chances are we're looking for an older vehicle.'

'That's a start, I suppose,' Harvey grumbles. 'But it doesn't narrow it down much.'

'And because of the size of the tyre, we think we're looking for an SUV or a four-wheel drive.'

'Any witnesses come forward yet?'

'We're still looking,' Chalk says with a note of regret.

'So what are you doing here? If you haven't found the vehicle and you don't have any witnesses, with respect, shouldn't you be out there looking instead of hounding me while I'm trying to eat breakfast?'

'Have you thought any more about what we talked about yesterday?'

Harvey's heart sinks. 'The press interview?'

'We still think it's our best hope of encouraging witnesses to come forward. Someone out there knows something. We just need to find them.'

'I don't know,' Harvey mumbles. 'Couldn't one of you do it? You know more about the investigation.'

'It's not the same,' Enright says, uncrossing her legs and leaning in towards Harvey, almost seductively. 'People want to hear from you and about the impact it's had.'

'But I wouldn't know what to say.'

Enright props an elbow on the table and rests her chin in her hand. 'Come on, Harvey. You'd just need to tell them a little about Gwyneth. What she's like and how devastated you felt when you found out she'd been left for dead on the roadside.'

'But most importantly, you need to appeal for anyone who might have any information to come forward. Sure, we could ask, but we're just a pair of coppers. If you asked, if you begged people, how could they resist? Coming from you, you could really prick their consciences,' Chalk adds, his eyes sparkling.

'I don't want to look like an idiot,' Harvey complains.

'You won't,' Enright assures him. 'We'll be there with you. You'll be great. I know you will.'

'The problem is, time is ticking, Harvey. We need to get this done like yesterday. Because the sooner it's done, the sooner we can catch whoever did this awful thing to your wife.' Chalk keeps his eyes fixed on Harvey, his gaze boring through him. 'You want to catch them, don't you?'

Harvey sighs. They're leaving him no choice, even though his gut is telling him it's a bad idea.

'Fine,' he says. 'If you really think it's that important, and it gets the pair of you off my back, I'll do it.'

Chapter 8

Everything moves so quickly once Harvey gives the go-ahead to the interview, and before he knows what's going on, he's in a hotel room with lights and cameras and people he doesn't know. He's had next to no time to prepare and is already beginning to regret going along with it. After all, it's not his job to catch criminals.

The room is like every other middle-grade hotel room Harvey's ever seen. Soulless and bland. A nondescript piece of modern art made up of a series of colourful splodges and splatters hangs on the wall in a gilt frame over the bed. A plastic plant sits in a tarnished copper pot by the door. An uncomfortable-looking beige sofa sits under the window, where net curtains waft gently in a breeze.

Harvey is greeted like a film star by an enthusiastic reporter with a mouth full of white teeth that are so perfect they must be fake. Too white. Too straight. Too dazzling.

She pumps his hand in a surprisingly firm grip and thanks him profusely for agreeing to the interview, before catching herself and adopting a sickening faux concern, offering simpering platitudes, as if she knows his wife. It's all so phoney. So transparent.

She invites him to sit in an armchair that's been set up in front of two TV cameras. A camera operator, an attractive woman with a dozen rings and studs in one ear, attaches a miniature microphone to his shirt and runs a wire down the inside of his jacket.

He's conscious he's sweating, but the more he tries to calm himself, the more he seems to perspire. He can feel it pooling under his arms and running down his back. The heat of the lights don't help, on top of the anxiety that started when the two detectives announced they'd set up the interview for later that day. He'd assumed he'd have a few days to prepare some thoughts and ready himself for the ordeal. How naïve. The only consolation is that he's not had to suffer a sleepless night worrying about it.

Chalk and Enright stand out of the way by the door, studying him. Watching him sweat. He has the distinct impression they're enjoying his discomfort.

There are seven people in the room, which makes it feel desperately crowded. Everyone's on top of each other. There's him and the reporter. The camera operator. The two detectives, and two more people he doesn't know. Someone else from the news station and someone in charge of media relations for the police, he thinks.

'Ignore the camera and focus on me,' the reporter instructs him, settling in a chair opposite, clutching a notebook, pen and a wad of typewritten notes that have been marked up with a yellow highlighter pen.

Harvey takes a moment to remember his lines. What was it the detectives wanted him to say? Something about appealing for witnesses to come forward. Or was it anyone with information? He doesn't want to mess this up or say the wrong thing. He'd hate to make a fool of himself.

He glances nervously at Chalk, who gives him a grin and a thumbs up, like a father at a school sports day encouraging his seven-year-old in the egg and spoon race. It all feels so alien. The reporter checks the camera operator is recording and begins.

'So, Mr Kerrison, Harvey, can you first let us know how your wife is doing?' she asks, tilting her head to one side and pouting sympathetically. 'Has she been able to tell you what happened yet?'

Harvey blinks, caught in the headlights. Don't they know? Hasn't anyone thought to tell them? He clears his throat. 'No, I'm afraid she's still unconscious, in a coma. She hit her head and has some swelling on the brain, so she's not been able to tell us anything yet.'

'I'm so sorry. I didn't know.' The reporter shoots a poisonous look at the media relations officer, who avoids the accusatory gaze by looking down at her own notes.

It's all a bit awkward.

'Perhaps you could paint a picture for us of what Gwyneth is like? What kind of person she is? What she enjoys?'

Where does he start?

'Right, well...' He glances at Chalk, who's scratching his chin again. 'Gwyneth is my everything,' he says, finally. A painful lump lodges itself at the back of his throat and his eyes grow moist with tears, but he really doesn't want to cry on TV. What would people think? 'She's the kind of woman who lights up a room when she walks in. People are naturally drawn to her and nobody has a bad word to say about her. She's perfect.'

That didn't sound too bad as it tripped off his tongue, apart from the clichés. He might as well have said she had a heart of gold and was the life and soul of the party.

'That's lovely,' the reporter says, nodding. 'It must have come as a huge shock when you discovered she'd been so badly injured?'

'Yes, it was a terrible shock. But she's fighting hard in hospital and I hope to have her home soon.'

'Have the doctors given you any indication how long her recovery might take?'

Harvey looks down at his hands in his lap. 'Like I said, she's in a coma. It could be days, weeks, or even months. It's impossible to say.'

'How awful for you.'

'It is tough, and I know it's going to be a long, hard fight, but knowing Gwyneth's determination and strength, I'm confident she's going to pull through this,' Harvey says, getting into his stride. 'There's no way a coma's going to defeat her.'

The reporter frowns, deep lines furrowing her brow. 'That's good that you have such belief, but...' she hesitates, glancing at the ceiling, as if searching for the right words, 'isn't it possible that there might be some lasting damage, especially as she has a head injury?'

Harvey tries to swallow, but his mouth is dry. He reaches for the glass of water at his side and takes a sip. It's a fair question, but he's been avoiding thinking about it. Could Gwyneth be left with permanent brain damage? How would he cope? She might need round-the-clock care, or be forced to spend the rest of her life in a wheelchair, or worse, bedridden, needing to be fed and bathed. The thought is unimaginable. What if it affects her memory and she no longer remembers him or their marriage? A shiver runs down his spine.

'That's a possibility,' Harvey says, 'but we'll have to face that issue when the time comes, if it comes.'

The reporter checks her notes. Pauses. Looks up. 'The police are still hunting for the driver. If you could address them, what would you say?'

Harvey lets out a silent sigh, grateful they're back on safer ground. It's a question he prepared for with the detectives earlier, although now he has to wrack his memory to recall the words they wanted him to use. There was a specific phrase they had him repeat over and over, but it's totally gone. Faced with the cameras and the bright lights, his mind's blank.

'We... errr... I... would urge anyone with any information about what happened to come forward and contact the police urgently.'

Was that it? Something like that. Close enough, anyway.

But the reporter looks disappointed. Did he say something wrong? She takes a breath and lets it out through her nose. 'Maybe you have a more personal message?'

Harvey looks to Chalk, who shrugs as if to say, *You're on your own, buddy. Make up something, but make it good.*

He has no idea what she's expecting him to say, but guesses she wants something less formal. More from the heart. 'Please, if you saw anything or know anything about the driver who did this to my beautiful wife, Gwyneth, come forward. Talk to the police. Even if it seems trivial, please pick up the phone.'

The reporter nods. 'Do you want to try looking straight into the camera,' she says, pointing at one of the ominous dark lenses staring, unblinking, at him, 'and speak to the public directly.'

It seems like an odd thing to do. It's bad enough speaking to a stranger about Gwyneth, but talking to a camera? He just wants this to be over so he can get back to the hospital.

'Someone must know something,' he says, his mouth dry with nerves. 'It's not going to make my wife better, or bring her out of the coma, but knowing whoever did this is still out there, thinking they've got away with it, is killing me.' A solitary tear falls from Harvey's eye and rolls down the side of his nose and onto his cheek. He wipes it away with his finger and sniffs. 'My wife could have died. I just want to see whoever did this to her caught and brought to justice.'

No one in the room speaks for what seems like the longest time. They're all staring at him, holding their collective breath. What's he done wrong now?

'That was brilliant, well done,' the reporter eventually says, beaming with delight.

'Was it?'

'So emotional. Really from the heart.'

Chalk strides forwards with a crooked smile. 'Great, Harvey. Thanks for doing that.'

'When will it be going out on TV?' Harvey asks the reporter, who seems suddenly distracted, jumping up and jamming her phone between her shoulder and her ear.

'Should be on the evening news tonight,' she says, 'if we can turn it around in time.'

'The deal is they have to share the interview with anyone who wants it,' Chalk explains. 'It saves you from doing multiple interviews.'

'But just locally?'

Chalk shrugs. 'It depends if it's a slow news day. We're hoping some of the national newspapers might pick it up. With your interview, it's a powerful story.'

A powerful story. Is that what he's become? He wonders bitterly if they'll still want to know in a year or two when they haven't caught the driver and Harvey's stuck at home nursing his brain-injured wife.

'Come on, let's get you a coffee, shall we?' DC Enright says, her expression icy. Harvey wonders if she ever smiles or what it would take to make her laugh. 'We can discuss the next steps.'

'It was nice to meet you.' The reporter shakes his hand as they head towards the door. 'I hope your wife gets better soon. Murray, before you leave, can we grab a quick soundbite?'

'Sure. Harvey, you go with Alison and I'll catch up with you at the cafe.'

As they leave the room and head for the lifts, Harvey finally stops sweating. He mops his brow with his handkerchief and runs a finger around the collar of his shirt.

'How was that?' Enright asks.

'It was okay, but I wouldn't be in a rush to do it again.'

'It takes some getting used to, doesn't it?'

'I don't think I'd ever get used to it.'

Something gnaws at the back of Harvey's brain, like he's forgotten something. He pats his pockets and feels the familiar lumps of his phone, wallet and keys.

'My coat,' he says, stopping suddenly. 'I left it hanging up in the room.'

He turns and hurries back, leaving Enright standing in the corridor.

He raises his hand to knock at the door but hesitates when he hears voices. They've obviously started their interview with Chalk, and he doesn't want to interrupt the recording. So he waits, with his ear to the door, listening for them to finish.

Although the voices are muffled, he can clearly make out the reporter's questions and Chalk's succinct answers.

'Has there been any progress in identifying the driver of the car?' the reporter asks.

'We're currently following up several lines of enquiry,' Chalk replies, giving nothing away.

'Such as?'

'I'm afraid, as the investigation is active, I'm not at liberty to reveal those details at this stage.'

'Have you at least been able to identify the make and model of the car involved?'

'As I said, we have a number of lines of enquiry we're pursuing.' Chalk's tone is defensive, and he sounds a little irritated by the question.

'Which is why you're so keen for any witnesses to come forward, I guess?'

'It would be helpful if any drivers who were in the area at the time could share with us any dashcam footage from their vehicles,' Chalk says.

'But you have no suspects at the moment?'

'It's still early days.'

'And what about Gwyneth's husband?'

Harvey stiffens, his heart beating a little faster.

'Is he a suspect?' the reporter asks.

Chalk hesitates for a beat. 'We're keeping an open mind at this stage.'

'So he *is* a suspect?'

'What's important is that we trace anyone who witnessed what happened yesterday afternoon.'

Harvey steps back, staring at the little spy hole in the door, shocked.

Is this why Chalk was so keen for him to appear in front of the cameras? To see if he'd slip up and give something away under the pressure? Anger ferments in Harvey's chest. And he thought Chalk was on his side.

The door opens suddenly, and the detective strides out, smoothing down his jacket. He startles when he comes face to face with Harvey, his eyes opening wide with surprise.

'Harvey, what are you doing?'

'I - I left my coat,' he mutters, pointing into the room.

The press liaison woman appears behind Chalk with Harvey's mac in one hand.

'Here you go,' she says with a smile, passing it around the detective, who's watching Harvey with narrowed eyes.

'Shall we chat?' Chalk says. 'Have a bit of a debrief?'

Harvey nods, shrugging on his coat. 'Sure,' he mumbles. 'I could do with a coffee after that.'

Chapter 9

Harvey and the detectives find a table in the window and order coffees and cinnamon buns. Chalk and Enright are buzzing, clearly delighted at how the interview went. But Harvey sits quiet and withdrawn, unable to share their excitement.

'If that doesn't have the phones ringing off the hooks, I don't know what will,' Chalk says, tapping his foot on the floor. 'Harvey, you were excellent. Really top notch.'

Harvey nods, but he's not happy he's been duped. He should have known better than to trust a copper. He's decided that in protest he's going to keep the detectives at arm's length from now on. He's done what they asked. Now they can get on with solving the crime themselves.

'You're a natural,' Enright says, nodding her approval. 'You came across so well. You even cried!'

He hadn't planned to shed tears, but when the reporter started asking him personal questions about Gwyneth, the emotion hit him in an unexpected wave, catching him totally by surprise.

'It's going to throw up so many leads, we'll have the bastard behind bars by the beginning of the week, I reckon.' Chalk's virtually rubbing his hands with glee.

Harvey smiles weakly. 'I hope so,' he says, finishing the last of his bun and licking his fingers. 'Do you think you could take me back to the hospital now?'

He spends the rest of the afternoon at Gwyneth's bedside, lost in his own thoughts. If Chalk really suspects he's guilty, why hasn't he arrested him? Because there's no evidence, that's why. Just because Harvey doesn't have an alibi to cover his movements for the period Gwyneth was walking home, it doesn't make him guilty. The problem is that the police are lazy and looking for easy answers. But this isn't the plotline of a cheap thriller, and it's not always the husband who did it.

By the early evening, he's had enough of the hospital and the sterile white walls of Gwyneth's room. The constant bleeping and whining of the machines has given him a headache. He decides to head home and return in the morning. After all, there's nothing to be gained from hanging around into the evening when she probably doesn't even know he's here.

The house feels empty and cold. He throws open the front door and switches on the lights, the aching heaviness of silence hitting him hard. The only sound comes from the infernal ticking of that damn George III clock in the hall. It's hideous, and it's noisy, and because it was one of Lionel's favourite pieces, it makes him hate it even more. He'd love to take a hammer to it and watch cogs and springs fly satisfyingly across the room. Bloody Lionel and his bloody clock.

As he kicks off his shoes and wanders into the lounge, contemplating whether he can be bothered to open a bottle of wine, he wonders if his interview is running on the news yet. He grabs his iPad and flops onto the sofa, tiredness washing over him.

He opens the *BBC News* website and is shocked to find the story is one of the top national headlines.

Husband's emotional appeal after hit-and-run leaves wife in coma

The article includes a short video featuring his interview which they've spliced together with a handful of photos of Gwyneth that Harvey gave to the police. Apart from how he looks - a little chubby around the face and with his shirt straining over his swollen stomach - he comes across better than he imagined.

They've used three different clips of him talking and some footage taken close to where Gwyneth was knocked down, showing the road and the brow of the hill on the fast corner where there's no pavement. They've even taken a close-up of the verge and a tyre track that's cut up the grass. There's also a short soundbite with DS Chalk, appealing for witnesses.

He reaches the end of the report and is about to watch it again when there's a knock at the door. It's late for visitors. With a huff of resignation, he tosses the iPad to one side and wearily hauls himself to his feet.

Sheryl Dubois is the last person he expects to find on the doorstep.

'I've just heard about Gwyneth,' she gushes, putting a liver-spotted hand to her chest. 'You poor thing. How are you coping?'

Sheryl lives in a large, detached, chocolate-box pretty cottage a stone's throw along the lower road. It's a magazine editor's dream with wisteria growing around the windows and crooked chimney stacks. She's not exactly a friend but they see her from time to time around the village when she always wants to stop for a gossip.

'You know, bearing up,' Harvey says.

'I wasn't sure if you'd eaten, so I've made you a lasagne.' She holds up a dish covered in foil. 'Got to keep your strength up.'

Why do people keep saying that to him?

Harvey's stomach rumbles. He's not had anything to eat since the stale sticky bun in the cafe with Chalk and Enright. He takes the dish and invites Sheryl in.

'Have you eaten? We could share it over a bottle of Merlot,' he suggests.

Sheryl waves a hand. 'No, I ate earlier. It just needs to go in the oven for thirty minutes to warm through.'

What a godsend. Harvey enjoys his food, but he's never been much of a cook. That's Gwyneth's department, although lately she's cut down his portion sizes and tried to make him eat salads and less red meat.

Sheryl follows Harvey into the kitchen and loiters by the table while he throws the lasagne into the oven.

'Is it true she's in a coma?' Sheryl asks.

'I'm afraid so.'

'Oh, gosh. Is she going to be... is she going to be okay?'

Harvey shrugs. 'I hope so. It's early days. She took a heavy hit to her head.'

'They said on the news it was a hit-and-run, just outside the village. I thought I heard sirens. If I'd known, I've have come straight over.'

It's a strange thing to offer. They've never been that close. She's a neighbour rather than a friend. In fact, he's not sure Gwyneth likes her that much. Sheryl can be quite full-on. A big personality who never holds back saying what she thinks.

She's another widow, who lost her husband seven years ago. He was a finance director at an engineering company on the other side of Kingstown, which is probably why they could afford such a stunning house.

'It's all been a bit of a whirlwind,' Harvey says, fetching a bottle of wine from the rack in the corner. He pulls out the cork with a satisfying pop.

'I thought you were brilliant on the TV.'

'Did I do okay?'

'I couldn't believe it was you at first. It was a bit of a shock. Look, if there's anything I can do while Gwyneth's in hospital, you must let me know. Anything at all.'

She moves closer and touches Harvey affectionately on the forearm as he's about to pour the wine, her perfume overpoweringly strong.

'That's kind but —'

'If nothing else, I can make sure you're eating properly. Can't see you going hungry, can I?' Her eyes crinkle at the edges when she smiles, and up close he can see she has a smudge of bright red lipstick on her front tooth.

'That's really not necessary.'

'I insist. It's the least I can do. You need to concentrate on getting Gwyneth better.'

'Okay,' Harvey concedes. He's not arguing with someone offering to bring him hot meals.

'I suppose it explains the shop, anyway.'

Harvey pours two glasses of wine and hands one to Sheryl. 'What about the shop?'

'It's not normally closed on a Thursday, is it?'

Harvey frowns. 'No, not normally.'

'I guess it was out of respect then.'

'Probably.' But it seems odd.

He sighs. Ruby is usually so reliable. He probably ought to investigate, in case there's an issue. Typical for something to happen while Gwyneth's out of the picture.

'What is it, Harvey? Is something wrong?'

'I don't know. Gwyneth's never been let down by Ruby before. I hope something hasn't happened.'

'Oh,' she says. 'You think there might be a problem? Well, look, I don't know much about the retail business, but if you were stuck, I don't mind looking after the place for a few days.'

Harvey has no doubt it's a genuine offer, and that Sheryl wants to help, but she's also one of those women who thrives in a crisis. He doesn't really want her getting involved and making matters worse. It's a problem he'll deal with himself.

'Thanks, but don't worry. I'll pop by tomorrow on my way to the hospital. I'm sure there's a simple explanation.'

At least he certainly hopes so. He could do without any more stress in his life right now.

Chapter 10

Harvey is up and out early the next morning to make a detour into the village on his way to the hospital. He feels duty-bound to check on the shop. He doesn't want to get his hands dirty with it, but is weighed down by the feeling that he probably should.

His route takes him directly past the spot where Gwyneth was knocked down. There's no avoiding it. As he approaches, his hands grow slick with sweat on the steering wheel. He tries to keep his eyes on the road and not let himself become distracted by the scrap of police tape tied around a tree trunk fluttering in the wind. Nor the unmistakable groove of a tyre mark cutting a muddy channel across a narrow grass verge.

He puts his foot down and accelerates away. If only it was as easy to escape the awful graphic images that seep uninvited into his mind of Gwyneth's broken body lying crooked in the road, blood seeping from a wound to her head.

As he reaches the outskirts of the village, he slows to a crawl and heads for the car park in the square behind the church. The only people around at this time of day are mothers on the way back from dropping their kids off at school, pushing buggies with toddlers in tow, and a handful of delivery drivers unloading outside the shops.

He parks up and heads for Gwyneth's antiques store, a dark and dusty premises in an old brick building with a hanging sign floating over the pavement.

Malone's Antiques and Collectables.

It irks him that the shop still bears Lionel's name, and although he can understand why it wouldn't have been practical to have changed it when he died and Gwyneth remarried, it's another irritating reminder of Gwyneth's past life.

Worryingly, the shop is in darkness and a closed sign hangs askew behind the glass in the door.

Harvey knocks and peers inside. There's no reply. It should have opened at eight-thirty, but it's possible Ruby is running late, so he gives it ten minutes, loitering outside checking his phone.

After ten minutes have passed, he gives it another five. Finally, he concludes she's not turning up.

Does it really matter? He has bigger problems to worry about. But then he hears Gwyneth's voice in his head, cross with him that he couldn't deal with this one problem while she's in hospital.

With a sigh, he makes a decision. He knows where Ruby lives. He might as well pop around to the house and see if he can find out what's going on, although there's bound to be a reasonable explanation. It's not as if she's going to have plundered the till and run off to the Caribbean.

Ruby Pettifer is as straight-laced and honest as anyone he knows. She dresses like the headmistress of a 1950s all-girls' school, prim and proper with a slight air of haughtiness. A serious woman who lacks any humour. She's a parish councillor and a former postmistress, at least before they closed the Post Office and made her redundant, although they've subsequently opened a counter in Sunni's newsagents after a backlash from the community.

Harvey hurries along Church Street, past the imposing early Norman church and its sprawling graveyard, heading for the row of cottages next to the old vicarage. Ruby's place is the one with swaying delphiniums struggling to hold their heads upright against a low stone wall.

He opens a squeaky gate, marches up the short, uneven cobbled path to the door, and knocks.

Inside, he hears the heavy tread of footsteps and the creak of floorboards. The door swings open and Ruby noticeably startles when she sees Harvey.

'I came to check on the shop for Gwyneth and noticed it hadn't opened this morning,' he says with what he hopes is a disarming smile. 'Is everything okay?'

Ruby stands as rigid as a soldier on parade. It's almost impossible to put an age to her. She could be a mature-looking forty-year-old or a sprightly pensioner.

She pulls her cardigan around her body and folds her arms. 'I've not been feeling well,' she says.

'I'm sorry to hear that. It's just that Gwyneth's been taken to hospital and —'

'Yes, I heard. How is she? Nothing too serious, I hope?'

'Actually, she has a nasty head injury.' He bites his lower lip. 'She's in a coma.'

'Oh?' Ruby's eyebrows arch in surprise. 'Is she going to be alright?'

Harvey shrugs. 'I hope so. In the meantime, I wanted to check if you would mind keeping an eye on the business, as I don't think Gwyneth's going to be around for a while. She's certainly not well enough to be overseeing the shop for the time being.'

'I see.'

'I can rely on you, then?' Harvey asks.

Ruby hesitates for a second or two, looking uncertain. He assumed she'd fall over herself to help. Ever Reliable Ruby is what Gwyneth used to call her.

'Ruby? Would that be okay?'

'Of course. I'll do my best.' She shoots him a tight-lipped smile.

'I really appreciate it, and if you're not feeling up to opening today, I have a friend who said she can help. If you let me have the keys, she can bring them back later.'

'That won't be necessary,' Ruby replies tartly. 'I was just on my way. I'll be over there in ten minutes.'

'Right, okay, that's great. And if you need anything, call me. There's plenty of stock at the house if you need me to run anything down?'

'It's fine.'

'Okay.'

'Goodbye then.' She shuts the door in his face and Harvey is left standing on the doorstep, not entirely sure how the conversation has gone. She agreed to look after the store while Gwyneth's in hospital, didn't she? Oh well, he's done his best.

He wends his way back to the car, mentally preparing himself for another day sitting at Gwyneth's side in that sterile white hospital room with the noise of the machines giving him a headache. How long is it going to last? A few days? Weeks? Months? Although he doesn't really have the right to moan about it. After all it's not him in that hospital bed with a swelling on the brain.

As he passes a florist's, several buckets of roses on display outside catch his eye. Gwyneth loves roses. Especially those Gertrude Jeykll ones she's always talking about. He ought to take her some. If nothing else, it'll lend a splash of colour to the room and maybe their scent will trigger a memory that sparks her back to life. He chooses two bunches of red blooms, their petals still tightly furled, and hurries back to the car.

Typically, the car park at the hospital is full when he arrives and it takes fifteen minutes, driving around and around, until he finds a space.

In the intensive care unit, everyone seems to be in a hurry and he has to dodge numerous harassed-looking doctors and nurses stomping up and down the corridor.

It's a little more serene where Gwyneth is being treated. He hesitates outside the door and watches Leanne fussing around his wife, making sure she's comfortable, and chatting with her like she's an old friend.

But if he'd hoped today was the day he'd arrive and find Gwyneth sitting up with her eyes open, having regained consciousness, he's disappointed. She's still lying with her eyes closed and a tube down her throat.

However, there is one noticeable change. She has a visitor. Harvey squints through the glass, trying to work out who it is. He doesn't recognise the woman in the frumpy brown dress and thick tights. She has wild, unkempt hair and is talking to Gwyneth as if she's awake.

He pushes the door open and strides in.

'Hello,' he says, but his smile evaporates when the woman turns to face him.

It's like looking at Gwyneth's older sister. The similarity is disarmingly striking, although where Gwyneth's hair is platinum blonde, her hair is black and streaked with grey. And she's much older, weathered with age, almost craggy, with wrinkles and creases framing her eyes and mouth, and a back that's starting to arch.

You'd think they must be related, especially as they share the same shaped nose and eyes. Even her mannerisms are the same. The way she tilts her head to one side as she studies Harvey and how she nervously curls her lip.

And then with the clarity of a lightning bolt on a stormy night, it hits him and everything becomes clear.

'I'm Harvey,' he says brightly, extending a hand towards her as he approaches.

She stares at him suspiciously through the thick lenses of a pair of cheap glasses which magnify her eyes, and almost trips over a bulging bag-for-life at her feet as she jumps out of her seat.

'Gwyneth's husband,' he adds.

She tentatively takes his hand.

'Hello,' she croaks with a nervous uncertainty.

'It's lovely to meet you. You must be Gwyneth's mother?'

Chapter 11

Gwyneth has never talked about her mother. They've been estranged for more than thirty years, but that's all Harvey knows. He doesn't know how or why. When they had those conversations early in their relationship about family, parents and siblings, and what life was like for them growing up, Gwyneth talked a lot about her father. Even by her own admission, she'd been a daddy's girl, close to him until his death when she was in her early twenties. But she rarely spoke about her mother.

He knows she went into a home after Gwyneth's father passed away, and had assumed, wrongly now it seems, that it was because she'd been ill or developed a long-term condition, like his own mother, whose brain had been ravaged by dementia.

The woman continues to eye him suspiciously, letting go of his hand and looking him up and down.

'I'm so pleased you came,' Harvey says. Close up, the similarities with Gwyneth are even more pronounced. The family resemblance is unmistakable.

'I heard about the accident on the news,' she says, her voice not so refined as Gwyneth's. Rougher and with the twinge of a northern accent.

'It was a hit-and-run. The driver didn't stop,' he tells her, although presumably she already knows if she saw it on the news. 'I'm sorry. This must have come as a shock. I know you've not seen Gwyneth for a long time.'

'No, but she's just as beautiful as I remember.'

Not so beautiful with a tube helping her breathe, her head swathed in bandages and her eyes puffy and black with bruising, but Harvey lets it go.

'Did you have to travel far?' he asks.

'From Newcastle.'

'Wow, how long did that take?' he asks, shocked.

She considers for a moment. 'About eight hours. I came as soon as I could.'

'Have the nurses explained about the coma?'

Gwyneth's mother nods. 'I bumped into a doctor. He said her brain was all swollen, and that's the reason she's not conscious.'

'They think she's lucky to be alive.'

'But she's going to be okay?' There are tears in her eyes.

'I hope so.'

'You don't need to worry. Now I'm here, I'm going to take good care of her and make up for all the time we lost,' she says. 'It's going to be my personal mission to get her better.'

'She's going to be so pleased you came. Gwyneth is always talking about you,' Harvey says.

'Is she?'

It's only a tiny white lie, but if it smoothes the path of their long overdue reconciliation, so what?

'I think she would have reached out sooner, but you know how it is.'

The woman nods sagely. 'It's silly really that we've let our petty differences get between us.'

Which is all she says about it, and even though Harvey would love to quiz her about why they lost touch, he bites his tongue.

'I'm sorry, this is really awkward, but what should I call you?' Harvey asks. 'I'm not sure calling you Mum is appropriate.'

'Freya's fine,' she says.

'Well, it's an absolute pleasure to finally meet you, Freya.'

'How long have you been married?'

'Three years.'

Freya raises a surprised eyebrow.

'Gwyneth's first husband passed away a few years ago, and I'm divorced. I think we were lucky to find each other when we did.'

Freya screws up her nose, as if the idea of it is totally distasteful.

'I always wondered whether she was married and had children. Whether she was happy.'

'She hasn't been able to have children. She and Lionel tried for a while, but it never happened for them. I think she came to terms with the fact she would never be a mum and threw herself into work instead. It's a shame. Gwyneth would have made a great mother.'

'That's sad,' Freya says. She nods to the two bunches of roses Harvey's forgotten he's carrying. 'You'd better give me those before they wilt.'

He lifts the blooms upright and sniffs the flowers. 'Roses are Gwyneth's favourite.'

Freya takes them from him and peels them out of their pretty pink paper wrap. 'Why don't you run along and see if you can find a vase and I'll arrange them for you.'

'A vase? Sure,' he says, with no idea where he's going to find one. He was hoping one of the nurses would sort it all out for him.

He turns and edges towards the door, wondering if anyone at the nurses' station might help, and almost bumps into Leanne as she breezes in. She has a bright smile plastered all over her face.

'How's the patient?' she asks, before noticing Freya. 'Oh, hello.' She glances uncertainly at Harvey.

'This is Freya. Gwyneth's mother.'

'Oh, right.' She seems surprised.

'Freya's not seen her daughter for a while. They sort of lost touch. It's a long story,' Harvey explains. 'Any idea where I'd find a vase for some flowers?'

'Try one of the porters.' Leanne's eyes remain fixed on Freya as if she's trying to work her out. 'They should be able to find something for you.'

Harvey heads out of the room and wanders around aimlessly, looking for someone to ask. But everyone seems so busy that eventually he gives up and returns empty-handed.

Freya and Leanne are chatting and laughing like they've known each other all their lives, rather than having been introduced only minutes earlier. That ability to find common ground with strangers within seconds of meeting is a female trait Harvey envies. It seems so effortless to them.

They're talking about the cost of parking at the hospital, of all things. How they ever stumbled on that topic in the few moments he's been gone is beyond him.

'They even make the nurses pay,' Leanne's saying, 'as if we have any choice.'

Harvey clears his throat. 'Sorry, I couldn't find a vase.'

Freya tuts and rolls her eyes at Leanne. 'Too late. I found this water jug. It'll do for now.' She's already arranged the roses artfully and places them on the wide windowsill. 'I know lots of people rave about roses, but I've never really liked them,' she says. Harvey's not sure whether the comment's directed at him or Leanne.

'I know what you mean,' Leanne says. 'I've always thought they were a bit commercial. I don't like the thorny stems either.'

The women share a laugh like they've formed a special club of two in his absence and he's not a welcome member.

'Roses have always been Gwyneth's favourite, ever since I've known her,' he says. 'I think she'd like them by her bed.'

He moves to the window, meaning to put the jug on Gwyneth's bedside cabinet.

'Leave them where they are.' Freya's bark is so unexpectedly ferocious, he jumps back, startled.

'I just thought —'

'They're fine where they are,' Freya says, with the authority of a head teacher.

'Leanne was saying that familiar smells might help Gwyneth recover more quickly,' Harvey adds, hoping to recruit the nurse onto his side.

Freya snorts. 'Nonsense. I think it'll take more than a few measly flowers.'

Measly? They cost him almost thirty pounds. They weren't cheap.

'It's important she gets the right stimulation,' Harvey continues, reciting the advice the doctors have been at pains to explain at every opportunity. 'I was going to play her some of her favourite music too. I've put together a playlist on my phone. Hopefully, some rousing pieces that she'll connect with. She loves a bit of Mahler.'

Freya pulls a face. 'Classical?'

'It's what she likes.'

'Okay.'

'Remember, Gwyneth can probably hear everything going in the room,' Leanne says, jumping in like a referee in a boxing match. 'But Harvey's right. Anything you can do to stimulate Gwyneth's senses and memories is going to help.'

Harvey's chest swells, pleased he's done something right, although why he feels the need to prove himself to Gwyneth's mother is a mystery. It's not as if he's a teenager anymore.

Freya wanders across the room and fiddles with the roses, before picking up the jug and taking it to Gwyneth's bed.

'Look, Gwyneth, we brought your favourite flowers. Don't they smell lovely?' she says.

We?

'Are you comfortable? Warm enough?' Freya asks. 'Do you need another pillow?' She turns to Harvey. 'Fetch her another pillow, will you? She's all slumped over.'

Harvey's mouth drops open, but before he can say anything, Leanne leaps to his rescue.

'She's fine as she is, Freya. I'd leave her for the moment.' Leanne smiles so disarmingly it's hard to see it as a rebuke.

'If you're sure? She doesn't look comfortable to me.'

'Honestly, she's fine.'

'Her lips are dry. Do you have something I can put on them?' Freya puts the jug of flowers down on the bedside cabinet, exactly where Harvey suggested.

'It's okay, I can do it,' he says, fetching a tub of petroleum jelly from a trolley in the corner. Leanne showed him how he should apply a thin layer every few hours. Just a little smear across her top and bottom lips around the tube fixed to her mouth, helping her breathe.

Freya snatches it from him, scoops out far too much and slathers it all over Gwyneth's mouth with her finger.

Harvey winces. 'Just a little,' he advises, peering over Freya's shoulder.

'I know what I'm doing.'

'Of course, sorry.'

Harvey steps away and slumps into the armchair that's been pushed up against the radiator under the window.

'What can I put on her hands?' Freya asks, dropping the pot onto the bed between Gwyneth's knees instead of putting it back where it belongs. Leanne hates that.

Harvey doesn't say anything, telling himself to be patient with her. She's Gwyneth's mother after all, and it's only natural she wants to make up for lost time. Even so, it's infuriating watching her take over.

'There's some cream in the bedside cabinet,' he says.

Freya digs around and retrieves a bottle of moisturiser. She squirts an enormous quantity into Gwyneth's palm and gets to work trying to massage it in, leaning awkwardly over the bed.

'Can I sit down?' she asks, nodding at the chair Harvey's collapsed in.

He pulls himself up with a sigh and drags it across the room, the legs scraping noisily on the tiles. He's left standing, watching Freya at work, not sure what else to do with himself.

In the last two days, he's been doing all these little jobs for Gwyneth. Keeping her lips and hands moisturised. Plumping up her pillow. Chatting to her. Damping her eyes with cotton wool buds, just like Leanne's shown him. Everything to keep her comfortable and prevent her from picking up an infection.

'I might grab a coffee then,' he says, 'if I'm not needed.'

Freya lowers Gwyneth's hand gently onto the bed. 'Sorry, I'm taking over, aren't I? I just want to feel like I'm helping.'

He's being childish. What difference does it make who puts cream on her hands or jelly on her lips?

'No, it's fine. You have a lot of time to make up. I'm happy you're here and able to help.'

Freya smiles at him and nods. Then picks up Gwyneth's hand and continues to massage the surplus cream into her skin.

Chapter 12

GWYNETH

There's a new voice. It's not Harvey. Or that other woman with the sweet sing-song tone who always sounds so happy.

Someone different. It's so hard to be sure because everything is so fuzzy and indistinct, but I think it's another woman. She sounds older. More intense.

She talks a lot, although I do not know what she's saying. It's like I'm lying under the water in the bath and all the sounds around me are dulled.

There's something about this unfamiliar voice that makes me anxious, though. I don't like the way she talks, sometimes in a hushed whisper, almost as if she's repeating an incantation or - and I know it sounds silly - a witch's spell. Even though I can't make out her words, she makes my skin tingle.

I can't shift the feeling. Every time I hear her voice, my heart beats a little faster and my breath becomes a little shallower.

And when a dark shadow suddenly looms above me, an ill-defined silhouette against the white domed ceiling of my world, its presence feels as threatening as a rumble of thunder on a sunny afternoon.

It's the woman, I'm sure it is. I hold my breath, terrified. I think she's talking to me. Does that mean she can see me? What's she saying? I wish I could make out her words, although I don't like her tone.

I squeeze my eyes shut. I don't want to see her or hear her, but she's talking urgently and I have a dreadful fear something bad is going to happen.

Please, leave me alone.

And then she stops. My world falls silent again, apart from the bleeps and clicks and huffs that are ever-present.

I prise open my eyes and the shadow above me has vanished.

Chapter 13

'Let me buy you lunch,' Harvey offers.

'You don't have to do that.' Freya is sitting at Gwyneth's bedside, holding her hand. She's barely let it go from the moment Harvey arrived.

'I thought it would give us a chance to get to know each other better.' It's been difficult to talk over the noise of the machines and the constant comings and goings of the medical and nursing teams on the ward.

Freya glances at Leanne as if seeking confirmation that it's okay to leave.

'Go on, eat,' she says.

The canteen is busy with a hungry lunchtime crowd and they're lucky to find somewhere to sit, grabbing a table vacated by two junior doctors who've just finished coffee and cake.

Freya sits with her arms on the table around her prawn sandwich like a sparrowhawk protecting its kill, head down, shoulders hunched. It's almost as if she's expecting someone to reach over and steal the food off her plate.

Harvey watches curiously as she nibbles at the bread like a mouse, her eyes constantly scanning the room. She has food stains that he hadn't noticed before down the front of her dress, an ugly mud-brown polyester garment that looks as if she's picked it off a rail in a charity shop.

'How long have you been trying to find your daughter?' Harvey asks.

'A long time. Years. I didn't know where to look.'

'She was Gwyneth Malone for a long time.'

Freya frowns.

'Her married name when she was with her first husband. If you didn't know that, you'd have had no chance of finding her.'

'I recognised her picture on the TV. She hasn't changed much. It was like looking in the mirror. What was her first husband like?'

'Lionel? I don't know. I never met him. She still talks about him, though. And we still have all his old clothes and belongings at the house.' Harvey rolls his eyes. 'Gwyneth refuses to throw any of it away.'

'Why?'

It's a question he struggles to answer. 'I think she still loves him deep down and she's worried that she'll be dishonouring his memory if she throws away his things.'

'That's crazy.'

'Tell me about it.'

'And how does it make you feel?' Freya asks, staring at him through her thick lenses, giving him the impression he's been placed under a microscope and is being studied closely.

'I don't know. Like she's not a hundred per cent committed to our relationship, I suppose. Sometimes I feel as though I'm sharing her with him, even though he's dead, you know?'

Harvey has never opened up about his feelings like this to anyone. Maybe it's because Freya's family, or that he doesn't really know her.

It's all true though. He worries that he's not enough for Gwyneth, that he doesn't measure up to her expectations or to her first husband, who she has firmly placed high on a pedestal. He worries she doesn't love him enough. That at any moment she's going to turn around and tell him so. But most of all, he worries he doesn't earn enough. After all, what he brings in from his counselling work is a pittance, and the divorce cleaned him out. It's no wonder some people think he must be living on his wife's charity and was only attracted to her because of her wealth. But it's not like that at all.

'That's sad,' Freya says, picking up crumbs from her plate with the end of one finger.

'Relationships are complicated though, aren't they? And just because someone's dead, it doesn't mean you stop loving them.'

Freya shrugs, as if she doesn't know what he's talking about.

'Did you ever remarry?'

She stares blankly at him. 'No,' she says, without elaborating. 'You were married before you met Gwyneth?'

'Things didn't work out with my first wife. We went our separate ways.'

Freya's eyes narrow. 'Because you had an affair with Gwyneth?'

'No, of course not. Actually, I was helping her through her loss after Lionel died,' he explains. 'My marriage was already over.'

'Helping? How?'

'I was her therapist. I specialise in grief counselling. Gwyneth was having a hard time coming to terms with Lionel's death and she came to me for support.'

Freya steeples her fingers over her plate. 'Is that sort of thing allowed?'

Why does everyone think they did something wrong, like he broke some kind of Hippocratic oath?

'No, it's not. We got together later. It's perfectly acceptable,' he says.

'Sounds dodgy to me.'

'We were in love. We couldn't help how we felt about each other.'

'I thought you said she was still in love with Lionel.'

Harvey takes a deep breath and lets it out slowly. 'Yes, but he's dead. Like I said, relationships are complicated.' He changes the subject. 'Tell me about you. How long are you able to stay?'

'I don't know. As long as it takes, I suppose.'

'It could be weeks before Gwyneth regains consciousness.'

'I've told work I need some time off. They'll have to cope without me.'

Harvey nods. 'That's dedication.'

'It's taken me all this time to find her. I'm not leaving in a hurry,' she says.

'And what do you do for work?'

'I'm in catering.'

'Oh, you're a chef?'

Freya chuckles. 'It's not that fancy. I'm a cook in an old folk's home.'

'Right. And where are you staying?'

Freya nudges her glasses up the bridge of her nose with her knuckle. 'I don't know yet.'

'I can point you towards a few hotels, if that's helpful?'

'I'll be fine, thanks.' She glances down at her plate.

'There are some decent hotels near the hospital,' Harvey says.

'I can't afford a hotel. It cost me enough in fuel just to get here.'

'Where are you going to stay? You can't sleep on the streets.' Harvey chuckles but Freya doesn't laugh.

'In my car.'

'Don't be stupid. You can't sleep in your car.'

Freya bristles. 'Why's that stupid? It's warm, it's dry, and it's free.'

'But it's your car. And where would you go? It'll cost you as much as a hotel in parking fees if you stay in the hospital car park,' Harvey points out.

'I'll find somewhere,' she huffs.

'No, I can't allow it.'

'You're not in charge of me. You can't tell me what I can and can't do.'

'I mean, you're Gwyneth's mother. She'd never forgive me if I let you sleep in your car, for pity's sake. Stay at our house. There's plenty of room.' The offer's out of his mouth before he can stop to think through whether it's really such a good idea or not.

But what's the alternative? He'd never forgive himself if he let her bunk down in her car. Anything could happen to her. It's absolutely the right thing to do. The only thing to do.

'It's kind of you, Harvey, but I couldn't possibly impose.'

'You wouldn't be imposing. And anyway, with Gwyneth not around, it would be good to have the company. I'm not taking no for an answer. You're coming home with me and you can stay as long as you like.'

Freya's eyes sparkle. 'Are you sure you wouldn't mind?'

'You're family, Freya.' Harvey reaches across the table and pats the top of her hand. 'And families look out for each other, no matter what.'

Chapter 14

'This it?' Harvey asks, nodding at the decrepit SUV that's been so badly parked it takes up two spaces. It's a wonder Freya hasn't picked up a ticket.

The car is a rust bucket, riddled with holes, its paintwork scratched and dented.

'It's all I can afford,' Freya says defensively, hooking a bunch of keys from the bottom of her bag.

It's a miracle the car made it from Newcastle. It looks fit for the scrapheap with one wing mirror hanging off, and at least one bald tyre.

Mind you, his own car, a twenty-year-old VW Golf, isn't in much better condition. It needs a new clutch and struggles to start when it's cold. He's been trying to convince Gwyneth to let him buy something newer and more reliable, but she's been resisting. She thinks it's a waste of money when she has a two-year-old Volvo sitting on the drive he could use. But it's not the same. He's always had his own car. It's about freedom and independence. He doesn't want to ask Gwyneth if he can borrow her car every time he wants to go out.

'Do you want to follow me?' Harvey says as Freya battles with the driver's door, which eventually opens with a loud creak. 'It's not far.'

They've been holed up together in Gwyneth's room all afternoon and Harvey's desperate to get home. The white walls have been closing in and the noise of the machines has brought on another headache.

Freya has barely let him within an arm's length of Gwyneth. She's insisted on doing everything, whether it's keeping her skin moisturised, playing her music or adjusting her pillows and position. Harvey's been pushed to the sidelines, bored out of his mind, mostly just staring out of the window and making excuses to visit the canteen to break up the day.

Freya is a cautious driver and approaches every roundabout and set of traffic lights as if she's never encountered such things before. By the time they make it to the house, Harvey is ready for a stiff drink.

They park side-by-side at the top of the gravel drive and as she climbs out of her car, Freya's eyes open wide with surprise. It's the same look of awe Harvey remembers feeling the first time he saw the house and took in the splendour of the converted barn with its grand sweeping drive and pair of olive trees in terracotta pots outside the double-height entrance doors.

From the outside, it's fashionable and modern and wouldn't look out of place on the front cover of an architect's marketing brochure. But inside hides a secret. Stepping through the front door is more like entering a museum than a home. Every corner, every wall, every shelf is taken up with an eclectic collection of historic artefacts. Gwyneth and Lionel's hoard of antiques, amassed over the course of their twenty-year marriage.

'Come inside and take a look,' Harvey says as Freya stands staring in wonder, clutching a bulging bag-for-life to her chest.

'Nice place,' she coos.

'Wait until you see inside.'

A foil-covered dish is sitting on the doorstep with a note taped to the top from Sheryl, their neighbour, sending her love and wishing Gwyneth a speedy recovery.

'What's that?' Freya asks suspiciously.

'It's from our friend, Sheryl. She lives down the road.' Harvey peeks under the foil to discover a chilli with rice, which smells divine. 'I think she's worried I'm going to starve to death while Gwyneth's in hospital.' He laughs, but Freya looks far from amused.

Balancing the dish in one hand, Harvey unlocks the front door. He throws the keys towards the bowl on the side, but they miss and strike the George III clock with an ominous thunk.

'Would you like a quick tour before I show you to your room?' he calls over his shoulder as he marches into the kitchen to put the chilli in the fridge.

When he returns to the hall, Freya's still standing by the door with her eyes on stalks, staring at the paintings and ornaments, vases and trinkets, old farm tools and even a suit of armour hanging on the wall.

As much as Harvey hates living with the constant reminder of Lionel, he still gets a thrill showing people around the house and watching their reactions. It's a unique property and something to behold. He loves taking first-time visitors from room to room, pointing out the tapestries and decorative plates, the chandeliers and marble busts, the gilt-edged mirrors and Chinese vases with their crazy cracked glazes, and especially the library filled with faded first editions and leather-bound folios of ancient works. Even all the furniture is historic. Dark mahogany wardrobes and dressers, intricately carved oak coffers, decorative chests of drawers and walnut writing tables.

'Pop your bag down and I'll show you around,' Harvey says, peeling Freya's bag from her grip and putting it on the floor by her feet.

He leads her into the lounge and through to the library, then the study, to the grand dining room with its impressive crystal chandelier and enormous mahogany table and chairs that take up most of the room. Into the kitchen, the most modern part of the house, and out through the folding doors onto the sun deck that overlooks the rolling lawn and beyond, across the valley to the woods on the horizon. Freya makes all kinds of appreciative coos and murmurs as she admires the decor.

'Come and see upstairs. You get an even better view across the valley,' Harvey says proudly.

But at the bottom of the oak staircase, Freya stops suddenly and points to a framed portrait on a Victorian walnut bow-fronted credenza.

'Is that Gwyneth?' she asks, her brow furrowed.

Harvey steps back and stands at Freya's shoulder. 'It is. Do you like it?'

'She looks much younger.'

'It was painted a few years ago. A gift from Lionel for her fortieth birthday.' Harvey thinks it's tasteless. Who has a portrait of themselves in their own home? It's the epitome of vanity. Plus, Gwyneth's eyes seem to follow you around no matter where you go, which he finds kind of creepy.

'I like the necklace she's wearing. It's pretty. Brings out the colour of her eyes.'

Harvey cocks his head. He doesn't know who the artist was, and although he despises the picture because of what it represents, he can appreciate the artist's talent. Freya's right, the necklace does bring out the colour of Gwyneth's eyes. The artist has captured it brilliantly.

The necklace is another piece from history. It's early nineteenth century and adorned with countless gemstones. Topaz, peridots, garnets, sapphires, emeralds and rubies, embedded in enamel and gold in delicate foliate patterns.

Lionel apparently acquired it at an auction in New York for an absolute steal and presented it to Gwyneth as an early Christmas present one year, not long after they were married. Gwyneth has since had it revalued for insurance purposes for an eye-watering sum of money, which is why she and Harvey keep it safely locked away.

'It's one of Gwyneth's favourite pieces,' Harvey says. 'Not that she wears it much. It's far too valuable.'

Freya blinks at him as if she's not sure whether he's joking or not.

'Let me show you where you'll be staying.'

'What's through there?' Freya points to a door at the end of the hall.

'Nothing. Just storage.' It's the only area of the house he's not shown her.

'Can I see?'

'There's not much down there.'

'It's a basement?' Her eyes light up.

'I wouldn't really describe it as a basement. It's where Gwyneth keeps the stock for her shop. Did you know she has a shop in the village?'

Freya shakes her head. 'I'd like to see.'

'The shop?'

'No, the basement. I'm curious. Unless, of course, there's something you're hiding down there?'

Harvey laughs. If she really wants to see the basement, why not? It's not particularly exciting.

'Okay, fine.' He reaches above the door for a key, throws it open and flicks on a light switch.

Technically, it is a basement, but Harvey thinks of it more of a lower ground floor. Lionel had it built when they were renovating the barn, with the idea that one day they might put a gym in there.

'Watch your step,' he warns Freya as he descends a steep set of concrete steps ahead of her.

Freya clutches nervously onto the handrail. She's going to be disappointed. The basement room is no bigger than an average-sized garage, the floor almost entirely covered in cardboard boxes containing an assortment of stock Gwyneth has acquired over the years for the shop. All kinds of collectables and ornaments. Although to Harvey's untrained eyes, most of it looks like junk. Certainly nothing he'd want to buy or own. But what does he know?

'There, you see? Just storage,' he says as Freya peers around the room.

He peels open the lid of the nearest box and pulls out a hideous Chinese porcelain dragon. 'Gwyneth's pet hobby,' he says dismissively. 'One day, I'll take you to the shop. It's only small, but Gwyneth enjoys pottering around down there.'

It's a reminder that he needs to check in with Ruby.

'I see.' Freya screws up her nose as she examines the dragon. 'And what about in there?'

She points to a solid, brushed metal door set into the wall below the staircase.

'That?'

'Yes, what's in there?'

'Nothing really. Do you fancy a cup of tea or maybe a glass of wine?'

'No,' she says, sternly. 'I want to know what's behind that door. Or maybe you really do have something to hide, Harvey?'

Chapter 15

'Of course I don't have anything to hide.' Harvey laughs. Freya is so suspicious.

'Then show me,' she demands. 'What's behind the door?'

'You know what a panic room is?'

She frowns.

'It's like the opposite of a prison cell. You lock yourself in to keep safe,' he explains.

'Yes, I know what a panic room is. Can I see inside?'

'If you really want. There's not much to see.'

He steps up to an electronic number pad on the wall next to the heavy steel door and punches in an eight-digit code. The lock clicks open.

'Is that a significant date?' Freya asks. 'I assume it's a date? Zero-seven-zero-seven-two-zero-two-one.'

Harvey glares at her. Wily old bird. She might be knocking on, but there's nothing wrong with her sight or her memory. 'Our wedding anniversary. The seventh of July.'

Freya sniffs. 'I wouldn't know. I didn't get an invite.'

'It was only a small do. We didn't invite many people,' he says.

As they'd both been married previously, they didn't think it was appropriate to make a big fuss. They weren't virginal twenty-somethings who needed a big church, a fleet of cars, a white dress or morning suits to celebrate their union. Nor did they want a big family affair. They held the ceremony in a small room at the back of a register office, invited a few close friends, and finished the day with a lovely meal in the village pub with locals and neighbours.

'I'm sure we'll find the time to make up for it when Gwyneth's better.'

Freya steps inside as Harvey hauls open the door.

Movement-sensing lights flicker on, illuminating up the small space inside.

'I told you there wasn't much to see,' Harvey says.

The windowless room really is tiny. Barely big enough to lie down in, not that you'd want to with its hard, concrete floor. The ceiling is claustrophobically low. Fresh air is pumped and filtered through a small, secure fan above the door.

Lionel had it built because he was paranoid about criminals and intruders, according to Gwyneth. The man's ego clearly got the better of him. He wasn't that rich.

'Where do you sit?' Freya asks, turning in a slow circle as she studies the room's plain interior.

'There used to be chairs down here, but we moved them out. We never thought we'd ever need to use it. Lionel used to keep tins of food and bottles of water down here, mind you, as if he was preparing for the end of the world.' Harvey laughs. 'Crazy old fool.'

'And what's that screen?' Freya points to a blank monitor on one of the walls.

'You can access the CCTV cameras around the house from down here.' Harvey's tempted to show her, but can't be bothered with the rigmarole of switching everything on. It's also a reminder that the camera covering the front door has slipped and is now pointing at the floor. It's another job he's been meaning to do.

'It seems a bit over the top.'

'That's Lionel for you.'

'And what's in there?' Freya points to a small door embedded in the wall.

'The safe where we keep some of Gwyneth's more valuable jewellery, and important documents.' As soon as he says it, he regrets it. Freya might be family, but he's not supposed to tell anyone about the safe or what's in it.

'It's creepy. I wouldn't like to get locked in here.' Freya shudders.

'Technically, it's not possible.' Harvey points to another keypad next to the door. 'It's always the same code to get out as it is to get in.'

'Even so.' Freya steps back into the basement, clearly unimpressed.

Harvey follows her out and pushes the door shut. It locks with a muted click. 'Satisfied now?'

'I don't know why you were being so secretive about it. It wasn't very interesting.'

'I told you there was nothing to see.'

'I'd like to go to my room now.'

'Sure. Follow me.'

He leads the way back up the stairs, pausing to lock the basement door and return the key to the top of the doorframe.

Freya follows slowly up the stairs to the first floor, taking the steps one at a time, as if she's afraid she might slip on the bare oak.

'This is our room.' Harvey pushes open the door to the grand main bedroom he shares with Gwyneth, with its enormous four-poster bed and en suite that's probably bigger than most people's family bathrooms. 'And just along the hall is where you'll be staying.'

He takes her to the guest room at the end of the landing, grateful that Gwyneth always keeps the bed made, just in case of unexpected visitors.

Freya sticks her head around the door and peers inside.

It's a bright and airy room at the back of the house with amazing views over the countryside. It's perfect for Freya.

'I think you'll be comfortable in here,' Harvey says. 'I just need to find you some towels.'

Freya has gone worryingly quiet. She nods but doesn't say anything.

'I'll find you a spare key and you can come and go as you please. '

But Freya doesn't thank him. You'd think she'd be glad of a roof over her head and a decent bed for the night.

'It's been a long day,' she finally says. 'I think I'd like a bit of a lie down.'

'Sure. Make yourself at home. I'll leave you to settle in. Can I get you anything to eat?'

'No.'

With a sigh of relief, Harvey withdraws from the room and pulls the door shut, glad of the space at last. They've spent most of the day together and he's had enough. He's already planning to open a bottle of wine while the chilli's heating in the oven.

He almost reaches the stairs when Freya calls after him. He stops and rolls his eyes.

'Harvey, are you still there?' she cries in the most pathetic voice.

'Yes, Freya. What is it?'

'Would you bring me a cup of tea? Milk, no sugar. I don't like it too strong.'

Harvey grinds his teeth. Who does she think he is, her bloody butler?

'Of course. No problem,' he calls back. 'Was there anything else?'

'No, that will be all. For now.'

Chapter 16

While Harvey waits for the kettle to boil, his mind wanders. It's been more than twenty-four hours since he faced the cameras, against his better judgement, and he thought he'd have heard something from those two detectives by now. Chalk and Enright were convinced it would throw up some significant leads, so why haven't they been in touch? When they were trying to persuade him to agree to the interview, they wouldn't leave him alone. Now, it's complete radio silence.

He makes Freya's tea in a mug, swirling the bag around in the boiling water until it's the colour of mahogany, and carries it upstairs to the guest room, resolving to chase Chalk in the morning. He deserves an update, even if there's nothing to report.

Harvey knocks at the door.

'Come.'

He grinds his back teeth, but there's no point letting Freya get to him. She's Gwyneth's mother and a guest in their house. He'll have to learn to make allowances for the way she speaks to him.

'I brought your tea,' he says, forcing a smile.

Freya's standing at the end of the bed, scowling at the duvet. It's all rucked up as if she's been rolling around on it. When she glances up and spots Harvey standing in the doorway with her tea, her face sours even further. 'A mug?' she sneers. 'I usually have tea in a cup with a saucer. Never mind. Put it down there.'

She points to the bedside table.

'Would you like me to put it in a cup for you?' Harvey asks through gritted teeth.

'It's too late now, but maybe you'll remember next time.'

'I'll do my best.'

'Now, about this room.' Freya presses her lips together so tightly her chin wrinkles like a walnut soaked in rum. 'I can't stay in here. The bed's awfully lumpy.'

'Oh?'

'I won't get a moment's sleep. And it's too hard. My back couldn't cope with it.'

Harvey bites his lip, stopping himself from pointing out that she'd been planning to spend the night in her car until he'd offered to take her in. Beggars can't be choosers and all that.

'You could try the room across the hall. It's smaller, I'm afraid, but maybe the bed's more to your liking?'

'No, no,' Freya says, shaking her head violently. 'It's east facing, so I'd get the sun in the morning and I'm such a light sleeper.'

Harvey shrugs, not sure what to suggest. He really doesn't want to go to the trouble of moving the beds around tonight.

'I think I'd be better off in your room, if you don't mind?'

'My room?'

'Yes, the bed looks much more suitable, and I noticed you have decent, thick curtains. I'm sure I'd sleep much better in there. Sorry, I know it's an inconvenience.'

An inconvenience? The woman's out of her mind, but what's he supposed to say?

'I suppose we could give it a go for a couple of nights,' he says wearily.

'Wonderful. Thank you, Harvey. That's good of you.'

She's out of the door like a shot, moving more briskly than she has all day.

'It's my pleasure,' he mutters with a heavy sigh of defeat.

'And can you bring my tea?'

Harvey's hands form tight fists. He takes a deep breath, counts to five and lets it out slowly. 'Of course,' he calls sweetly.

When he catches up with her, she's sitting on the end of his bed, bouncing up and down. 'Yes, this is going to be much better,' she says with a grin. 'It's such a lovely room, isn't it? So spacious and airy.' She glances at the ceiling and the gnarled exposed oak beams, twisted with age and riddled with a million tiny woodworm holes.

Harvey puts her mug on the cabinet on his side of the bed, bemused by how easily she evicted him from his own room.

'And one more thing. Would you mind bringing up my bag? I don't have a lot. I packed in a rush.'

'Right. Was there anything else while I'm going down again?'

'No, that will be all.'

Harvey storms out of the room, down the stairs and angrily snatches up her supermarket bag-for-life she dumped in the hall, a bundle of wool and a pair of knitting needles poking out of the top. Who knows what else she's brought with her. For someone who's supposedly packed light, it weighs a ton.

When he returns to the room, he's surprised to find Freya at the wardrobes, going through Gwyneth's clothes.

'What are you doing?' Harvey snaps, dropping her bag by the bed.

'I told you, I packed in a hurry and didn't bring many clothes. I thought I'd borrow some of Gwyneth's. I'm sure she wouldn't mind. She has some lovely things, and fortunately we're about the same size.'

She pulls out hanger after hanger of dresses, skirts, blouses and trousers, studying each for a second or two before tossing them in a heap on the bed.

Gwyneth has always dressed fashionably. Even when she was at her lowest ebb in the wake of Lionel's death, she took pride in her appearance. She's never let age dictate what she could or couldn't wear. She creates her own style and executes it with panache. The thought of a stranger, even if it is her own mother, going through Gwyneth's clothes like she's sifting through secondhand stock at a jumble sale, brings Harvey out in a cold sweat.

'I'm sure she wouldn't mind if you borrowed one or two things,' he says. 'But please, look after them.'

'I might try a few things on and then turn in. It's been such a long day.'

It certainly has.

'Are you not hungry?' Harvey asks. His mind's been on the chilli Sheryl left on the doorstep since he arrived home.

'A cup of tea will do me fine. Unless you have a couple of biscuits?' she asks hopefully.

'I'll see what I can find. Let me grab a few of my things first and make some room for you.'

Sulkily, Harvey plucks out a few clean shirts, a pair of trousers and some underwear from his closet, and marches with them into the guest room. He hangs the trousers and shirts on the back of the door and collapses on the edge of the bed with his head in his hands.

If he had any idea that Freya was going to be this difficult, he's not sure he'd have offered her a bed. But now she's here, he can't exactly kick her out. He's going to have to grin and bear it. After all, she dropped everything to be with her daughter the moment she heard she was seriously ill. She drove all the way from Newcastle without a moment's hesitation and was prepared to sleep in her car to be with her. Maybe he shouldn't be so churlish. It's not going to be forever.

'Harvey, are you there?' Freya's voice carrying through the house grates on his nerves like a rusty hinge squeaking in the wind. 'Any sign of those biscuits?'

Chapter 17

GWYNETH

I have it!

I know where I am. Finally. Or at least where I think I am.

It's been troubling me since I woke in this colourless world full of noise, muffled voices and people constantly moving around.

It was the smell that I recognised. Crisp and clinical. Harshly astringent. A chemical stench of disinfectant that made the back of my nose tingle.

I must be in hospital. It's the only thing that makes sense. All these people must be doctors and nurses, but why I'm here, I'm not entirely sure.

I wonder if it has anything to do with that car I keep seeing in my nightmares, accelerating towards me through the blinding brightness of a low-hanging sun. I think I may have been in some kind of accident.

I'm also hearing more clearly. The voices are less muffled. Or maybe I'm becoming more used to them. Occasionally, I can even pick out the odd word or two. One in particular I've heard a few times.

Coma.

What if they're talking about me and I'm not dead after all? What if I'm right and I am in hospital, trapped in a suspended state of unconsciousness?

What if I'm trapped in a coma?

I've seen films about people in comas, alive but totally unresponsive to the world around them, sometimes for weeks or months on end. A terrifying stupor in which they're left dangling somewhere between life and death.

Is that me?

'Gwyneth, can you hear me?'

The voice is so soft, so soothing, and yet it startles me, making my heart gallop.

'Mother?'

'My darling.'

A stone hardens in my throat and tears come to my eyes. Above me, a shadow looms. Someone leaning over me. Over my bed?

'Is it really you?'

She squeezes my hand. I can actually feel it! The warmth of her fingers, the pressure of her palm against mine. I try to squeeze back, but my muscles don't respond. It's as if the signal from my brain is being diverted long before it reaches my limbs.

I hope I'm not paralysed. That really would be a living hell.

'I'm here, my sweet. There's nothing to be afraid of.'

My eyes grow bleary and my body is wracked with sobs.

I try to snatch back my hand.

No, that can't be right!

What deception is my mind playing on me now? It has to be some kind of trick. Because as much as I want it to be my poor, beautiful mother, I know beyond doubt it cannot be her.

No matter how much I want it to be true, it's simply not possible.

Chapter 18

Harvey wakes refreshed but confused, until he remembers he's in the guest room and that Gwyneth's in a coma and her mother is staying under his roof and has kicked him out of his own bed.

The guest bed was surprisingly comfortable. He certainly didn't notice any lumps or bumps. He stretches, runs his tongue over his furry teeth and listens to the silence of the house. The birds singing outside. A bee at the window, banging against the glass. But nothing to indicate Freya is up and about. She's probably still asleep, exhausted after a long day. It was a mammoth twenty-four hours for her, travelling from the northeast and spending the day with her estranged daughter, reunited after so long and in such surreal circumstances.

After he showers in the family bathroom, dresses and heads down for breakfast, there's still no sign of Freya. Not that he minds. It's like having the house back to himself. He thought they'd travel into the hospital together this morning, but there's no point waking Freya when she could do with the rest.

Maybe when she's not so tired, she won't be so spiky with him.

Harvey leaves her a note, scribbled on the back of an old envelope he fishes out of the bin, and heads into Kingstown on his own. She has her car. She can join him later.

There's still no change in Gwyneth's condition. She's still lying in bed with her eyes closed, while the machines chirrup and hum around her. If anything, the bruising around her eyes looks worse today, the swelling more pronounced, a dark purple tinge giving way to a rainbow of blue, green and yellow.

'Anything overnight?' he asks Leanne.

She shakes her head. 'Nothing yet, I'm afraid.'

All he wants is the twitch of an eye. The flutter of a finger. A groan. Something to reassure him that his wife is still there inside her body.

He pulls up the chair and begins moisturising Gwyneth's hands, massaging her skin tenderly, a job he missed out on yesterday when Freya arrived and took over. Her fingers are limp. Her skin dry. It's like touching a model of his wife. A facsimile that's perfect in every way, but not her.

'Don't forget to talk to her,' Leanne reminds him. 'Let her know you're here.'

It's the one thing he's struggled with. There's something inherently weird about talking to Gwyneth while she's lying on a hospital bed, totally catatonic. The sterile surroundings don't help, nor the constant comings and goings of doctors and nurses. He feels self-conscious and a little stupid, even though he knows it's something positive he can do that might pull her out of the coma.

'Your mother totally took over yesterday,' he says, with half an eye on Leanne, who nods her encouragement. 'But I suppose I shouldn't blame her. She's not seen you for so long.'

Harvey stares into Gwyneth's face, watching for the slightest tick that might signal she can hear him. A microscopic muscle spasm. Anything.

'She told me she was actually planning on sleeping in her car last night.' He laughs and runs a hand over his face. 'I know you wouldn't have wanted that, so I told her she was welcome to stay at ours. I put her in one of the guest rooms, but apparently the bed's too lumpy, so I had to give up our room for her, can you believe?'

Gwyneth's expression remains blank. Vacant. Harvey sighs. How long is this going to go on for? Days? Weeks? Months? He's not sure he can stand it, especially if he has Freya to contend with on top of it all.

'She's certainly a forthright woman, isn't she? Not afraid to speak her mind to get what she wants.' He chuckles to himself. It seems funny now, thinking back to how she was last night and how she talked him into giving up his bed. He shouldn't let her brusque manner get to him so much.

'And of course I was in trouble because I made her tea in a mug instead of a cup.'

115

Leanne shoots him a look of surprise. He rolls his eyes.

'I know, you couldn't make it up,' he says. 'Anyway, she was impressed with the house, I think. You should have seen the look on her face when I gave her a tour.'

Gwyneth looks so pale and washed out, her hair all messy under the bandages around her head, blonde strands sticking up at strange angles. Ever since he's known her, she's worn it in a sophisticated bob, like those women in the 1920s with their scandalously short skirts, cutting loose in the jazz clubs of the world, smoking cigarettes and sipping gin cocktails. She's always been refreshingly stylish, a woman who could still turn heads even though she's approaching her mid-fifties. It's why, he supposes, it's such a shock to see her like this.

Eventually, Harvey runs out of things to say. He's never been an easy conversationalist like Gwyneth, who can talk to anyone for hours on end, even if they've only just met. He pushes back the chair and pulls out his phone, finding a game of solitaire to while away the hours.

Later that afternoon, he's dozing in the chair, his phone in his lap, when he hears the hiss of the door opening. His eyes spring wide open.

'Gwyneth?' he gasps, confused.

It looks like her and yet he instinctively knows it's not. It can't be, and besides, the woman striding into the room is less polished, her walk more of a loping

116

amble than the way Gwyneth floats effortlessly. And yet she has the same icy white-blonde hair and is wearing Gwyneth's clothes.

'Hello, Harvey,' she says with a crooked smile.

'Freya? What on earth have you done to your hair?'

Chapter 19

Freya puts her hand to her head. 'This?' she says, running her fingers through her tangled blonde mop. 'Do you like it? I fancied a change.'

Last night, her hair was jet black, streaked with grey. Now it looks almost identical to Gwyneth's. It's weird.

And it's not just the hair. She's dressed from head to toe in Gwyneth's clothes. A loose-fitting white blouse with cream trousers and a royal blue chunky-knit cardigan draped over her shoulders. To top it all, she's wearing Gwyneth's vintage white metal faux diamond necklace.

'Wow, you look different,' Leanne says with an annoying hint of admiration. 'Love what you've done with your hair. You two could pass as sisters.'

Freya flushes with embarrassment. 'You think so? Well, Harvey said I could borrow some of Gwyneth's clothes.'

Borrow some of her clothes, not dye her hair and dress like they're identical twins. The woman's lost the plot. Harvey's so shocked, he's lost for words.

Maybe she's having some kind of breakdown.

'Sorry I'm late in. I couldn't wake up. Must have been all the travelling,' she says, shooing Harvey out of the armchair and drawing it closer to Gwyneth's bed. 'You should have woken me.'

She swings Gwyneth's blue and white canvas bag off her shoulder and dumps it at her feet, the tatty bag-for-life gone for now.

'I figured you needed the sleep,' Harvey says, unable to take his eyes off his mother-in-law. He has no idea where she found hair dye. It's certainly not Gwyneth's. Her hair colour is totally natural.

'I guess. Although it was a bit hot in your room.'

'I'm sorry to hear that,' Harvey grumbles.

'Anyway, I'm here now, so you can take off, if you like?' Freya puts Gwyneth's hand to her cheek. A gesture of intimate tenderness that irks Harvey far more than it should.

'I'm fine,' he protests.

'Don't be silly. You've been here all morning. You must be bored out of your mind. I can take over. Get some rest.'

Here we go again. Harvey's being pushed away when his place is here at his wife's side.

'Really, I'm happy to stay. I was just about to do her eyes.'

'I'll do it. Go,' she orders.

What's the point in arguing? He is bored and there's no point staying to squabble with Freya. Perhaps it would be better if they staggered their visits anyway, so they see less of each other and break up the monotony of sitting with Gwyneth.

'Okay, fine. But I'll be back early evening and we can swap over.'

'Yes, yes, whatever,' Freya says dismissively, as if she can't wait to get rid of him.

There's no point hanging around the hospital, so Harvey drives home. There are plenty of jobs he could get on with around the house.

But when he arrives thirty minutes later, he's confronted by another surprise from Freya.

Harvey takes great pride in keeping their lawn in pristine condition, but at the top of the drive, it's been churned up into a muddy mess where someone has clearly driven over it as they've turned their car around.

Freya. Who else would be so careless?

Angrily, Harvey inspects the damage. Does the woman have no respect? There's plenty of room on the drive to turn around, so why has she cut across the grass? His blood boils.

But it gets worse when he steps inside.

The kitchen looks as though a small bomb has gone off. There are dirty dishes strewn across the counter and dumped in the sink. There's even a plate and a dirty mug left on the kitchen table, along with a carton of milk and a tub of butter spread, while the worktops are coated in crumbs.

Furious, Harvey throws the dishes into the dishwasher, puts the milk and butter back in the fridge and wipes down all the surfaces.

When he's done, he marches upstairs to check his bedroom, the room he graciously gave up for Freya last night out of a misguided sense of doing the right thing.

With a feeling of dread, he pushes open the door and is hit by an overpowering cloud of perfume. Gwyneth's perfume. As if Freya has been spraying it liberally around the room.

The bed hasn't been made, the duvet left coiled in a crumpled pile on top of the rucked-up sheet, and piles of Gwyneth's clothes are lying all over the floor. Blouses and dresses, skirts and cardigans, mindlessly abandoned as if a whirlwind has blown through the house and stripped everything out of the wardrobes.

It's unbelievably thoughtless, and frankly, insulting. Harvey's thrown open his house to Freya, and this is how she treats his hospitality? It's an absolute outrage.

He finds worse still in the en suite, where he follows the sound of running water. A bath tap has been left on, flowing idly, and damp towels are scattered across the floor, soaking up soapy pools of water. The basin and mirror above it are splattered with toothpaste and the cold tap is dripping.

Harvey surveys the mess and shakes his head in despair. It's unforgivable. You wouldn't leave a slum in this state. If he'd had any idea this was the way she'd treat their house, there's no way he'd have invited her to stay. But now she's here, what's he supposed to do? He doesn't want to risk falling out with her when they've only just met, but this can't go on. It'll drive him mad.

He thinks about clearing up the mess while Freya's out, but stops himself. She's the one who has to live with it and what's to say she won't do it again tomorrow, anyway? He withdraws from the bathroom, pulling the door closed behind him.

Maybe he's brought it on himself. After all, he told her to treat the house as if it were her own. It's going to be a long, trying few days at this rate. Or weeks. Months even.

With a sigh of resignation, Harvey heads back downstairs on weary legs, remembering there's a bottle of Australian Shiraz open in the kitchen. It's still early, but maybe one glass will help to take off the edge.

Chapter 20

When he's finished the bottle of wine, Harvey feels considerably better, before remembering he'd promised to return to the hospital later to take over from Freya. But he can't drive now. He's had far too much to drink, although it's not as if Gwyneth's going to notice if he's there or not. They say she's aware of everything going on around her, but he's not convinced.

The alcohol has also had a calming effect on his nerves and he's concluded that it would definitely do more harm than good to say anything to Freya about the mess he found when he returned home. With Gwyneth seriously ill, they both have more important things to worry about than a little mess around the house. It was thoughtless of Freya not to clear up after herself, but he's sure there was nothing malicious about it.

His more pressing concern is what he's going to eat. He devoured the chilli Sheryl brought yesterday and now the fridge is empty and there's not much in the cupboards. Not that he'd know what to do with it. Catering has always been Gwyneth's domain. She's cooked for him every night they've been married, as well as looking after the shopping, although it comes delivered now by a man in a van straight from the supermarket.

Harvey's never needed to learn to cook because he's never had to. He's always had someone to do it for him. After his mother, it was various girlfriends. Then his first wife, Debbie, who was a master in the kitchen. And now Gwyneth. For the short periods he's been on his own, he's lived on takeaways and beans on toast.

He could pop to the pub and see if they have a free table, but since they remodelled it into a trendy gastropub, you have to reserve weeks in advance, especially at weekends. The other alternative is to pick up fish and chips from the village, but that's not really an option as he's been drinking and is well over the limit to drive.

Then he remembers the new Indian restaurant that opened a few months ago and makes home deliveries. He's sure a menu came through the post recently.

He's digging through the kitchen drawers trying to find it, when there's an unexpected knock at the door. Irritated at the interruption, he stomps into the hall, but is thrilled to discover Sheryl on the doorstep with the answer to his prayers.

'You do like shepherd's pie, don't you?' she says with a sheepish grin, holding up another dish wrapped in foil.

'You're a lifesaver. Come in.'

'And a little something to cheer you up.' In her other hand, she has a small, label-less half-bottle of opaque cherry red liquid. 'Homemade sloe gin. Highly prized. Gifted to only my favourite people,' she announces.

'Sheryl, you shouldn't have.' Harvey takes the bottle and holds it up to the light.

'I know, but I wanted to cheer you up. It must be awful for you. It's the least I can do while you're on your own. How's Gwyneth?'

'The same. No better. No worse. Are you on your way out?'

'What? No, I was just passing,' she says. 'Why?'

'Oh, you look like you're dressed up, that's all.'

She laughs nervously. 'This?' She steps back and looks down at the ankle-length, sleeveless summer dress, which is pinched in at the waist, showing off her athletic figure. 'It's nothing.'

Harvey notes she's also wearing full make-up. Letterbox-red lipstick and dusky eyes. He wonders if she's secretly seeing someone. She'd be a great catch for someone, especially with that stunning cottage and all the land she owns.

'I was about to open a bottle of wine, if you fancy a glass?'

'Go on, then. Just the one.'

While Harvey uncorks an expensive bottle of Bordeaux he'd been saving, Sheryl switches on the oven to heat the pie.

They sit at the kitchen table and Harvey passes Sheryl a large glass of wine. She takes a ladylike sip and purses her lips in appreciation.

'You probably haven't heard the big news,' Harvey says.

'Don't tell me the police have actually caught the driver who hit Gwyneth?'

Harvey snorts with derision. 'No, at least not that they've told me. It's crazier than that. Gwyneth's estranged mother has turned up out of the blue.'

Sheryl's eyes widen. 'I didn't know they were estranged. I assumed she was dead.'

'Apparently, she's been looking for Gwyneth for years. When she saw the news, she drove straight to the hospital from Newcastle,' Harvey says.

'Bloody hell, that's a long way to come.'

'It was a bit of a surprise, to be honest. But not as much as suddenly finding out I had a house guest.'

'She's staying with you?' Sheryl whispers, placing her glass on the table with a look of mild alarm, and glancing towards the door as if Freya might come ambling in at any moment.

'She's not here right now. But what else could I do? She was threatening to sleep in her car. Anyway, the weirdest thing is that she turned up at the hospital this morning with her hair dyed blonde, like Gwyneth's, and wearing Gwyneth's clothes. They look like twins, apart from the age difference.'

Sheryl's mouth falls open in surprise. 'You're kidding?'

'Oh, and I've had to give up my bed for her because apparently the guest bed is "too lumpy".' He draws inverted commas in the air with his fingers.

Sheryl laughs. 'I would have told her where she could shove it, mother-in-law or not.'

'You're probably right. I left her at the hospital with Gwyneth this afternoon, but when I came home, you should have seen the state of the place. She'd left dirty dishes everywhere. Wet towels all over the floor. She'd even left the bath tap running.'

'What are you going to do?'

Harvey sighs and takes another large mouthful of wine. 'I can hardly throw her out onto the street, can I? And it's not as if it's going to be forever.'

Sheryl raises a perfectly shaped eyebrow. 'You hope.'

'Bloody hell, don't say that.'

Sheryl chuckles. 'Now she has her feet under the table, she might never leave.'

'Kill me now!'

'Couldn't you have offered to put her up in a hotel or an Airbnb for a few nights?'

'It's a bit late now.'

Sheryl shrugs. 'Rather you than me.'

The timer on the oven pings and Sheryl finishes her wine.

'Another?' Harvey asks, holding up the bottle.

'I'd better not. I need to get back. I'll let you eat in peace. The pie should be warmed through by now. I'll let myself out.'

127

Harvey pushes his chair back and stumbles drunkenly as he catches his balance. 'Thanks again for the food and the gin.' He nods at the bottle on the side. 'I'll enjoy a glass of that tonight.'

'Look after yourself, Harvey.' She shoots him a thin smile. 'I'll pop in again in a few days.'

'You could always visit Gwyneth in hospital. It would be good for her to hear another voice she recognises.'

Sheryl tugs at her ear, her gaze drifting around the room. 'I don't know. I'm not great with hospitals.'

'Just for half an hour?'

'Maybe. I'll see,' she says.

'I'd really appreciate it.'

'I have to go.' And then she's gone, fleeing from the house like it's on fire.

Surely the prospect of visiting his comatose wife in hospital isn't that appalling? Nobody likes hospitals. They're full of sick people. But it would be so good for Gwyneth to have some different visitors. Some friends as well as family. Although he can't force Sheryl to do something she doesn't want to do.

The shepherd's pie tastes as good as it smelt, and Harvey tucks in with relish.

It's strange being in the house without Gwyneth. They've hardly spent a day apart since they were married and have always sat down to eat together.

It took a while to feel comfortable when he first moved in, but over time the house began to feel like home, even though he's surrounded by memories of Lionel, who had the old barn renovated to his specifications and decorated to his taste. There's even a photo of him, looking young and dashing, taken when he was in his late twenties, in a frame on the sideboard in the dining room. Watching what's going on, a slight sneer of disapproval on his face. Like most of Lionel's things, Harvey hates it.

There's no doubting Harvey is a cuckoo in the nest. An interloper who's breezed into Gwyneth's life, filled Lionel's still-warm brogues and shamelessly lies in his bed. He's tried to persuade Gwyneth to sell up and move. Start again somewhere new where he doesn't feel Lionel's warm breath on his neck in every room, but she won't countenance it. In fact, when he first mooted the idea, she laughed. Thought it was a joke. She's never going to leave.

And so, Harvey's had to make adjustments, come to terms with living in another man's shadow, and constantly reminding himself that the house is nothing more than bricks and mortar, timber and steel. A material structure of no significance other than providing warmth and shelter. Although, there aren't many days when he isn't reminded that Lionel's ghost still walks with them.

Harvey has his fork halfway to his mouth, dripping potato and gravy onto his plate, when the front door crashes open, heralding Freya's return. He winces and closes his eyes briefly, willing himself to remain calm. His heart skips. His throat tightens.

She appears in the kitchen doorway in Gwyneth's clothes, creased and misshapen, hanging off her scrawny old bones, her newly dyed hair looking as if a flock of birds has been nesting in it.

'I thought you were coming back to the hospital to take over?' she snaps.

'A friend popped around and we opened a bottle of wine. Sorry.' He tops up his glass, sensing he's going to need it. 'Would you like some?'

'What are you eating?' Her eyes, comically enlarged behind her glasses, narrow as she stares at his plate.

'Shepherd's pie. There's plenty left if you'd like some.'

'Where did it come from?' Freya asks suspiciously.

'Sheryl brought it around. She's worried I'm not eating properly.'

'That woman from down the road?'

Harvey straightens and pulls his shoulders back. 'Yes. Do you have a problem with that?'

'I have a problem with you inviting strange women into the house while your wife is fighting for her life in hospital,' Freya hisses.

'She's not a strange woman and Gwyneth's not fighting for her life. She's in a coma. She just needs time.'

'Oh, you're a doctor now, are you?'

Harvey sighs. He doesn't need this right now.

'I'm just saying.'

Freya stomps across the room, snatches a plate from the cupboard, and a fork from the drawer. Then, to Harvey's horror, she grabs his plate and scrapes half of what's left onto her own.

'Good, is it?' she asks.

'Yes, it is, actually. If you want some, there's plenty left in the oven keeping warm.'

Freya stands at Harvey's side and scoops up a minuscule amount of food onto the end of her fork and puts it to her lips. Harvey sits back with his wine, amused at the ridiculous performance. He could almost predict what's going to happen next.

'Urgh,' Freya says, screwing up her eyes and pulling a face of disgust. 'That's horrible.'

It's so childish. Absolutely pathetic.

Freya spits a chunk of minced beef onto her plate, a long string of drool trailing from her lips.

'All the more for me then,' Harvey says, slurping more wine.

Freya marches with her plate to the bin and scrapes it off with a flourish. Then, she opens the oven, pulls out the dish and pours that into the bin with it.

'Don't want to be giving yourself an upset stomach,' she says. 'It was rank.'

Harvey slams his fist on the table, making his plate and cutlery jump. 'Freya! You had no right.'

She dumps the dish on the side. She doesn't even put it in the dishwasher.

'And what's this?' she asks, picking up the bottle of sloe gin.

'Put it down!' Harvey demands.

Freya pops open the stopper with her thumb and puts the bottle to her nose, sniffing suspiciously.

Harvey pulls himself out of his chair and charges angrily towards her, snatching the bottle from her hand.

'What is it?' she repeats.

'Sloe gin. Sheryl made it,' he huffs, securing the stopper.

'She's always bringing gifts, isn't she? Don't you think that's odd?'

'She wanted to cheer me up, that's all,' Harvey says, although he doesn't know why he feels the need to justify himself.

Freya tuts. 'Yes, I bet she does.'

'There's nothing untoward going on,' he growls. 'I love Gwyneth and I'd never do anything to hurt her.'

Freya's eyebrows shoot up. 'Well, I'm watching you, Harvey. I'm not having you running rings around my daughter while she's ill. Take the day off tomorrow. Don't bother going to the hospital. I'll take care of everything, like I've had to do for most of today.'

Harvey's blood burns like acid. 'Thank you very much, but Gwyneth is my wife and I'll take care of her. Why don't *you* take the day off?'

'I've come all this way. I'm not deserting her now. Think about what I said, Harvey. I'm going to bed.

Hopefully, you'll have sobered up and calmed down by the morning.'

Chapter 21

Harvey wakes abruptly with his heart pounding so hard in his chest, he can feel it against his ribs. His eyes spring open, but it's so dark he can't see a thing. He rolls over, checks the clock on the bedside cabinet and groans when he sees it's still the early hours of the morning. But something's woken him and now adrenaline is racing around his body like a shot of pure caffeine. He's sure it wasn't a nightmare. So what was it?

He sits up on his elbows and listens.

There are voices talking. A deep, incoherent rumble, followed by a slightly higher-pitched murmur. Indistinct and indecipherable. It sounds like people in the house. His heart thumps even louder.

He throws off the covers, trembling, and flicks on the bedside light. It's too bright. It hurts his eyes, and he has to squint for a few moments until his pupils become accustomed to it.

Burglars? The house is a veritable gold mine with all the antiques on display. It's why they have all the security alarms and cameras.

Unless he forgot to set them last night. He flushes with a panicked heat. Did he remember after his run-in with Freya? His temper was so frayed, his patience so tested that he can't remember, especially after drinking the best part of a bottle of wine over the course of the evening.

Oh, god, what does he do? Call the police? But what if it's nothing?

The timbre of voices changes. A different man speaking now. Deeper and more resonant, giving a long monologue. But to who? It's odd. It's not the anxious, hushed voices he'd expect to hear from burglars, unless of course they think the house is empty.

Harvey tiptoes to the door. Reaches for the handle. Pulls it open with a wince, praying the hinges won't squeak or the floorboards creak.

The voices become louder. Booming. Too loud to be people in the house. It sounds as if they're being amplified through a speaker.

Confused, he sneaks past the master bedroom. The door's shut and there's no sign that Freya's awake. No lights on. No sound or movement. She must be sleeping through it all.

At the top of the stairs, he hesitates, cocks his ear and relaxes, certain now it's not intruders and that the voices are coming either from the TV or the radio. But it's still odd. Why would either be on in the middle of the night and so loud it echoes through the house, reverberating through the floorboards?

Harvey descends the stairs and follows the sound towards the lounge. Flickering light plays under the door, music now in place of the voices. He eases open the door and stares in surprise at the TV, which is on and the volume ear-achingly loud.

The remote's on the table in front of the long sofa by the fire. He snatches it up and clicks the television off, the silence instantly deafening as the room falls into semi-darkness, lit only by a lamp in the corner.

Harvey hadn't been in the lounge last night, so it wasn't him. And anyway, when he went to bed, he checked all the lights were off, just as he does every night, worried about electrical fires starting in the old, oak-framed building.

The only explanation is that Freya must have gone into the lounge later in the evening after he'd gone to bed, a suspicion confirmed when he spots a whisky bottle on the floor next to a glass stained with a telltale amber residue. It's not just any whisky either. It's his favourite. The bottle Gwyneth bought him for Christmas. And now it's half-empty. Clearly, Freya has no idea how much it costs, knocking it back like it's cheap vodka rather than an expensive, limited edition Scottish single malt.

Furious, he snatches up the bottle and glass. He wouldn't have put it past Freya to have deliberately left the TV on loud to wake him, so he would come to investigate and find the whisky. To see what she's done. To score petty points.

He should never have invited her to stay, but he's too trusting. Too willing to help others. It's no wonder he became a therapist. Unfortunately, his innate desire to help people has backfired spectacularly this time. She's going to have to go, but how's he going to get rid of her? As Sheryl said, now she has her feet under the table, she might never leave. Harvey shudders.

On the chair next to the sofa, there's more evidence that Freya has spent the evening in the lounge. She's left behind a ball of wool with two knitting needles. He thinks it's the same ball of wool and needles he saw poking out of the top of her bag earlier. There's also the beginnings of what looks like a woollen sweater she's been knitting.

He picks it up and examines it at arm's length. It's tiny. Barely a foot across the shoulders. A child's garment? But who's she knitting it for? She's not mentioned any children in the family, and as Gwyneth is her only child, there can't be any grandchildren. It's a mystery, unless there's another side of the family Harvey's not aware of, which would be great news. It would be an incentive for Freya to leave.

He carefully lays the jumper back down under the ball of wool and needles, exactly where he found it, and storms out of the room with the whisky bottle and glass.

He puts the whisky back with the other bottles of spirits in the utility room, behind the bottle of sloe gin Sheryl brought around earlier, and drops the glass in the dishwasher. If she'd asked, of course he'd have let her have a glass of whisky. It's the fact she helped herself and the presumption she can take what she wants that annoys him.

Wide awake now, he knows he'll never get back to sleep, so he heads to the freezer and finds a tub of toffee caramel ice cream. He scoops out three large spoonfuls into a bowl and sits at the kitchen table, eating it while contemplating what to do about Freya.

He's tried to do the right thing, inviting her into his home, but he didn't know she'd take such liberties. She's rude and obnoxious. Disrespectful. Ungrateful. Entitled. And the worst of it is that he's been so careful to make her feel welcome. Yet this is how she repays his generosity?

Sheryl's words of warning keep echoing around his head.

Now she has her feet under the table, she might never leave.

What if Sheryl's right and she decides life's too cosy here? How's he ever going to get rid of her?

The only solution is to lance the boil. He needs to tackle it head on and tell Freya straight that she's outstayed her welcome. It's not going to be an easy conversation, but it's one that needs to be had. He can't go on like this.

He'll do it first thing in the morning. Make it clear that she has to go. And if it comes to it, he'll even offer to pay for a hotel for her, like Sheryl suggested.

One thing's clear though. There's no way he's going to allow her to stay in the house another day longer. It's time for Freya to pack her solitary bag and leave.

Chapter 22

Harvey lies in bed staring at the ceiling. The sun is up, the birds are singing in the garden, an aircraft drones high overhead and a woodpecker attacks a tree with a staccato machine-gun-like chatter. But inside the house, it's quiet and still.

When he went back to bed at around four in the morning, his mind was made up. He was going to tell Freya things weren't working out, and that she had to leave. He was going to look up some inexpensive B&Bs near the hospital, and if necessary, offer to pay for her accommodation. Anything to get her out of the house.

But now, with his head thick with sleep and a dull ache behind his eyes, he's having second thoughts. It's one thing to decide in the middle of the night that he wants her gone. It's an entirely different matter to tell her to her face that she has to go. That he's throwing her out when they clearly have plenty of room in the house.

It all seemed so straightforward last night, but what's he going to say? She has to go because she helped herself to his best whisky? That just sounds petty. Even complaining that she's left the house in a mess and churned up his lawn sounds churlish.

Can he really justify kicking an old woman out onto the street? What if something happened to her? What if she was attacked or raped? He'd never forgive himself.

Harvey groans and runs a hand over his face. The clock on the bedside table blinks that it's gone ten. He can't believe he's slept so late. He should be at the hospital with Gwyneth by now. Freya's probably there already. He can almost guarantee she was up early this morning to beat him in.

That's another thing. What was Freya thinking, telling him he isn't needed to help with Gwyneth's care? She's been treating him like he's an irritation who's always in the way ever since she turned up. But he's Gwyneth's husband. He should be there at her side, in sickness and in health. She'd do well to remember that.

On his way downstairs to see if he can rustle up some breakfast, he stops outside Freya's room. *His* room. The door's ajar, but there's no sound coming from inside.

'Freya? Are you in there? Can I come in?'

He pushes the door open, anticipating a scene of carnage. Clothes all over the floor. Dirty dishes piled up on the carpet. Wet towels hanging off the four-poster. But he's surprised to find the room clean and tidy.

All of Gwyneth's clothes appear to be back in the wardrobe, the bed's been made, and the window left open a crack, flooding the room with fresh air. Harvey blinks in surprise. Maybe he's been too quick to judge.

His eye catches Freya's old bag-for-life shoved under the bed, and he's drawn to it like a bee attracted to nectar. He still knows almost nothing about her and is curious. Where's she been all these years? How and why did she lose contact with her only daughter? Maybe some answers are to be found in her bag.

He hooks it out, slides it across the carpet, and drops to his knees to peer inside.

He finds a smelly, rolled-up towel. A moth-eaten cardigan screwed up and shoved down the side. A freaky looking plastic doll with one eye missing and her blonde hair pulled out in patches. And an old wooden box inlaid with pearl. When he opens it, a ballerina springs up and pirouettes to a strangulated tune that plays too slowly. It's creepy as hell. Harvey shuts the box and pushes it to one side.

There's a pair of rusty scissors with oddly notched blades and a hairbrush matted with black hair. And at the bottom of the bag, he finds an opaque plastic box with a lid fastened shut with four hinges. He peers at it, curious. It's not heavy, but it rattles. There's something inside.

He flicks open the hinges, removes the top, and recoils in horror. Inside are at least half a dozen flattened, desiccated frogs and toads of various sizes, all blackened, almost as if they've been burnt.

He snaps the lid back on and throws the box back into the bag with the rest of Freya's belongings, unsettled. It's weird.

He shoves the bag back under the bed and leaves the room, with the door ajar like he found it. He doesn't want Freya to find out he's been snooping.

Still disturbed from what he's just seen, he makes his way slowly down the stairs, his appetite suppressed for a change. He was going to see if he could find some bacon and eggs, but he's gone off the idea. He might just have toast and butter and grab a coffee from the canteen at the hospital later.

But as he reaches the hall, he stops dead in his tracks. Something's not right. Something is out of place, but he can't immediately put his finger on what. He looks around, taking it all in slowly. By the front door, the George III clock is still ticking. On the credenza at the bottom of the stairs, Gwyneth's awful portrait that Freya was admiring has been knocked and stands slightly askew. But that's not it.

Harvey's eyes roam over the shelves and the paintings, the various tarnished shields, pikes and blunted swords, rusted hoes, picks and shovels hanging from the walls, and the suit of armour suspended over the basement door.

And then he sees it. A gap between an ivory figure of a Venus with Cupid and a decorative plate on a stand.

Something is missing on the shelf between them, but he can't recall what. He narrows his eyes and casts his mind back.

It's that hideous double-handed vase. He picked it up once, curious, and Gwyneth snatched it out of his hands, horrified. She told him it was a double gourde, popular in China as a symbol of the unity between heaven and earth, and that it could fetch as much as four thousand pounds at auction. He was shocked.

Now it's gone and Harvey has a pretty good idea who's taken it. He shakes his head sadly and lets out a long sigh. Just another thing he needs to talk to Freya about when he sees her next.

In the kitchen, he drops two stale pieces of bread in the toaster and thinks of roundabout ways he could persuade Freya to leave without ordering her to go.

What if he told her they had building work scheduled, and the house was going to be uninhabitable for a few weeks? Or that he's discovered toxic mould growing in the attic? An infestation of rats? Cockroaches? That the sewers are backing up?

The piercing scream of a smoke alarm snaps him back to the moment. Thick, black smoke is pouring out of the toaster. He pops it up, coughing, and unplugs the machine before running around with a tea towel, waving it wildly to chase away the smoke. He throws open a window and eventually the alarm stops.

It's too late to save his toast. It's burnt to a crisp. Totally cremated. He carries the two charred slices to the bin, flips open the lid and drops them in. He's about to walk away when a glimpse of porcelain at the bottom of the bin liner catches his eye. A familiar shape and colour.

He reaches in and pulls the shard out, followed by another six pieces, the ragged remains of Gwyneth's double gourde. Four thousand pounds worth of antique destroyed. He lays the fragments on the counter and tries to piece them together like building a three-dimensional jigsaw, wondering if it's even worth gluing them back together. But there are splinters and small shards missing, presumably lost when the vase was dropped.

In a fit of frustration and anger, he throws the pieces back in the bin and slams the lid shut.

Freya's done this. Either deliberately or accidentally.

It doesn't really matter. She's not even had the courtesy to leave a note.

Four thousand pounds lost in a split second.

That's it, she has to go. As far as he's concerned, she can find herself a hotel or sleep in her car. He doesn't care. He just wants her gone. She's weird, she's disruptive and now she's costing them money.

Harvey snatches up his keys, pulls on a pair of shoes, and storms out of the house with a renewed determination. He's going to the hospital, and he's going to confront Freya.

He's going to tell her time's up. She can't stay any longer. She has to go.

And this time, he means it.

Chapter 23

During the thirty-minute drive to the hospital and what has become the daily battle to find a parking space, Harvey works himself into a fizzing ball of rage. He's beginning to wonder if Freya has played him from the start, knowing full well he'd never allow her to sleep in her car. She could probably afford a hotel, or at least a B&B, for a few nights - she certainly managed to afford the fuel to travel from Newcastle - but she's manipulated him into letting her stay under his roof by playing on his good nature.

He stomps through the hospital lobby, pushing his way irascibly through a sea of visitors, patients in wheelchairs and fraught-looking medical staff, and straight to the intensive care unit on the third floor, stopping only briefly to take a breath when he reaches Gwyneth's room.

He's practised a speech in his head on the way over and he wants to get his words straight. He doesn't want Freya twisting what he has to say and weakening his resolve.

He peers through the glass. Freya is sitting in the armchair in her usual position by the bed, while Gwyneth lies as motionless as a pebble on a beach. Freya's chatting to her, her words tumbling from her mouth casually, delivering a one-sided monologue about who knows what. She's probably dripping poison about Harvey into Gwyneth's ear, telling her what a terrible husband he is. How Sheryl's been popping around with food and gifts while Gwyneth's back has been turned, making it sound like something it's not.

While she talks, Freya's hands work frantically at a pair of knitting needles, the sweater she'd left in the lounge last night slowly taking shape in her lap. It all looks so cosy. So comfortable.

'Harvey, you finally made it,' she says, glancing up with a smile as he barges in. She glances at her watch. 'I thought you'd be here before now.'

'I need a word.'

'Oh?' Her smile slips and a veil of concern falls across her face.

'Outside, please.'

'If you have something to say, you can say it to me here. We shouldn't keep secrets from Gwyneth, should we?'

Harvey would rather not have this conversation in front of his wife, especially when he's about to call her mother out for her appalling behaviour. He certainly doesn't want to cause her any stress that might undermine her recovery.

'I'd prefer to speak outside,' he says coolly, determined not to let Freya call the shots.

But she doesn't make any attempt to move. She remains seated while she knits, the tic-tac, tic-tac of her needles causing a prickle of irritation across Harvey's skin.

Fine. Maybe it's not a bad idea if Gwyneth hears what he has to say.

'It's not working out,' he says, folding his arms.

The trace of a smile plays across Freya's lips, like she's taunting him.

'And I don't think it's a good idea for you to stay at the house any longer.' There, at last, he's said it. It's out.

Finally, Freya's hands stop moving, her needles poised in the air.

'Oh, Harvey. Is this about the vase? It is, isn't it? I'm so, so sorry.' Her face crumples. 'I was going to tell you tonight and apologise. I feel awful. I don't know what to say. It just slipped out of my hands. I didn't mean to drop it. Was it worth a lot of money? You must let me replace it.'

The unexpected apology and her contrite tone knock him momentarily off his stride. He never expected her to own up to the breakage, let alone offer to pay to replace it. As if she could afford it.

'It was an antique,' Harvey mumbles.

'It was such a beautiful vase, I only wanted to take a closer look, but I'm a total butterfingers.' She puts her knitting down, reaches into the stripy canvas bag she's borrowed from Gwyneth, and retrieves a worn fabric wallet. Flipping it open, she pulls out a crumpled ten-pound note and holds it out at arm's length. 'Here, take this,' she says, waving it at him. 'Will that cover it?'

Harvey stares at the dog-eared note in disbelief. Ten pounds? Is that what she really thinks it was worth? He's lost for words.

'I'm afraid it's all I can afford at the moment,' she adds, staring up at him pitifully from behind her thick glasses.

'It's not about the money,' Harvey sighs, although that's only partly true. It's four thousand pounds, maybe more, gone in a slip of her fingers. She shouldn't have touched it. 'It's the fact you put it in the bin and hoped I wouldn't notice.'

'I would have told you, but you were having a lie-in and I didn't want to wake you.'

'I've made my mind up. I want you to move out.'

'But I've said I'm sorry and I'll replace your silly vase. And anyway, it was your idea. You insisted I stayed with you and now you're throwing me out? What would Gwyneth say about that?'

'Maybe when Gwyneth's better and we have her home again, you can stay for a few nights. How about that?'

Freya glances down at her hands, her knitting slowly sinking into her lap. A solitary tear runs down her cheek and settles on the end of her chin. 'I've upset you, haven't I?'

'I could help you find a guest house or a cheap hotel that's closer to the hospital,' Harvey suggests.

'But I can't afford it,' she cries, like a kitten with an injured paw.

'We'll pay. You don't have to worry about the money, and you'll be closer to Gwyneth. You can pop in and see her whenever you like without having to worry about the drive from the village.'

'I don't mind the drive. And I enjoy living at the house with you, getting to know you better.'

'Don't you think you'd be more comfortable in a hotel?' he says.

'Not really.'

'You'll have your own space.' He's trying to be positive about it, so why does he sound so unreasonable?

'Is it because I asked you to give up your room?' she sniffs, her voice thick with emotion.

'No, of course not.'

'It's just that I couldn't have slept in that bed.'

'It's not that.'

'What then? You can't stand the sight of me? Is that it?'

'Freya, you're being silly. I just thought we'd both be happier with a bit of space, where we're not always under each other's feet.'

'Don't you think you're overreacting? No one died.'

'It isn't about the vase,' Harvey growls. 'It's... everything.'

151

Freya shakes her head, her newly bleached, frizzy blonde hair rocking from side to side. 'Everything?'

Does she really want him to spell it out for her and explain that the reason he wants her gone is that he finds her weird and more than a bit creepy, especially since she dyed her hair blonde and started wearing Gwyneth's clothes, and he discovered what she was keeping in her bag under the bed? That the way she's taken over Gwyneth's care in the hospital is unbearable? That the sound of her voice makes him want to pull out his own teeth? That he hates the way she treats their house like it's a hovel? That she's rude, abrasive and manipulative?

Why can't she take a hint and leave?

'Take last night, for example,' Harvey says.

Freya raises a quizzical eyebrow, her glasses slipping down her nose.

'You left the television on so loud, it woke me up,' he says, but as the words trip from his lips, he hears how ridiculous they sound.

'The television?'

'And you helped yourself to my best whisky.'

'I only had a little to help me sleep. I didn't think you'd mind.'

'You could have asked first.' Now he sounds like a petulant child, unwilling to share his toys.

'You were asleep. But it won't happen again. I promise. And I'll buy you a new bottle.'

He screws his eyes shut and shakes his head. It's not about the whisky. Or the television being left on. Not really. 'The thing is, I was still in shock after Gwyneth's accident and when you said you were going to sleep in your car —'

She looks at him the same way Simba looked at his dead father in *The Lion King*, with a profound sadness that claws at his melting heart. 'I told you, I couldn't afford a room. I wasn't lying.'

'The thing is, you might be my mother-in-law, but we're strangers. You didn't even know Gwyneth was married until a few days ago.'

Freya shrugs. 'What better way to get to know each other then?'

Harvey pinches the bridge of his nose, the tension building behind his eyes, a throbbing headache threatening.

'I've never stayed anywhere as nice as your house,' Freya continues, lowering her voice to barely a whisper, emotion catching in her throat. 'It's beautiful. You're so lucky. It's amazing how the sun falls across the garden first thing in the morning and the sound of the blackbirds last thing in the evening is idyllic,' she says, looking wistfully over his shoulder. 'It's not like living in the city. You have so much space. You should see my flat.' She snorts. 'I have to sit on my bed to watch TV and if I want to make a cup of tea, I can reach the kettle without moving.'

Harvey's resolve crumbles like a sandcastle facing the onslaught of an incoming tide.

'I hate it there,' she continues. 'The mould in the bathroom isn't good for my lungs.' She coughs, a chesty, hacking cough that wracks her body.

Harvey closes his eyes and opens them slowly.

'I suppose...' he begins.

'Yes?' Freya nudges her glasses up her nose and stares at him like a puppy that's been beaten by its owner and is clinging to the hope that she's still loved.

'Really, don't you think you'd be better off in a hotel where they'll make your bed every morning and bring you clean towels?' Harvey tries one more time.

'You know I'm quite a decent cook? What if I started cooking for you as a way of showing my gratitude? I mean, you need to look after yourself while Gwyneth's away, and you can't keep relying on that neighbour friend of yours. Have you even eaten anything today?'

'Well, no, not really.' He gave up after burning his toast and was so incensed after discovering the broken vase in the bin that he drove directly to the hospital to have it out with her.

'You need a decent breakfast, Harvey. Didn't you know it's the most important meal of the day? And I'm not talking about any of that rabbit food either. I'm talking about a cooked breakfast that will set you up. Sausages, bacon, eggs, mushrooms, hash browns, beans, tomatoes, black pudding.'

As Freya reels off the list, dwelling on each item, Harvey's mouth waters and his stomach growls. Gwyneth never lets him have a fry-up. She says it's bad for his health, but what's the point of living if you can't enjoy the pleasurable things in life, like good food?

'I'm worried you're not eating a proper meal in the evening, either. I make a mean chicken curry. And do you like toad-in-the-hole?'

Wow, toad-in-the-hole. He's not had that in years.

'With gravy?' he drools.

'Of course, but not that granulated stuff. I prefer to make it from scratch. And what about liver and bacon? Do you like onion rings?'

Maybe it wouldn't be so bad to let Freya stay for a few more days, especially if she started pulling her weight around the house. And he could definitely use a cook while Gwyneth's in hospital.

'Why don't I swing past the shops on the way home and grab us something for tonight?' she says. But then her face falls. 'Do you fancy a roast as it's a Sunday? Although I'd need to borrow some cash. I'm skint at the moment.'

'Of course.' Harvey hunts in his pockets for his wallet and produces a twenty-pound note, which he shoves into Freya's hand. 'Here,' he says. 'Is that enough?'

'I'll pay you back.'

Harvey waves a hand dismissively. 'Don't worry about it. There's no need.'

Freya's face cracks into a wide smile. She shoves it into her wallet with the crumpled ten-pound note she'd tried to hand Harvey.

She folds up her knitting and stands, stretching her back. 'Do you mind keeping an eye on Gwyneth for half an hour?' she asks. 'I need to pop to the loo and I might grab a cup of tea while I'm at it.'

'Of course,' Harvey says, with the sinking feeling he's been outmanoeuvred by Freya once again. 'Take your time.'

When she's gone, he stands at the foot of Gwyneth's bed in shock, wondering how he arrived so fired up and determined to kick Freya out, only to be talked so easily into letting her stay. He's even handed over money.

Maybe she's right, and they just need a little more time to adjust. He shrugs off his coat, slumps into the armchair by the bed, and grabs his wife's warm, dry hand.

'What do you think, Gwyneth? Am I doing the right thing?'

Chapter 24

GWYNETH

What is that sound? It's driving me crazy.

Not the bleeps and the clicks or the wheezing puffs that are ever present and which I hardly notice now, but something intermittent. It comes and goes.

Clickety-clackety-clickety-clackety.

Sometimes that woman talks over it in a drone, a never-ending monologue of who knows what. But all I can hear is that sound that sets my teeth on edge, like someone rapidly tapping two pencils together.

When it stops briefly, I hold my breath, hoping it has ended, but usually it starts up again just as quickly, as if whoever is doing it is feeding on my false hope, giving me a brief respite and beginning the torture all over again.

What *is* it?

I hate it, not just because it irritates me, but because it touches something deep in my soul. A raw memory that stings at the slightest touch. I only wish I could remember what it is. It's on the tip of my tongue and still tantalisingly out of reach, like hearing a famous actor talking on the radio and yet being unable to picture their face or recall their name.

If only I could work it out.

Clickety-clackety-clickety-clackety.

Pause.

Clickety-clackety-clickety-clackety.

It's utter torture. Maybe if I will it hard enough, using the power of my mind, I can make it stop. A kind of telekinesis.

And finally it does, followed by a scraping sound that could be a chair being pushed back on a tiled floor. More murmurings. Indistinct voices. Movement. The brush of clothing. A cough. A sniff.

Then, out of nowhere, it comes to me.

I'd punch the air with joy if only I could lift my arm.

But my delight is almost instantly replaced by dread and fear.

A chill runs from my head down to my toes and my skin prickles. Someone's taunting me, tapping into my deepest neuroses. I tremble uncontrollably.

My head thrashes from side to side as if I'm caught in a nightmare I can't wake from.

Knitting needles.

How could I have forgotten that sound? The memory is so vivid and so visceral it's almost real.

Please, I beg. *No. Don't. Stop. Get off me. Leave me alone.*

Chapter 25

It's been a Sunday night tradition since Harvey and Gwyneth were married that he's allowed to pop into their local pub, The George, for a couple of quick, early evening pints, and he can't see any reason he shouldn't do so this evening. God knows, he needs a drink after the week he's had.

The pub used to be an old coaching inn, but has had all its soul and character ripped out in recent months after it was converted into a gastropub, catering for a different crowd who are drawn by the allure of a Michelin-starred chef and a fancy menu. It's not really a drinkers' pub anymore, but thankfully there's still a corner at the end of the bar where Harvey can sit and have a pint in peace.

'Bloody hell, I heard what happened to Gwyneth,' Nigel, the landlord, says, pulling a pint for Harvey with the lazy ease of a man who's been behind the bar for the best part of thirty years. 'I'm so sorry. How is she?'

'She's been better.'

'I heard she was in a coma.'

Harvey sups his beer, wipes his mouth with the back of his hand and nods. 'She was knocked out cold when the car hit her and she hasn't come round yet.'

'But she's going to be okay?'

Harvey shrugs. 'I hope so, but I don't know how long it's going to take. It could be weeks or even months before she comes out of it.'

'That's awful. Do they know what happened?'

'Some idiot driving too fast didn't see her.'

'And they didn't stop? I can't believe anyone could be that callous. What kind of sicko hits a pedestrian and drives off without stopping?' Nigel shakes his head sadly. 'I don't know what the world's coming to. I hope when the police catch the bastard, they throw the book at him.'

'I'm just concentrating on getting Gwyneth better at the moment, and trying not to think about it.'

The pub's packed with people, most of them eating in the restaurant. A team of waiting staff marches up and down carrying plates of food and trays of drinks like an army of worker ants, while the noise of chatter and laughter fills the building like the drone of a thousand bees. It was never this busy before the renovations.

'If there's anything I can do to help, just shout,' Nigel says.

'Sadly, there's not much anyone can do at the moment. We're just praying for a miracle.'

Nigel shoots him a grim smile of condolence as a young couple walk in and approach the bar tentatively. Strangers. Harvey would recognise them if they were from the village. He knows most of the faces around here these days.

They're looking for a table, but Nigel has to break it to them they're fully booked, and they walk out, despondent. How times have changed.

'Busy in here tonight,' Harvey says, glancing around.

'I'm not complaining.' Nigel leans forwards with both hands on the bar, the sleeves of his branded polo shirt riding up his arms to reveal an armful of faded tattoos. A reminder that he used to be a Royal Marine, one of those who's seen actual combat and lost friends after yomping halfway across the Falkland Islands. Not that he likes to talk about it. 'Are you eating properly while Gwyneth's in hospital? Want to see if I can rustle you up a plate of something? We don't have any tables, but if you're happy eating at the bar?'

'Thanks, but there's a meal waiting for me at home.'

Nigel's forehead crumples with a frown. 'Oh?'

'Gwyneth's mother turned up out of the blue after she saw the news. She's staying with me for a few days.'

Nigel laughs. 'So you've been stuck looking after the mother-in-law? How's that working out?'

Harvey rolls his eyes. 'Don't ask. I've never met her before.'

'How come?'

'She and Gwyneth have been estranged for years. It was only because it was on the news that she came.'

'I wonder what Gwyneth's going to make of that.'

'I could hardly turn her away, could I? Mind you, she's been a complete pain in the ass since she's been here. She's kicked me out of my room and taken my bed. Last night I caught her helping herself to my best whisky. And this morning I found out she'd broken one of Gwyneth's expensive vases.'

Nigel chuckles, which brings a much-needed smile to Harvey's face. He's not had much to smile about lately, and it is pretty funny when you think about it.

'How long's she staying?'

'Who knows? She's driving me mad. It doesn't help that we're spending most of the day together in the same room at the hospital, where she's doing everything. She's totally taken over and won't let me do anything.'

'Sounds like you need to lay down the law. Stand up for yourself.'

Harvey sighs. 'I tried. I told her she wasn't welcome anymore, but somehow she's talked me round with the promise to cook roast chicken tonight.'

'Rather you than me,' Nigel says with a grimace. 'I can't imagine living with my mother-in-law. I'm pretty sure we'd end up killing each other.'

'I keep telling myself it's not going to be forever.' Harvey shudders. The thought of Freya never going home brings him out in a cold sweat.

Today was typical of how it's been going. Even though he thought they'd ironed out some of their differences, Freya's still been pushing him away when it comes to Gwyneth's care. He can't go near her without Freya shooing him away or telling him he's doing something wrong. He's beginning to wonder why he's bothering to go into the hospital every day if he's not allowed to do anything.

'What's happening with the shop while Gwyneth's out of action?' Nigel asks.

'Ruby's holding the reins. She knows what she's doing. At least, I hope so. She's been doing it long enough.'

'Ruby? Oh, right.' Nigel looks surprised.

'Why? What is it?'

'Nothing.'

'No, come on. What's on your mind?' It's obvious he's hiding something. It's written all over his face, and in the way he's turned away, busying himself unloading clean glasses from the dishwasher behind the bar. 'I know there were a couple of days earlier in the week when she was ill and couldn't open up, but I've talked to her and she's fine now.'

Nigel hangs two tankards on hooks above the bar, his hairy pot belly popping out from under his shirt.

'Ill? Is that what she told you?'

'Why, what have you heard?' Harvey asks suspiciously.

'Just a rumour. That's all. I'm sure there's nothing in it. Idle chit-chat. You know what pubs are like.'

'Nigel, will you just spit it out and tell me? Please. Is there something I need to know?'

Nigel sighs, leans across the bar, and lowers his voice conspiratorially. 'It's just that a few people were saying that Ruby was caught with her hand in the till and Gwyneth found out.'

Harvey stares at him as if he's gone mad. 'Are you insane? Ruby Pettifer? The most honest woman in the village?'

Nigel shrugs. 'I'm only telling you what I heard. People are saying that Gwyneth had threatened to sack her.'

'No, she would have mentioned it!' But then, Gwyneth knows he has zero interest in the shop and never talks to him about the business. He's made his feelings about it clear. He thinks she should sell up and retire.

It's funny, Ruby never said anything when he spoke to her at the house the other day. But then, would she mention something like that, especially as it was obvious Harvey had no idea? Now he thinks about it, she was behaving strangely when he spoke to her. He put it down to her eccentricity. She's a cold fish at the best of times, but what if there's some truth in what Nigel's saying? What if Gwyneth had caught her stealing and sacked her? It would explain why she was so surprised when he asked her to go back.

Harvey guzzles down his pint, lost in thought. Does he need to confront Ruby again? He really doesn't have the time or the inclination. Maybe he'll leave it until Gwyneth's well enough to deal with it. That's probably for the best.

'One for the road?' Nigel nods at his empty glass.

Harvey glances at his watch. 'I'd better not. Cheers, Nigel.'

'Sure?'

No, he's not sure. He could happily stay and lose himself in inebriation tonight, letting the alcohol chase away all his worries and woes. About Gwyneth. About Freya. About Ruby. But Freya's likely to be at the house by now, cooking for him. And he doesn't want to leave her alone too long. Who knows what kind of carnage she could cause.

'Got to get back for my dinner,' he says.

'With the mother-in-law? Good luck.' Nigel gives him a knowing wink.

'Thanks, I think I'll need it.'

Chapter 26

Harvey has been deliberately avoiding the scene of the crash. He's driven past it a few times, but always with his gaze averted, speeding by with his head down, not wanting to dwell on what happened there. But as he climbs into his car to head home and spend the evening with Freya, he makes a snap decision. He can't avoid it forever. Maybe it will help him come to terms with Gwyneth's if he sees for himself whether there was anything she could have done to avoid being hit.

It's only a five-minute journey from the pub, past the bottom of the drive and back towards the village. As he draws closer, his palms sweat and his heart rate rises.

He gives a woman on a bicycle a wide berth, checks in his mirrors that she's still upright as he pulls back in, then slows as he approaches the rising bend where Gwyneth was apparently found bleeding in the road.

His heart beats faster still as a vision of Gwyneth flying through the air in slow motion, her face twisted in shock and horror, flashes through his mind.

To think she could have died. She probably should have died by all rights. It was only by the grace of god that she survived.

A car flies past in the opposite direction, travelling far too quickly, a reminder, as if he needed one, that it's a fast road and Gwyneth should never have risked her life walking along here.

He indicates and pulls over, braking sharply. He kills the engine and sits for a minute, listening to the sound of his breath and the thud of his heart. Does he really want to do this?

He releases his seatbelt and elbows open the door, almost taking out the cyclist he overtook a few moments earlier. She swears at him and he raises a hand in apology. His mind is so preoccupied, he didn't even check his mirrors. Stupid. Careless.

Other than a ribbon of police tape flapping wildly in the wind, marking the spot, there's not much to look at. A low wall of ragged, dirty stone built to prevent the road from subsiding into a sheer drop to a wooded ravine. A painted white line, partially obscured by dirt. A single tyre track cutting up a grassy verge. And when he looks closely, he's sure that's a trace of blood on the wall. A dark brown mark that could look to anyone who didn't know what had happened here like natural mineral seepage from the stone itself.

All of it paints the story of what happened here in a few brief seconds, a near tragedy which has cast long shadows.

In his mind, Harvey pieces together the chain of events. Gwyneth walking home facing the oncoming traffic. A car approaching at speed. A squeal of tyres. An anguished scream. The dull thump of flesh and bone meeting immovable metal and plastic.

Nausea swells in Harvey's stomach. Why did he need to come here this evening, when he's been avoiding it all week? The beer? Curiosity? Anger? Or maybe a combination of all three?

He looks back the way he came at the sound of another car and steps onto the verge in front of his Golf, not wishing to go the same way as his wife. That really would be an irony.

A dark-coloured saloon is approaching at a steady speed, unusually for this section, not too fast. The driver is taking the corners with care. Harvey keeps his eye on it as it draws closer, light reflecting off the windscreen making it impossible to see inside.

He expects the saloon to pull out around his own car and for the driver to maybe shoot Harvey a curious look, wondering what he's doing, but he doesn't. The car's slowing down, coming to a stop with its indicator light blinking.

Doors fly open and the two detectives, Murray Chalk and Alison Enright, step out.

He groans. He's barely heard a word from either of them since they talked him into giving an interview to the media. What are the chances they would be passing at the precise moment Harvey stopped to spend a few moments of contemplation at the scene?

As Chalk strides up to him, his arm outstretched and his suit jacket flapping open, Harvey takes a step backwards, conscious of the alcohol on his breath.

'I didn't expect to see you here, detective. I thought you'd finished with the scene?'

Chalk scrutinises him. 'I could say the same thing. What are you doing here?'

Harvey shrugs. 'I was passing. Curious, I guess.'

'It's a dangerous place to stop. You should be careful.'

'I've been avoiding it until now, but I wanted to see where it happened.' Harvey points to the wall. 'Is that where she hit her head?'

'We think so, yes. We're confident that she was hit head-on by a driver heading towards the village. You've probably noticed there's a tyre track but no skid marks.'

Harvey glances at the verge and the single channel that's been carved through the mud by a car tyre. 'In other words, the driver didn't brake?'

'Or apparently make any other attempt to avoid your wife. Either they didn't see her until it was too late, or...'

'Or?'

'She was driven at deliberately.'

Harvey shakes his head. 'But why? Who would want to hurt Gwyneth?'

'That was what I was hoping you might help us with.'

'That's a crazy idea. I don't know anyone who'd wish her ill. I told you before, she doesn't have any enemies,' Harvey says. 'Anyway, I thought you were supposed to be the detectives.'

Chalk shoots him a humourless grin, tight-lipped and sour. 'If you have any information you've not previously mentioned, now would be the time to let us know.'

'Like what?' Harvey doesn't like the insinuation that he's sitting on information. He's done everything they've wanted, hasn't he? He did that interview with the press and faced the cameras. What more do they want? Blood?

'Anything that you think might be relevant, no matter how minor.'

Harvey scratches the back of his neck. 'I can't think of anything. Anyway, what about the media appeal? You said it would throw up some new leads. So?'

'We're working on some new lines of enquiry.'

Harvey arches his eyebrows. 'Such as?'

'You know I'm not at liberty to discuss that with you.'

'I'm Gwyneth's husband,' Harvey says, raising his voice. 'I think I have a right to know.'

'It's standard procedure. We have to keep our cards close to our chest until we make an arrest,' Chalk says. As he folds his arms, he rucks up his tie.

'You're close to making an arrest?'

'I didn't say that.'

Harvey turns and walks away, frustrated. He paces up and down the road, fighting a wave of emotion. Tears threaten his eyes and a hard, uncomfortable lump forms in his throat.

'You still think I had something to do with it, don't you?' he snarls, marching back up to Chalk and jabbing his finger in his face. 'Because it's always the husband, isn't it?'

'Nobody's suggesting that.'

'You think that just because my wife has a big house and a healthy bank balance, I tried to kill her? But it's nonsense,' Harvey yells, the alcohol getting the better of him. 'I love her. She means everything to me.'

Chalk stares at him impassively, totally unmoved.

'This your car?' he nods at Harvey's Golf, parked precariously on the side of the road.

'It's not much but, yes, it's mine. Why?'

'Do you have access to any other vehicles?'

'There's Gwyneth's car, but I rarely drive it.' Harvey narrows his eyes.

'What's the make?'

'A Volvo.'

'A four-by-four?'

Harvey takes a deep breath and answers slowly. 'Yes.'

'We'll need to look, to rule it out.'

'And what about Ruby Pettifer? That's who you should talk to,' Harvey blurts out. He's not sure why he didn't think to mention it a moment ago.

'The woman employs to run her antiques shop?'

'She's been stealing from the till. I found out tonight that Gwyneth had to let her go.'

'She sacked her? But you only just found out tonight? That's strange. Who told you?' Chalk asks.

Harvey scuffs his foot along the ground, toeing a stone from side to side. 'I heard it in the pub.'

'Gwyneth didn't tell you herself?'

'No.'

'Why do you think that was?'

'I don't know. It's her business. I don't have much to do with it.'

'But if she'd found out someone was stealing from her, wouldn't you have expected her to have at least mentioned it?'

'Yes, probably. But she didn't. I don't know why, but it doesn't mean it isn't true. You should check it out.'

'Don't worry, we will. In the meantime, Mr Kerrison, why don't you leave the investigating to us and concentrate on getting your wife well again.' Chalk's tone couldn't be any more patronising.

'I just want you to catch whoever did this. Is that too much to ask?'

'I understand your frustration, but we're doing everything we can. When would be convenient to look at your wife's car, so we can eliminate it from our enquiries?'

'I was on my way home. You might as well come with me now, if you really want,' Harvey huffs. He might as well get this over and done with. After all, he has nothing to hide.

'That would be helpful, Mr Kerrison. Why don't you lead the way and we'll follow?'

Chapter 27

Harvey is surprised Freya's car isn't parked outside the house. He thought she'd have been back hours ago and cracking on with dinner. She must have been delayed at the shops, or more likely, lost.

He cranks on the handbrake and watches in his rear-view mirror as the two detectives come to a halt a few metres behind him.

They've jumped out of their vehicle and are swarming around Gwyneth's Volvo before he has the chance to haul himself out of his seat and lock the door.

'Satisfied?' he asks, as Enright takes pictures on her phone of the treads on all four wheels.

Chalk nods, taking a good look around, admiring the neatly mown lawns, beautiful gardens and converted barn that would be the envy of most people.

'Landed on your feet here, didn't you?'

Harvey prickles. 'Excuse me?'

'I'm sorry. I thought the house belonged to your wife and her first husband before you met?'

'What does that have to do with anything?'

'It's just an observation, Mr Kerrison.' Chalk smiles smugly.

He's trying to make a point, but there's no mistaking the envy in his tone. There's no way someone on a police officer's wage could ever afford anything like this.

Even Lionel didn't have it handed to him on a plate. He had to work hard to turn it into what it is today. Harvey has seen pictures from way back when it was nothing more than a neglected farm, the barn so dilapidated it looked as though it was on the verge of collapse. It took years of hard work and a lot of money to turn it into a home, by all accounts.

Harvey is under no illusion that he's lucky to have inherited such a wonderful life. But it's not all one-sided. Harvey helped Gwyneth through a dark period in her life when she couldn't see a way forward, when she was all but ready to give up on her own future. And together, they found love. It's a precious thing. They saved each other.

Enright starts to wander, eyeing the place up with the hard-nosed scrutiny of a suspicious copper. She ambles down the drive and turns back to study the house. Then drops to her haunches, looking at the lawn.

'Boss, come and have a look at this,' she says.

Chalk holds Harvey's gaze for a second or two before breaking away and joining her.

'Someone's made a bit of a mess of your lawn.' Chalk points to a criss-cross of muddy tracks that has churned up the grass.

Harvey rolls his eyes and tuts. 'My mother-in-law, Freya. You'd think the drive was wide enough for her to turn around without having to go cross-country.'

'Mother-in-law?'

'She's staying here for a while. Just until Gwyneth's better.'

Chalk hitches up his trousers and squats next to Enright. He takes a pen from the inside of his jacket and prods at the mud.

'Something wrong, detective?' Harvey asks.

'What car does she drive?' Chalk asks.

'It's an old SUV. A Nissan, I think. Makes my car look like a royal carriage. Why, do you think —'

'Where is she now?'

'She's supposed to be here. She promised to cook tonight, but she's probably lost, knowing her.'

Chalk tilts his head quizzically.

'She's come from Newcastle,' Harvey explains. 'She drove down when she heard Gwyneth was in hospital.'

Chalk stands, pulls out a notebook from his pocket and scribbles something in it. 'I see,' he says. 'We'd like a word with her as soon as possible.'

'To eliminate her from your enquiries?'

Chalk glances up and fires Harvey an acidic look. 'To see if she might have any information pertinent to our investigation. Mind if we wait?'

Actually, he does. Their presence is suffocating, especially the way Chalk keeps looking at him, as if he's waiting for him to slip up. It doesn't matter what Harvey says, Chalk seems convinced that he tried to kill Gwyneth. It's absurd.

'It's been a long day, detective. Could you come back another time? Or I'll ask her to contact you,' Harvey suggests.

'It would be a shame to miss her if she's due back at any moment.' His smile is a challenge, daring Harvey to contradict him. 'And you said her name was Freya?'

'That's right.' Harvey nods. 'Freya...' He wracks his memory for her last name before realising he doesn't actually know it. He's never asked. And she's never told him. 'I think it must be Grainger. That was Gwyneth's maiden name and I don't think she's ever been married.' In fact, he doesn't know an awful lot about her at all.

Chalk writes down the name and draws an emphatic line under it. 'And when did you say she arrived in the area?'

Harvey scratches his head. All the days have blurred together. 'It must have been Friday morning. The day after I did the interview for the TV. She was already at the hospital when I arrived the next morning.'

'Newcastle's a long way to come.'

'I guess she was worried about Gwyneth.' Should he tell them they've been estranged for thirty years?

Is it relevant? No, let them do their own detective work. It's not up to him to fill in the blanks for them. Not while he remains a suspect.

'I don't suppose you have an address for her?' Enright asks.

'In Newcastle? No.'

'But she's staying here with you for the foreseeable future?'

Harvey hopes Chalk doesn't notice his grimace. 'That's right. If you need to speak to her, the chances are she'll either be here or at the hospital.'

'That's good to know.'

Enright's phone rings. She turns away to answer it.

'Get on well with your mother-in-law, do you?' Chalk asks.

'Do you?'

This time when Chalk smiles, there's a humour behind his eyes. 'No, not really.'

Harvey shrugs. 'You are going to catch the driver who did this, aren't you?' he asks.

'We're doing our best.'

'Because Gwyneth could have died.'

'I'm well aware of that, Mr Kerrison.'

'Are you? Then shouldn't you be getting out there and doing some proper investigating. Finding who actually was responsible.'

'Rest assured, we're doing everything we can and we will catch them.'

'Boss?' Enright strides back towards the two men, the phone held away from her ear, her face pinched with concern.

'What is it?'

'I think you'll want to hear this.' She hands him the phone, which he snatches with a hint of irritation.

'Hello? Right, yes. I see. Are you sure?'

Enright stands with her hands hanging loosely at her side and an enigmatic smile on her face.

'What's in there?' Enright nods towards the barn.

'A glorified shed. It's mostly full of Gwyneth's old crap. And her first husband's stuff she can't bring herself to throw out.'

Enright presses her lips together and nods. Behind her, Chalk hangs up. He spins around and presses the phone into her hand, his expression darkening. 'We need to go.'

'I thought you wanted to speak to Freya?' Harvey says, with a mixture of surprise and relief.

'Something's come up.' The two detectives hurry towards their car. 'Let her know I'd like a word.'

'Yeah, sure.' Harvey's reply is lost to the double thud of two car doors slamming closed.

Wheels spin. Stones and dirt kick up. And the vehicle shoots down the drive.

Harvey stands watching, bemused, as they disappear, the brake lights flashing briefly before they join the main road and accelerate away.

He takes a deep breath, filling his lungs, and lets it out slowly, his shoulders relaxing. He doesn't like the police being here, prodding around and shoving their noses into his business. It makes him anxious.

His stomach rumbles with the hollowness of hunger and, as if on cue, Freya's car turns onto the drive and speeds towards him. She pulls up sharply, the old Nissan skidding to a dramatic halt.

'Who was that?' she asks as she clambers out of the car, her brow furrowed.

'The police.'

She freezes, clutching Gwyneth's canvas bag to her chest. 'What did they want?'

'To speak to you, actually.'

'Me? Why?'

Harvey shrugs. 'I don't know. They didn't say,' he lies. 'Did you find the supermarket? I'm starving.'

'Eventually. You can carry the bags in. I'll put the oven on and make a start on dinner.'

She hobbles into the house, discarding her bag in the hall, as if she owns the place.

Harvey ambles towards her car, lowers himself to the ground and inspects the tyres. They're caked in mud and dirt. The rubber is cracked around the edges and the treads are almost bare in places. He doubts they're legal. No doubt she'd claim she can't afford to replace them.

He sighs. He has no idea what he's looking for or even why he's looking. It can't have been Freya who drove at Gwyneth because she was at home at the time, in the northeast. Eight hours away by car.

That's a pretty solid alibi. At least it would be if she can prove that's where she was.

Chapter 28

Harvey drops his knife and fork onto his empty plate, his stomach full, and pushes himself away from the table. Freya has surpassed herself. The meal was sublime. She'd prepared a succulent roast chicken with crispy, salty skin, crunchy, floury roast potatoes that melted in the mouth, thin carrot rounds, juicy savoy cabbage, and thick, unctuous gravy. If anything, she's undersold her talents. She really is an excellent cook.

'That was delicious,' he says.

Gwyneth would never indulge him like that. On the rare occasions she's cooked a roast, she's served such meagre portions that he's gone to bed hungry.

He wipes his mouth with a napkin and takes a large mouthful of wine. He let Freya choose the bottle and although she picked out one of the expensive French reds he and Gwyneth had been saving for a special occasion, he didn't say anything. He didn't want to trigger another fight when they've finally worked out how to be civil to each other.

'I'm glad you enjoyed it.' Freya pushes the left-overs of her tiny portion to one side. 'I hope you still have room for pudding.'

'Pudding?'

'Sticky toffee pudding. I'm afraid it's shop-bought. I didn't have time to make it myself.'

'I love sticky toffee pudding.'

'And I picked up some bits for a cooked breakfast in the morning,' she says, looking pleased with herself.

'Wow, you really are spoiling me.'

'It's the least I could do. I know we haven't had the easiest of starts.' She bows her head, unable to hold Harvey's gaze.

'Anyone who can cook like that is welcome to stay,' Harvey beams.

'Although the supermarket is so much more expensive than up north. The prices are definitely higher.'

The not-so-subtle hint isn't lost on Harvey. 'Of course, you must let me know how much you spent and I'll pay you back.'

Harvey pulls out his wallet and hands Freya a wad of notes.

'Does that cover it?' he asks.

'I should think so.' She shoves the money in the back pocket of the jeans she's borrowed from Gwyneth's wardrobe, then scratches at a mark on the tablecloth with her thumbnail. Eventually, she asks, 'When the police were here earlier, what did you tell them about me?'

'Nothing much. I don't really know anything about you.'

'Why do they want to talk to me? I don't know anything about Gwyneth's accident.'

'They're talking to everyone. They have this crazy idea that someone might have deliberately driven at Gwyneth.'

Freya stiffens, her spine snapping straight. 'I thought it was an accident? You said it was probably someone distracted by their phone or their sat-nav.'

'I don't know. They won't tell me anything. All I know is that there were no skid marks on the road which they think suggests the driver didn't brake.'

The colour drains from Freya's sallow cheeks and she blinks rapidly, her eyelashes fluttering like agitated moths behind her thick lenses.

'Why would anyone want to hurt Gwyneth?'

'I wish I knew. Sometimes people do crazy things for no reason.'

'They can't think it was me,' Freya says, with a tremor in her voice. 'I wasn't even here.'

'I told them that.'

'I'd never hurt her.' Freya slams her palms on the table so hard the plates jump. She scowls at Harvey. 'Never ever in a million years.'

Harvey's head jerks backwards, startled by her sudden outburst. 'Don't let them rattle you. They're just doing their job.'

'Not very well. They should have caught that driver by now. How difficult can it be?'

Harvey folds his napkin and lays it on the table. He crosses his legs and looks Freya directly in the eye. 'Can I ask you a question?'

'It depends.' Freya blinks again and nudges her glasses up her nose.

'Why did you and Gwyneth stop speaking?'

Freya's face is unreadable. 'I don't really know, if I'm honest.'

'Something must have happened or been said. Families don't stop speaking to each other without good reason.'

She shakes her head. 'It was such a long time ago, I'm not sure either of us remembers.'

Can that be right? Families fall out all the time, sometimes for the most absurd and trivial reasons, but there's always something behind it. A perceived slight. A misplaced word. A misunderstanding blown out of all proportion. But there's always a trigger.

'It's a shame it's taken something so horrendous to bring the two of you together again,' Harvey says.

'I'd have come sooner, but I didn't know how to find her. She just disappeared. All those wasted years. All that time worrying about what had happened, whether she was happy or if she was even still alive. As soon as I saw her picture on the TV though, I knew it was her.'

'It's brave that you came straightaway without stopping to think how it would be after all this time,' Harvey says.

'Brave? I don't think it was brave at all. Now, what about that pudding?' She jumps out of her chair and heads for the fridge.

'I'm sure I can manage a little.' Harvey pats his bulging stomach.

'Do you really think someone was trying to kill Gwyneth?' Freya asks as she takes a sticky toffee pudding from the fridge and studies the cooking instructions on the back.

'She's not the sort of person to make enemies, so I wouldn't have thought so. I still think it was an accident. Someone driving carelessly. Not that it makes it any better.'

Freya purses her lips. 'You must have given it some thought, though? Is there anyone you can think of who has a grudge or a grievance against her?'

The only person who springs to mind is the unlikeliest. Ruby Pettifer might have been facing the sack, but she doesn't seem capable of doing anyone any harm, let alone deliberately running them down in her car. Not mild, timid, wouldn't-say-boo-to-a-goose Ruby. 'No, not really,' he says.

'There must be someone.'

'She and Lionel were in the antiques trade for years. I suppose it's possible she could have made one or two enemies over a business deal gone wrong? But it seems unlikely.'

Freya removes a plastic bowl from a cardboard carton, peels off a cellophane lid and pops the pudding into the oven. She turns back to Harvey and crosses her arms, a frown creasing her forehead. 'There's one obvious suspect, of course.'

'Who?'

'The person who stands to gain the most if she was dead.'

Harvey scowls, not sure what she's getting at.

'Well, if Gwyneth dies, you get to inherit all of this, don't you?' She makes a sweeping gesture with her arm. 'The house. Everything in it. And the business. I bet Gwyneth's sitting on a tidy sum after her first husband's death as well, isn't she?'

Harvey's jaw tightens. If this is Freya's idea of a joke, it's not funny.

'Don't be ridiculous. I don't stand to gain anything other than losing a wife,' he snarls.

'The house is in joint names, is it? And the bank account? The business?'

'You don't know what you're talking about.'

'That's quite a motive.'

'Shut up. You know I'd never do anything to hurt Gwyneth.'

'I hardly know you, Harvey. How would I know what you're capable of or not? It's why the police were here earlier, isn't it? They were checking up on you. They know you have a motive. Now they need to establish a means and opportunity.'

'How dare you.' Harvey stands, knocking the chair over. It thuds noisily onto the tiled floor. Freya jumps.

'Where were you when Gwyneth was knocked down?' Freya's eyelids flutter like she's asking the most innocuous question, rather than accusing him of attempted murder.

'Here at the house, sorting through some of Lionel's old things in the barn, if you must know. Not that it's any of your business,' he snaps.

'Oh, so no witnesses?'

He stares at Freya in utter disbelief. Where has this vile poison come from? He's shown her nothing but hospitality, and this is how she speaks to him? In his own house?

'It's funny you should mention the police being here. They took a great deal of interest in the tyre marks you've left across my lawn. They seemed to think they might be a match to the tyre marks at the scene of the accident.' Harvey raises his eyebrows. 'They think it was an SUV or a four-by-four that struck Gwyneth, but you might have noticed I don't own one.'

'Harvey,' she smirks, 'I was in Newcastle as you well know. It couldn't possibly have been me, could it?'

'The police will want to check your story.'

'Apart from anything else, I don't have any reason to want her dead. We've only just found each other.'

189

'I don't care about the house or Gwyneth's money,' Harvey yells. 'I just want her to be well again.'

'How much *is* the house worth exactly? I bet you've had it valued.'

'How dare you. Get out!' he screams. 'Just get out of my sight. I should never have invited you to stay. If I'd known what an evil, mealy-mouthed, sour old woman you really are, I'd have thought twice.'

The triumphant expression Freya was wearing a moment before vanishes like a spring dew on a sunny day. She blinks at him rapidly, startled.

'I - I'm sorry, Harvey,' she stammers.

'I said get out. I don't want to hear another word.'

'I didn't mean it,' she cries. 'You didn't think I was being serious, did you? I was only joking.' Tears stream down her face.

Her whole demeanour has changed so suddenly, like one of those tricks where a magician whips off a tablecloth and leaves everything on the table still standing. Harvey's not sure what to think.

Was she joking? Has he overreacted?

Freya bolts out of the kitchen, wailing. She slams the door behind her, leaving Harvey to wonder what the hell just happened.

Chapter 29

They both said things they shouldn't have, but Freya shouldn't have provoked Harvey like she did, accusing him of wanting Gwyneth dead, even in jest. And Harvey shouldn't have overreacted. He's not ready to face her the next morning and he stays in his room until he hears her leave for the hospital.

Anyway, he has an appointment with a client at ten, and despite all the drama going on in his own life, he doesn't want to let him down by cancelling. Especially as Tim has troubles of his own, still struggling to come to terms with his wife's death in hospital, two months on. She was only thirty-four and being treated for a late-stage miscarriage, seventeen weeks into her pregnancy, when she developed blood poisoning that wasn't detected by the doctors. Five days later, she was dead. It's no wonder her husband's bereft.

Harvey dresses in a smart shirt, puts on a tie and heads down to his study to fire up his computer. Most of his consultations are done via video conferencing calls these days. Technology has revolutionised his industry.

He pats down what's left of his thinning hair, pulls his chair closer to the desk and logs onto the call. Tim is already online, waiting. His ghostly outline appears in a box on the screen but it's impossible to make out his features as he's sitting in front of glass patio doors and the sun is streaming in behind him, back-lighting him, like in those TV interviews with rape victims and anonymous whistleblowers whose identities have to be protected.

'Morning, Tim. How are you feeling today?' Harvey adopts his counsellor's persona, lowering his voice to make it sound deeper and more authoritative. Wears a concerned expression. Friendly, but not jovial. He's dealing with vulnerable people and the last thing they expect from him is frivolity.

'Probably better than you this week.'

Harvey frowns. 'What do you mean?'

'How's your wife? It's Gwyneth, isn't it? I saw the piece on the news. I'm really sorry.'

Harvey is momentarily thrown. He's always been careful to maintain a separation between his personal and professional life and doesn't want his clients confused about their relationship. His job is to provide the mental and emotional therapy they need to navigate their lives, not to be their friend. So he tries to be friendly, without giving them the impression that they've become friends. And that means not talking about his own life.

The only time he allowed himself to get too personal, to give too much of himself away, he ended up marrying his client. He needs to be careful not to develop a reputation.

'Thank you, she's okay, although it's been a difficult few days.' Harvey doesn't mention that on top of dealing with his wife in a coma, he's had the stress of her estranged mother turning up unexpectedly. That's been the real kicker.

'How is she?'

Harvey squirms in his seat. It's airless in his study and he starts to sweat. 'Still in hospital, but she's in good hands.'

Tim sucks air through his teeth and rocks back in his chair.

'It's a completely different situation to what happened with Alison,' Harvey hurriedly adds.

'I heard she's in a coma.'

'Yes, but we're hoping to have her home in a few weeks. Now, tell me about your week.'

'I thought Alison was coming home too.' Tim sighs. He does a lot of that. An exasperated exhalation of despair.

He and Alison had only been married for six years. To lose her at such a young age while she was pregnant with their first child is heartbreaking. An absolute tragedy.

'How have you been managing this week?' Harvey presses.

'I don't know. I seem to spend a lot of time just sitting staring at the walls, imagining she's going to walk through the door at any moment, and then it

193

hits me all over again that she's gone and she's never coming back. It's just... I don't know... it just knocks the wind out of me every time.'

'That's perfectly normal.'

'Was that how you felt when you found out what happened to Gwyneth?'

'Yes.' Harvey gives a taut smile. 'But we're not here to talk about me. This is your time. Let's not waste it.'

The truth is that it was a brutal, mind-numbing, terrifying blow that knocked the sense out of him for sure, but Gwyneth's not dead. She's not out of the woods, and who knows if there will be any lasting damage, but she's still fighting and there's every chance she'll get better.

Harvey has caught himself catastrophising a few times, imagining what it would have been like if she had been killed. If the police officers who'd called at the door last week told him she was dead. Whether the grief would have hit him hard. How he would have coped.

He's thought about what it would be like to wake up every day without Gwyneth. The hollowness of the house. The emptiness of their bed. The silence without her voice. What about birthdays and Christmases, anniversaries and special occasions? They'd be forever tainted by death and loss.

'I was just interested, that's all,' Tim fires back, a curtness to his tone that sometimes surfaces.

'Have you tried any of the coping strategies we discussed? Journalling or meditation?'

'I'm not sure they're helping much.'

'Okay, well if that's not working for you, another thing you might like to try is scheduling some grief time. Put aside a set time when you can actively reflect on your grief, which should reduce those feelings of being overwhelmed throughout the day,' Harvey says.

He can see Tim's head nodding thoughtfully. 'I guess I could do that.'

'Because grieving isn't about letting go of the people we love, but rather finding a way to carry forward their memory and what they meant to us.'

'What does Gwyneth mean to you?'

Harvey bites his bottom lip. 'Tim —'

'It would help me to know how you'd deal with it if Gwyneth had died.'

Harvey has no idea. He might have spent much of his career helping other people come to terms with their grief, but he has no first-hand experience of such an abrupt, unexpected and devastating loss. Everything he knows, he's learnt from books.

'Everyone grieves differently, Tim,' he says, 'so I don't think it's helpful to look to other people and their coping strategies.'

But Tim's not listening. 'It's a miracle she survived at all, isn't it? I mean, it's a fast bit of road. She was lucky not to be thrown down the bank and into the undergrowth.'

Harvey stares at the screen, frozen, the walls of the study closing in around him. 'How do you know the road?' he asks, drawing his words out slowly and deliberately, trying to pick out Tim's face in the shadows. Tim doesn't live anywhere near the village and yet he speaks as if he has intimate knowledge of the scene.

'I saw it on the TV,' he says. 'On the news.'

Harvey allows himself a wry smile. Did he really think Tim had driven to look for himself like one of those mawkish rubberneckers on the motorways who slow down to stare morbidly at a crash?

'I suppose it was a miracle,' he says.

'Was it a drunk driver or something?'

'Tim, I appreciate your concern, but really, I can't talk about it with you, okay? The police are investigating and I'm sure they'll find who did it.'

'I hope they do. Can you imagine hitting someone and not even stopping to help them? It's awful.'

'Shall we talk about you now? It's what you're paying me for,' Harvey says through gritted teeth.

'Right, yeah. It's just I thought you'd appreciate having someone to talk to about it.'

'You're diverting.'

'What?'

'You're deliberately steering the conversation away from Alison. I get it. Your pain must be unimaginable, but the sooner you deal with your feelings, the sooner you'll be able to process what's happened and look towards the future.'

'You mean suing the bastards at the hospital?' he says with a bitterness so venomous it could curdle milk.

'Getting angry and blaming other people isn't the answer. We've talked about this.'

'I'm not letting them get away with it.'

'I understand that. But no one deliberately set out to harm Alison. Not intentionally. They might have had a lapse in concentration or overlooked symptoms, but the doctors were doing their best and they made a mistake. Can you accept that?'

'I don't know. Maybe,' Tim says with the reluctance of a sulky child. 'Do you think someone deliberately set out to hurt *your* wife?'

'Please, Tim. I've told you, I don't want to talk about it.'

'You said talking was good.'

'This isn't about me!'

'But what if someone drove at her intentionally and meant to hurt her?'

'It was an accident. Pure and simple. Just like Alison's death. No one planned for her to die. Gwyneth was in the wrong place at the wrong time. She shouldn't have been walking home along that road, I've told her a million times, but she did it anyway. And now we are where we are and we both have to deal with the consequences. So, now can we get back to you? You're going to give grief scheduling a try, right? What about any hobbies or interests? Is there something you can throw yourself into to help you cope with your downtime?'

Tim's quiet for a moment and Harvey worries he's spoken too harshly. Eventually, he draws a breath and says quietly, 'I like to take pictures.'

'Great! Photography can be really therapeutic and might even help you express how you're feeling about Alison's passing.'

'I guess. I suppose I could try it if you think that's a good idea. What about you? What do you do to unwind?'

'At the risk of repeating myself, these sessions aren't about me. We're here to focus on getting you better.' Harvey draws in a deep breath, trying to centre himself.

'I do feel much better since we've been talking.'

'That's good.'

'I have one question, though.'

'Go on.' Harvey nods.

There's a brief lag on the line. The sound momentarily breaks up and the picture freezes.

'Are you still there?' Harvey asks.

'Harvey? Can you hear me?'

'Yes, you're back. Go on.'

'You said your wife is in a coma. Do you think she's aware of what's going on around her? Do you talk to her? I suppose it's a bit like being in a really deep sleep, isn't it?'

Harvey's chin falls onto his chest. It's hopeless. This isn't going to work out.

'This obsession with my wife's accident isn't helpful, Tim. We should be concentrating on you.'

'I'm sorry. You're right. Forgive me.'

'In fact, do you know what? I can't do this right now.'

'What do you mean?'

'It's too much. I want to help, I really do, but I have too much on my plate to play games. I've made it clear I don't want to talk about my personal circumstances. That's not what we're here for, but that's all you seem to be interested in.' Harvey taps his fingers furiously on the table next to his laptop.

'I said I'm sorry.'

'No, I think given the circumstances, it would be better for us both if we stopped working together.'

'What are you talking about? Harvey, what are you saying?'

'I think it would be better if you found a different therapist. I can recommend a few names for you if you'd like —'

'No! I don't want a different therapist. I want to work with you,' Tim cries.

'I think my... situation has become a distraction from the work you need to do on yourself. I'm sorry, Tim, but my mind's made up. I can't see you again.'

'I need you, Harvey. I was a mess before we started working together. Please, don't be like this.'

'It's for the best.'

'It's not. If I spoke out of turn, I'm sorry. It won't happen again. I really felt as though we were making progress. And if you dump me, I don't know what I'll do.' He sounds like he is on the verge of tears.

'There are plenty of other good counsellors who can help you with your grief.'

'Not like you, there aren't. I need you. And I'm not speaking to anyone else. I refuse to let you palm me off like this.'

'I'm afraid you don't have any choice,' Harvey says, and disconnects the call.

Chapter 30

Harvey powers off his laptop and pushes his chair back, convinced he's done the right thing. While he doesn't like letting down clients, there have to be boundaries, and Tim has ridden roughshod over them, even after being warned. He's become obsessed by Gwyneth's accident and it's a distraction. It's best for both of them that they go their separate ways.

Of course, it wouldn't be an issue if he hadn't agreed to that interview with the press and the story hadn't been splashed all over the TV and internet. And now everyone knows his business, although it doesn't seem to have brought the detectives any closer to catching the driver, which was the whole point of it.

He glances at his watch. He ought to think about heading to the hospital to see Gwyneth soon, but it means facing Freya again and after last night's row, the idea of it fills him with dread. Instead, he finds a distraction in sorting through some paperwork in his study.

After twenty minutes, he's in need of coffee and something to eat, and heads into the kitchen where he's confronted with the detritus from Freya's breakfast, as if she was expecting the cleaning fairy to magically appear and tidy up after her.

Harvey had to clean up after her last night as well when she'd cooked and then stormed off, pretending to be upset. Not that he bought a single one of her crocodile tears.

Wearily, he opens the dishwasher. Inevitably, it hasn't been emptied from last night, and with a sigh, he puts away clean pots, pans, crockery and cutlery, wondering if Freya is this slovenly in her own home or whether she's just taking liberties because she knows Harvey will do it.

From the bottom rack, he picks out Sheryl's white dish she brought over with the shepherd's pie. He ought to take it back and thank her properly. She's been so supportive since Gwyneth's been in hospital. A real friend in need. But some women are like that, thriving on a crisis, especially when it's someone else's. And there's nothing quite like a vulnerable man in distress to bring out the charitable side of a lonely widow.

He heads out to the car with Gwyneth's voice echoing through his mind, nagging him to walk. Sheryl's house isn't far, but why walk when you can drive? And it's not as if he's making a special journey. He'll be stopping off on his way to the hospital.

Sheryl's house is a chocolate-box cottage with wisteria rampant around the door, and a well-maintained garden with symmetrical, rounded flower beds bursting with roses and colourful lupins.

Her face lights up when she finds Harvey on the doorstep. She smooths her skirt and pats down her hair.

'You should have warned me you were coming. Look at me,' she laughs nervously. 'What a frightful mess. I've not even had a chance to put on any make-up.'

It's a blatant lie. She's wearing eyeliner and her lips are scarlet with a brush of gloss. She's the kind of woman who never goes anywhere without make-up, even around her own home.

'The pie was amazing, thank you,' Harvey says, offering her the clean dish.

Sheryl's cheeks flush. 'I'm glad you enjoyed it.'

'You needn't have gone to the trouble.'

'I couldn't have you starving, could I? Come in, come in,' she says, stepping to one side. 'Do you have time for a coffee?'

'Well...' He ponders for a second or two. The alternative is heading into the hospital, confronting Freya, and dealing with the fallout from their fight. 'Go on, then. But only if you're having one.'

He follows her into the kitchen and watches as she fills the kettle. The house is deceptively large, although with its exposed oak beams and low ceilings, it retains a homely feel. It's immaculate, like something from those property pages in the Sunday supplements, although decorated in pastel pinks and mauves, it's a little feminine for Harvey's tastes. Regardless, the cottage must be worth a few million, especially with several acres of surrounding fields where Sheryl grazes her horses, and a small wood he can see from the kitchen window, which he's pretty sure she also owns.

When he and Gwyneth were first married, she told him all about the neighbours and how much their houses were worth, who was sitting on a fortune and who was living beyond their means.

Sheryl's husband, she told him, worked in banking, until his untimely death on the golf course, just shy of his sixtieth birthday, when he dropped dead of a massive stroke. He left everything to his wife, including the house. She might be lonely, but she is most definitely not short of money.

'How's Gwyneth?'

'The same.'

'That woman's a fighter. You mark my words, she'll be home in no time.'

'I hope so,' he says. 'It's not the same without her around.'

Sheryl coos sympathetically. 'You're being so brave. Just remember, if you need anything, I'm always here.'

He knows she means it genuinely. All he has to do is ask, and she'd tie herself in knots to help him out.

'And what about the Wicked Witch of the West?' The kettle bubbles and pops.

'Who?'

'Sorry. Your mother-in-law, Freya.'

Harvey chews his lip. 'Don't ask.' He rolls his eyes theatrically. 'I told her I thought it was for the best if she moved out, and even offered to pay for a hotel, but she laid such a guilt trip on me I agreed to let her stay for longer.'

'Oh, Harvey.'

'I know. I'm too soft for my own good. And then last night, it turned nasty. Can you believe she accused me of marrying Gwyneth for her money? And that I was the driver who tried to kill her?'

'The cheek of it.' Sheryl shakes her head. 'I don't know how you stand having her living there. I'd have told her where to shove it by now.'

'I'm afraid I lost my temper. Then she claimed she'd been joking and hadn't meant a word of it. But I could see it in her eyes. She meant everything she said. And now I don't know what to do. I'm supposed to be on my way to the hospital, but Freya will be there and I don't want to pick up where we left off in front of Gwyneth.'

'She clearly doesn't know you very well, but it's hardly surprising.' Sheryl folds her arms and casts her gaze down to her feet. When she looks up again, she's wearing a serious expression, her brows knitted. 'Harvey, there's something you need to know.

I wasn't sure if I should mention it. I don't want to cause any more trouble.'

Harvey studies her face, his mind racing. 'What?' he asks. 'If you have something to say, just tell me.'

'It's about Freya.'

'Go on.' Harvey swallows. It's hard to believe the situation with his mother-in-law could be any worse or their fledgling relationship any more strained.

'The thing is, I know it's none of my business and I shouldn't have been looking, but I couldn't help myself and after how that woman's treated you, I think you have a right to know.'

An icy chill spirals down Harvey's spine. 'Please, Sheryl, just say it.'

'I was going to do a bit more digging, so I was a hundred per cent certain, you know? I don't say it to be vindictive. After all, I hardly know her.'

It feels like standing under a mountain, listening to the distant rumble of an avalanche about to engulf him. 'Sheryl?'

'I don't think Freya is who she claims to be.'

The kettles reaches its climax in a hissing explosion of steam, and clicks off. Silence fills the room. Harvey blinks at his neighbour, her words filtering slowly through his brain. He gives a slight shake of his head. 'What do you mean?'

'Freya isn't Gwyneth's mother. It's impossible.'

Harvey stands motionless as if he's waiting for the punchline of a feeble Christmas cracker joke.

'I'm sorry, Harvey. There's no easy way to tell you
this, but Gwyneth's mother died more than twenty
years ago.'

Chapter 31

Laughter bubbles up from Harvey's chest. This has to be a joke. He looks deep into Sheryl's eyes, waiting for her to break into a smile. To join him in an awkward, nervous chuckle. But she doesn't. She's deadly serious.

'How can she be dead?' he mumbles.

'I wasn't sure whether I should say anything. I didn't want you to think I was interfering, but something felt off when you were telling me about her, you know? That she said she'd lost touch with Gwyneth for so long and suddenly she appeared at the hospital. It didn't make sense. So I started doing some research.'

'Research?'

'Looking through family records, mainly.'

Harvey shakes his head, confused.

Sheryl leans back against the counter with a sigh, as if it's all perfectly obvious. 'I've always been interested in family history,' she says. 'I've mapped out my entire family tree going back six generations. It's fascinating what you can find out, and it's not difficult if you know where to look, especially as everything's online these days. Birth records. Marriage certificates. Deaths.'

Harvey's never been interested in that sort of thing. The only time he's looked into his past was when he was set an assignment at primary school to trace his family tree and his mother gave him as much information as she could remember. Names, dates of birth, marriages and deaths. Who was related to who and how. And he'd drawn it carefully as the branches of an actual tree on the back of a scrap of old wallpaper his father had left over from decorating the living room. He was amazed at how many cousins he had and never knew existed, and how far the branches of the tree extended, even within three generations. It was mildly interesting, but not something he'd ever considered pursuing further. Not like Sheryl.

'I started looking into Gwyneth's family,' she continues. 'I hope you don't mind? It is a bit naughty of me without her permission. It took a bit of investigative work, but eventually I found Gwyneth's birth certificate, which gave me her parents' names.'

'Gwyneth's never really talked about her parents. I know her father died when she was in her early twenties and something happened between her and her mother that caused them to lose touch, but that's all she ever told me. I assumed it was something trivial that blew up out of proportion. That's what families are like, isn't it?'

Sheryl shrugs. 'It might be easier if I show you,' she says, with a glint in her eye, clearly pleased with herself.

Harvey follows her into a small study with books lining two walls. A hardwood, leather-topped desk is tucked under a window overlooking the back garden and green, rolling fields.

Sheryl flips open a laptop on the desk and taps at the keyboard. After a few moments, she pulls up an official-looking document. Then steps out of the way so Harvey can see the screen.

'There,' she says, pointing at what appears to be Gwyneth's birth certificate. 'You see? Her parents are Yvonne and Victor Grainger.'

She's right. Gwyneth's mother's name is there in black and white. Printed in ink. Unmistakable. *Yvonne*. Not Freya.

He blinks and swallows, the enormity of what Sheryl has uncovered hitting him hard. Freya's been lying to him all along.

'Yvonne passed away more than twenty years ago when she was sixty. Here, I found the death certificate.' Sheryl pulls up another document. Indisputable proof that what she's telling him is true and that Freya can't possibly be Gwyneth's mother because she's been in her grave for two decades.

'If Freya's not her mother, who the hell is she?' Harvey growls shock and confusion giving way to burgeoning anger.

And more to the point, what does she want? Why has she turned up at the hospital pretending to be someone's she not, and what's she hoping to achieve?

Acidic bile rises from Harvey's stomach, his head as light as a helium-filled balloon. 'Oh, god, she's at the hospital now, with Gwyneth. She could be planning anything,' he says.

He's been so gullible. Why did he never think to challenge her? She told him she was Gwyneth's mother, and he accepted it without question. But she looks so much like Gwyneth, even before she dyed her hair blonde and started wearing his wife's clothes. That can't be a coincidence.

So what's her motive? Is she planning some kind of elaborate con? Or something more sinister?

'I ought to call the police,' Harvey mutters as a wave of embarrassment and shame washes over him. He's always thought of himself as worldly-wise. Not the kind of man to be taken in by a common fraudster.

He knows all about the unscrupulous scams that catch the unwary. The phone calls that try to talk you into letting scammers access your computer and bank accounts. The text messages purporting to be from a son or daughter who've found themselves in trouble and urgently need money wired to their account. The emails supposedly from billionaire princes in Nigeria who need help releasing enormous sums of money from off-shore bank accounts.

He'd never fall for any of those. Why has he been so easily taken in by this fraudster?

'I agree. I think you should explain to the police exactly what's going on. God knows how many others she's conned,' Sheryl says.

Is that what's happening? Have he and Gwyneth fallen prey to a serial criminal who's picked on them because they've been left vulnerable and unsuspecting after the hit-and-run?

'I should have seen she was lying,' Harvey snaps, angry with himself for being such an idiot.

'You can't blame yourself.'

'Can't I?'

'Harvey, it's not your fault. You've been under enormous stress.'

'I let a complete stranger into our lives. Into our home. What was I thinking? If she's laid a finger on Gwyneth, I'll kill her. I knew I shouldn't have done that interview.'

He had no idea when he agreed to talk to the press how much personal information he'd end up giving away. It's played straight into Freya's hands, if that's even her name. She had their names, where they live, where Gwyneth was injured and even the hospital where she was being treated. It wouldn't have taken Sherlock Holmes to track them down and exploit them when their defences were laid low.

All Freya had to do was turn up, looking like a frail old lady, and convince the hospital she was a family member. Probably no one at the hospital checked her identity either. They all took her at her word and she was never once challenged, which makes them all guilty.

Sheryl flinches. 'You don't think she's planning to hurt Gwyneth, do you?'

'I don't know what she's planning, but I'm going to find out, and I'm going to put an end to it.'

How dare she take advantage of them like this, when his wife's fighting for her life in hospital. When he's distracted by more important things.

Whatever Freya has in mind, whether it's to rob them blind or something more heinous, now he's onto her, he's going to make her pay. And he's going to enjoy every second.

Chapter 32

Harvey ought to alert the police and let them deal with Freya, but she's made the attack on them so personal, he can't let her get away with it without confronting her. She's gatecrashed their lives, tricked her way into their home and even made Harvey feel as if he's unwelcome at his wife's bedside.

He will call the police, but first he's going to look her in the eye and tell her exactly what he thinks of her. He's going to take great pleasure in telling her she's an evil, contemptuous, bloodsucking monster and watch her squirm as he reveals he knows the truth. That she's a fraud. A charlatan.

His gut instinct is to head to the hospital, to hunt her down and have it out with her. He can't wait to hear her pathetic excuses as she tries to convince Harvey he has it all wrong, but it's too late for that. He's going to destroy her and make sure she's never able to do the same to anyone else again.

But there's something even more pressing he needs to do first. He's going to remove every trace that she's been in the house. He wants all the reminders of how stupid he was to let her into their lives gone.

He turns back towards home, his car skidding to a halt on the gravel drive. He hurries inside, puffing as he marches up the stairs and heads into Freya's room - *his* room. Something else she's stolen from him.

At least she's had the decency to make the bed, although there's a pile of Gwyneth's crumpled clothes lying by the wardrobe which haven't been hung up.

Harvey walks slowly around the bed as if he's a detective hunting clues to catch a killer. The room smells musty, and there's a nauseating hint of stale sweat in the air. He throws open the wardrobe doors and peers inside, raking through Gwyneth's dresses, skirts and blouses. He scours her drawers and checks the bedside cabinets, but Freya's left nothing of her own. Like a cuckoo in the nest, she's assumed Gwyneth's life, stolen her clothes and her appearance, used her cosmetics, and left scant evidence of her own miserable existence. There's not so much as a pair of Freya's dirty knickers lying around.

Harvey throws back the duvet on the bed and looks under the pillows. Then, with a grunt, lifts the mattress. Below the slats, he spots Freya's tattered bag-for-life and shivers. He hooks it out with his foot and pushes it across the floor. He knows what's inside and has no desire to look again. Even the thought of that plastic box full of dead frogs makes him shudder.

215

He initially planned to return Freya's things to her at the hospital, dumping them theatrically at her feet as he yelled at her to never show her face again. But now he's having second thoughts. It would be much more satisfying to burn the bag and watch it crackle and melt. A far more fitting end to Freya's time with them.

He's about to drop the mattress back onto the bed when something else catches his eye. Another bag, in the shadows, pushed closer to the wall. He recognises it as the grey holdall he shoved there a few weeks ago after he and Gwyneth returned from a weekend away in the Cotswolds. He'd been meaning to put it back in the loft where it belongs but had forgotten all about it. It should be empty, but it's clearly been filled with something bulky from the way it's bulging at the seams.

He lowers himself to his knees and drags it out by its shoulder strap. He puts it on the bed and tears open the zip.

One of their expensive fluffy blue towels spills out. So that's her game, stealing the towels? He wonders what else she's pilfered, and as he pulls it out angrily, he's shocked to discover a delicate blue and white Chinese vase that's supposed to have pride of place on a shelf in the lounge wrapped inside it.

Beneath it, another thick towel has been wrapped around a beautiful glass plate Freya's taken from the wall in the library and one of Gwyneth's favourite broaches is swathed inside one of her T-shirts. At the bottom of the bag, sheathed in a tea towel, he finds an oil painting of an old sailing boat on choppy waters under a leaden sky that's come from one of the guest rooms.

Did she really think he wouldn't notice they were missing? And what was she planning to do with them? Sell them on eBay? Try her luck at an auction house? Doesn't she realise they're all unique pieces that are going to raise eyebrows if they turn up on the market?

At least it answers one of his questions about Freya's motivations. She's nothing more than a common thief.

He lays each of the items out on the bed next to the bag and snaps a picture of the haul on his phone as evidence, his bubbling. Did she really think she could waltz into their home and take what she liked? It's the gall of it, the brazen way she's lied and cheated to win their trust, that angers him the most.

He rushes back to the car, ignoring the twinge that catches him beneath the sternum as he huffs down the stairs, and breaks most of the speed limits on his way to the hospital.

When he reaches the intensive care unit, having foolishly thought it would be quicker to take the stairs than the lift, he's out of breath, sweating heavily, his legs wobbly.

He's buzzed onto the ward and marches past the nurses' station with determination, fuelled by anger.

He crashes into Gwyneth's room and immediately spots Freya standing by one of the bleeping machines at Gwyneth's side. She jumps guiltily away from whatever it was she was doing.

'You!' Harvey splutters, stabbing a stubby finger in Freya's direction. 'How could you?'

Freya's eyes widen with shock as she clutches at her chest.

Seeing her standing there, wearing his wife's clothes, her hair bleached ridiculously blonde like Gwyneth's, drives Harvey into a further rage.

'Harvey,' she says, 'what on earth's wrong?'

'You know what's wrong.' He advances towards her, eyes burning. He could kill her with his bare hands.

'I don't,' she pleads, innocence written across her face.

She's good, but she's had a lot of practice at pretending to be someone she's not.

'You lied to me. You made me believe you were Gwyneth's mother.'

'Harvey, I...'

He glances at the machine by Gwyneth's bed, suddenly aware of the cacophony of bleeping, whirring and clicking.

'What were you doing?' he asks, a spike of suspicion and fear running through his veins.

'Nothing.'

'When I came into the room. Were you doing something to the machine? You were touching it. I saw you.'

'No, I wasn't.'

Was she trying to kill Gwyneth by tampering with the equipment? Has he arrived in the nick of time? If he'd been five or ten minutes later, would his wife already be dead?

'Stay away from her,' he growls. 'I'm warning you.'

'Harvey...'

'You're sick. And you're evil.'

'What?' she gasps. 'Why are you saying such horrible things?' Her glasses have slipped halfway down her nose, making her eyes appear even larger than normal. She's the picture of frailty and innocence. But he's seen through her act and he's not falling for it anymore. She's a cancer eating slowly and insidiously away at their lives, trying to destroy them.

There's only one way to deal with it. To cut it out.

'I found the bag,' Harvey says, his voice wavering with emotion.

'What bag?'

'The vase? The glass plate? The painting? What were you going to do? Strip the house bare piece by piece? Take everything you could lay your grubby hands on? What else have you taken?' He'd told himself he'd deal with her calmly and rationally, but his emotions rage like wildfire, and he's virtually yelling at her.

'Oh, that.' Freya bows her head and sighs. 'I'm sorry,' she mumbles.

'What else?' Harvey repeats, the veins in his neck pulsing.

'Nothing, I promise.'

'And all the time you've been alone with Gwyneth, what have you been doing in here? Looking for her bank cards? Hoping she'll wake up so you can squeeze her for her PIN number? Plotting how you'll kill her when you've got what you wanted?'

'Of course not!' Freya's head jerks up. 'Don't be stupid,' she laughs.

It's the final straw. She's played him for an idiot all this time and now she's laughing at him?

He flies at her, his hands wrapping around her scrawny neck, forcing her head against the wall.

She grasps his wrists, trying to pull free, while her eyes bulge in fear and alarm. But Harvey has only one thought. He's going to kill her.

'Did you really think you'd get away with it?' he screams in her face, spittle flying from his mouth.

Freya makes a panicked, croaking noise. Her jaw works, but no sound comes from her mouth.

'Do you have no conscience? My wife almost died, but you just saw an opportunity, didn't you? How do you sleep at night?'

She kicks him in the shins, but he barely feels it. Her body is so bony and light, it's like holding up a chicken carcass.

'You have some nerve waltzing in here, pretending to be Gwyneth's mother when you've never even met her before. You sad, deranged, manipulative witch!'

He squeezes her neck harder, his arms trembling. He didn't come here to kill her, but maybe he'd be doing the world a favour if he did. Saving the next innocent family from falling for her duplicity. After all, she's nothing but a scourge on society.

'I hope you rot in hell,' he yells.

He doesn't hear the clatter of the door being thrown open, the thunder of feet or the shouts of alarm. At least not until powerful hands grab his arms and shoulders and pull him away.

'Let her go,' a man roars in his ear.

Arms wrap around his chest and his world is suddenly filled with noise, panic and violent tugging as his hands are wrested from Freya's neck, and he's dragged backwards, his feet kicking, powerless to resist.

He watches in slow motion as two nurses rush to Freya's side, catching her as her legs buckle and her hands fly to her throat. They guide her to the chair with such compassion and kindness. If only they knew what she was really like.

'She was trying to kill my wife,' Harvey shouts in protest as porters and security guards pull him to the door. But nobody's listening to him.

His instinct is to fight, but there are too many of them. They're too strong.

'Call the police!' someone shouts.

When he realises the futility of resisting, his rage slowly calms. He stops kicking and his body goes limp.

'Alright, alright,' he says. 'I'm calm. You can let me go.'

They stand him up but keep a tight grip on his arms.

'Are you done?' a security guard asks.

'Just get the police here, will you?'

'You *want* me to call the police?'

'It saves me from having to do it. That woman,' he nods at Freya, who's slumped in the chair with the two nurses at her side, 'tried to kill my wife. I want to report an attempted murder.'

'Wait!' Freya looks up, her dress dishevelled, her hair even more of a tangled mess than normal. 'Let me speak to him. Alone.'

She stands and staggers across the room.

'Madam, I don't think that's a good idea,' one of the guards suggests.

'It's okay. He's not going to hurt me,' she croaks, her voice husky and weak. 'There's something I need to tell him. Alone.'

Harvey sneers. 'Save it for the police. I'm sure they'll be fascinated.'

'I owe you an explanation. I'm sorry I lied to you. You're right, I'm not Gwyneth's mother.' She hangs her head in shame.

'It wasn't just me. You lied to everyone in the hospital.'

She shakes her head. 'No, I told them I was family. That's the truth.'

'More lies, Freya. When are you going to stop with this charade? The game's over.'

'I'm not lying. It's the truth. I'm not Gwyneth's mother. I'm her sister. And I can prove it if you don't believe me.'

Chapter 33

Harvey stares at Freya in shock. 'Her sister? I don't believe you. She doesn't have a sister.'

'It's the truth.'

'What on earth is going on here?'

As one, Harvey and Freya turn towards Leanne.

She usually has the face and temperament of an angel, so it's disconcerting to see her turn up looking so flustered and angry. She brushes past the security guards restraining Harvey and marches towards Gwyneth's bed, casting a concerned eye over the blinking numbers on the machines.

A flush of embarrassment heats Harvey's cheeks. He shouldn't have lost control, especially in front of Gwyneth. Leanne warned him she could hear everything going on in the room and that they all needed to maintain a calm environment.

Harvey tries to pull free, but the security guards won't let him go. Not yet.

Leanne folds her arms stiffly across her chest. 'Who is going to explain?'

Freya's head droops. 'I'm afraid it's all my fault, nurse.'

'She lied to us,' Harvey blurts out, sounding like a petulant child. 'She told everyone she's Gwyneth's mother, but it's not true.'

Leanne's gaze flicks from Freya to Harvey and back again, like a reluctant observer at a tennis match.

'Freya?' Leanne says.

'It's true. I'm not Gwyneth's mother,' she whispers. 'She's my sister. I'm sorry.'

'So she says,' Harvey huffs.

'Quiet! And for goodness' sake, let him go,' Leanne snaps at the security guards.

They exchange a look, uncertain what to do. 'He assaulted that woman. We were about to call the police.'

'I'll deal with it,' Leanne says sternly.

'Are you sure?'

'Just let him go,' she demands.

The guards shrug and finally release Harvey's arms. 'If he causes any more trouble, call us, okay?'

Harvey rubs the feeling back into his arms and shoulders as the guards depart, and Leanne suggests they go somewhere more private to talk.

She marches them out of the room like two naughty schoolchildren and finds a quiet office off one of the main corridors.

They stand facing each other, reminding Harvey of the night Gwyneth was brought into hospital and he stood with the detectives, Chalk and Enright, in a similar office as they questioned him.

'Would you like to explain why you thought you could come onto my ward and assault Freya?'

It's worse than being summoned to the head teacher's office. Leanne's probably young enough to be his daughter, but she speaks to him like he's a spotty teenager caught smoking behind the bike sheds.

'Sorry,' he mumbles. He probably overreacted, but he couldn't help himself, especially when Freya laughed at him. 'But she's been lying to us all. She's not who she says she is.'

'I never lied,' Freya protests. 'You assumed I was Gwyneth's mother when we first met. I know it was wrong, but I was too embarrassed to correct you. I didn't even know who you were.'

It's not the way Harvey remembers it. He's sure she introduced herself as Gwyneth's mother when he found her at his wife's bedside, but there was a lot going on. He was still trying to come to terms with his wife being in a coma, their lives changed forever. Everything about the last week is a blur.

'You're a liar,' Harvey shouts.

'Alright, let's keep this civil, shall we? I'd rather not have to involve the police,' Leanne warns him.

'I think we should.' Harvey folds his arms, mirroring the nurse's defensive stance. 'Let's get them in here to sort this out.'

'I can explain everything.' Ugly red marks are developing around Freya's throat. 'Honestly, I didn't come here to cause trouble, no matter what you think.'

'I caught you red-handed.' Harvey glowers at her. 'You've been stealing from us.'

'I haven't stolen anything.'

'I found the bag,' he screams.

'Enough!' Leanne holds up her hands, separating them, like she's parting the Red Sea. 'Freya, he has a point. Why didn't you say something instead of letting us all go on thinking you were Gwyneth's mother?'

'I don't know. I suppose I thought it didn't matter. I was more concerned about Gwyneth.'

'Ha!' Harvey snorts. 'And anyway, there's one tee-ny problem with your story. Gwyneth doesn't have any sisters.' He rocks back on his heels with a self-satisfied smile. Let's see Freya wriggle out of this.

'Oh? Is that what Gwyneth told you?' Freya whimpers, pulling an expression of hurt and disappointment.

'No brothers. No sisters. She was an only child,' Harvey confirms. If she'd had a sister, she would have told him, but it's just more lies and deceit.

'I'm sorry she didn't tell you about me, but I'm not surprised. I was nine when she was born. A happy accident, I've always thought. But it was more than Mother could cope with. I was a teenager when she sent me away. I had to start a new life with a foster family and never saw Gwyneth again. At least not until I saw her picture on the news.'

Harvey claps slowly, an ironic applause for an implausible story. 'And you expect us to believe that?'

'I'm telling you the truth.'

'You wouldn't know the truth if it spat in your eye,' Harvey hisses. 'I've heard enough. If you won't call the police, then I will. You can explain it to them.' He digs into his pocket for his phone, and looks up the number for Chalk, the detective investigating the hit-and-run.

'I can prove it.' Freya meets his gaze defiantly. Her eyes are rimmed red and moist with tears. She should be on the stage.

Harvey calls her bluff with a shrug. 'Fine. Do it.'

Freya digs into the bag slung over her shoulder, lifts out a ball of wool and a pair of knitting needles, and retrieves a folded slip of paper.

'I grabbed this on my way out in case I had to prove who I was at the hospital to get in to see Gwyneth,' Freya explains as she thrusts the slip of paper at Harvey. 'As it turned out, I never had to show it to anyone. Until now.'

Harvey unfolds the paper and turns it up the right way, scanning the words printed on the certificate with a sinking feeling.

'It proves I am who I say I am,' Freya says.

Harvey swallows a hard lump in his throat.

'I'm Freya Grainger, born in London in November 1962 to parents Yvonne and Victor Grainger,' she says, as if he can't read for himself.

'How do I know it's genuine? I bet you can buy fake birth certificates like this online,' he says, waving the piece of paper at her dismissively.

Freya gives him a withering look. 'It's not a fake.'

Leanne takes the certificate and reads it for herself. 'It looks genuine to me.'

'Well,' Harvey splutters. 'It still doesn't explain what you're doing here.' And if it's true, why didn't Gwyneth ever mention she had a sister?

'I told you, I came to see Gwyneth. We've been apart for almost fifty years and I'd lost hope that I'd ever find her.' Freya reaches for a chair at the desk. She rolls it across the floor and sits.

'And how fortunate that you discovered she'd done so well in life,' Harvey sneers, unconvinced. What about the things she'd stolen that he'd found hidden in the bag under the bed? 'I bet you couldn't believe it when you found out she had a big house in the country.'

Freya shakes her head sadly. 'It's not like that.' Her voice catches in her throat. 'Being taken away from my family was the worst thing that ever happened to me. I've dreamt for so long about being reunited with them, but after Mum and Dad died, there was only Gwyneth left. I'd almost given up hope of finding her. I know it's a strange thing to say, but it was a stroke of luck she was hit by that car and the story was on the news. Otherwise, I might never have found her.'

'It wasn't lucky. She nearly died,' Harvey points out.

'I didn't mean to sound flippant. But she's going to be okay, isn't she, nurse? Because I couldn't stand it if she died before I had the chance to speak to her again, and to tell her how much I've missed her. How much I love her. Bad circumstances have brought us together again. I just want a second shot at happiness.'

Oh, please.

Harvey rolls his eyes, but when he looks at Leanne, she's fighting back tears. She sniffs and throws her arms around Freya, wrapping her in a warm hug.

'Oh, honey,' she snivels. 'I'm sure she knows you're here. You've been so good with her, talking to her and looking after her.'

Which is exactly what Harvey was supposed to be doing until Freya turned up and pushed him aside.

'How do you explain the bag under the bed?' he asks.

Freya pulls away from Leanne, removes her glasses, and wipes her eyes with the sleeve of her sweater. 'Bag?'

'The bag you filled up with antiques you were going to steal.'

'Oh,' she says. 'That.'

'Yes, *that*.'

'I shouldn't have taken them, but I didn't think Gwyneth would mind. She has so many lovely things.'

'She does.'

'I was going to put them all back. I wouldn't really have taken them.'

'A likely story. Let's see what the police have to say about it.'

'Harvey!' Leanne chides. 'You can't call the police to report your own sister-in-law. And anyway, they might have something to say about the fact you assaulted her.' She glares at him from under the hood of her brow.

'I don't want to report the assault,' Freya says, picking at her fingernails. 'As far as I'm concerned, it's water under the bridge. Harvey was upset, that's all. The main thing now is getting Gwyneth better.'

'Harvey?' Leanne's still glowering at him.

He huffs. The problem is, nothing has actually been removed from the house, as far as he's aware. Just because Freya took a few things and put them in a bag, it doesn't technically constitute theft, does it? 'Fine. Forget the police. For the moment.'

'And if you think it's for the best, I'll leave,' Freya says. 'I'll go home tonight and you'll never hear from me again.'

'No, you can't leave. What about Gwyneth?' Leanne looks horrified. 'You've waited all these years to be reunited. You can't walk away now.'

'Harvey doesn't want me here. He's made that clear.'

Harvey rolls his neck as his stomach rumbles noisily. Why's he suddenly being painted as the bad guy?

'You can't let her leave,' Leanne says. 'It's not fair. Maybe you two need to start over, now you know the truth.'

'What do you think, Harvey? I'm willing to try again if you are.' Freya smiles weakly.

Harvey bites hard on his lower lip. They've backed him into a corner. He can hardly refuse, can he? 'I don't know.'

'You know, I make a mean treacle tart.' Freya's eyes glisten behind her thick lenses. 'I could knock one up tonight for us to share, if you'll have me back,' she says.

Treacle tart is his absolute favourite. How did she know? But having her back in the house? He's not so sure. Although, the advantage of keeping her near is that he'd be able to keep a close eye on her. And what more harm can she do, now she knows he's onto her?

Eventually, he lets out a long sigh of defeat. 'Alright,' he says. 'You can stay.'

Freya and Leanne grin at each other.

'For now, at least,' he adds.

Chapter 34

Freya's story is leakier than a sieve. Even if she is Gwyneth's long-lost sister, which Harvey still doesn't entirely believe, it doesn't explain why she took those antiques and hid them in a bag under the bed. Or lied to Harvey about being Gwyneth's mother.

He doesn't trust her, and although the last thing he wants is for her to be living under the same roof, he needs to keep her close. Let her think she's won him around. Then he can find out what she's really planning, while keeping one step ahead of her.

He spends the rest of the day monitoring her every movement. They share an uneasy truce as they tend to Gwyneth and try to bring some semblance of normality back to her care. Harvey is under no illusion that as closely as he's watching Freya, Leanne is watching him.

That evening, Freya follows Harvey home in her beaten-up SUV. They park side by side and Harvey holds open the front door for her with a forced smile, although the way she looks at him, with a mixture of fear and suspicion, makes it clear she doesn't trust him. It's almost as if he tried to kill her earlier.

For a moment, he thought he might. When the red mist descended and he had his hands around her throat, he could have done it. He nearly did. The marks around her neck are likely to be testament to it for several days. But he's calmer now, intent on playing a longer game.

'I'm happy to cook tonight,' Freya announces. 'And I think I may have promised treacle tart for dessert.'

'There's not much in the cupboards. I've not had the chance to even think about shopping.' He's not had to. Sheryl's been bringing him meals while he's been in and out of the hospital.

'Don't worry, I'll rustle something up. I'm sure I can find something in the freezer. I assume you have some eggs and flour? An old tin of treacle?'

Harvey shrugs. 'I think so.'

'Then why don't you put your feet up?' Freya suggests. 'I'll crack on with dinner.'

They exchange smiles but there's no hiding the fragile atmosphere between them as they both juggle with the pretence of normality, although there's nothing normal about their situation.

'Are you sure?'

'Of course. I'll bring you a glass of wine, if you'd like?'

'I'll be in my study then,' Harvey says. 'There are a few work things I need to catch up on.'

When she shoos him away, he doesn't argue. He has a difficult phone call that he'd rather not have to make, but Tim's been bombarding him with voice-mails, texts and emails all day. He can't put it off any longer.

He ambles into his study, closes the door, and sits at his desk. Then dials Tim's number and waits anxiously for the call to connect.

Tim answers breathlessly, as if he's been out for a run or just climbed the stairs.

'Harvey?'

'Tim, you have to stop trying to contact me. I've made my position clear and I'm afraid I'm not changing my mind. It's no longer going to be pos-sible for me to work with you. I'm sorry,' he says, rubbing the tension out of his brow with his free hand.

'Don't say that.'

'My decision's made. I have the names of some colleagues I could recommend —'

'I don't want to work with anyone else,' Tim yelps. 'I want to work with you. You understand me. You know what I'm going through.'

'It's nothing personal.'

'So why are you doing this to me? As if I haven't gone through enough in the last few months.'

'It's a professional decision with your best inter-ests at heart.'

'No, it's not. I need you, Harvey. I can't cope with-out you.'

'Listen, you've made tremendous progress since our first session, but now it's time for a change.'

'Why? I don't understand what I've done wrong.'

Harvey sighs silently. 'Why don't you give Graham Turner a call? He's a brilliant therapist and comes highly recommended. I can give you his number —'

'I don't want to talk to anyone else!' Tim screams down the line so loudly Harvey has to hold the phone away from his ear.

'Please, don't raise your voice at me.'

'You know what? I'm glad about what happened to your wife.'

'Excuse me?'

'You heard me. I'm glad Gwyneth ended up in hospital. I hope she dies.'

Harvey's stunned. 'What?' he splutters.

'I said, I hope she dies and then maybe you'll know what it feels like to lose someone you love. To know the pain. The emptiness. The gut-wrenching agony.'

A rage swells in Harvey's chest. It takes all his willpower to hold it in check. 'I know you're still hurting, Tim, but you don't mean that.'

'I do. I mean every word, you sanctimonious, pompous twat. Well, fuck you and fuck everyone you care about.'

'Tim —'

'No, shut up and listen for once. You sit there on your high horse, preaching about something you know nothing about, telling me I should journal my feelings and channel my grief into something positive. And for what? What good do you think it's done? It's not brought Alison back, has it? So what's the point of carrying on? Life without her isn't worth living.'

'You have everything to live for. You have your whole life ahead of you. New adventures to discover. And you will find happiness again.'

'Oh, fuck off, Harvey. What do you know about it? The worst you've had to deal with is your wife ending up in a coma. But she'll survive, won't she? She'll be home before you know it and you'll put it all behind you and carry on as if nothing's happened.'

She will if there's no permanent damage to her brain, but they won't know for sure until the swelling goes down. For all Harvey knows, Gwyneth could be left unable to talk, walk or do anything for herself. And then what? Is he expected to be her carer and her husband?

'I could do without the lecture, thank you,' Harvey says, bristling.

'Do you still think it was an accident? What if someone was trying to teach you a lesson? Someone who wanted you to know what it's like to have to identify their wife in the morgue?'

'I've told you, I don't want to discuss it. It's not appropriate,' Harvey says.

'I know which hospital she's in. How difficult do you think it would be to blag my way in to see her?'

Harvey's blood runs cold, not only at the implicit threat, but because he knows how easy it is for a stranger to talk their way into the intensive care unit. Freya's proved it.

'Are you threatening me?'

'Threatening you? Of course not.' Tim laughs cruelly. 'Why would you say that?'

'This conversation is over. Do you want these contact details or not?'

'Fuck you. Just remember, I know where you live.'

Harvey pulls the phone away from his ear and disconnects the call, stabbing at the screen with a trembling finger. *Was* that a threat? It sounded like one. He probably ought to report it, but what are the police going to do? Nothing. He tries to convince himself that it's just Tim letting off steam. At least it confirms Harvey's done the right thing. Hopefully, it was just empty threats and Tim's frustration boiling over. He'll calm down in time.

When there's a knock at the door, Harvey almost drops the phone.

The door creaks open and Freya shuffles in with a large glass of red wine in one hand.

'Are you alright?' she asks. 'You look like you've seen a ghost.'

Harvey tosses the phone down and pushes it away as if it's toxic. 'I had to make a difficult call, that's all.'

The smell of something delicious coming from the kitchen makes his stomach rumble. As usual, he's starving.

'Dinner won't be long. I've found some bits to throw into a stir-fry. I hope that's okay?' Freya says.

'Sounds good.'

'And there's a treacle tart about to go into the oven,' she adds with a coy smile.

'You found some eggs then?'

'I had to improvise a little, but I think you'll like it.'

Harvey's never thought of himself as a comfort-eater, but food has always brought happiness to his life. Especially something as sickly sweet as treacle tart, which his mother used to make him when he was a child. After that call with Tim, it's just what he needs.

They eat informally in the kitchen. Harvey sits at the head of the table with Freya at his side, opposite Gwyneth's usual place.

The stir-fry is a triumph, not least because the fridge is virtually empty. He has no idea where she found the ingredients.

'I defrosted some chicken that was in the freezer,' she explains as Harvey shovels a huge forkful of food into his mouth. 'And there was a bag of frozen veg, plus some dried noodles in the cupboard. Hope it's okay.'

'It's better than okay. It's wonderful.'

'I'm glad you like it. My way of saying I'm sorry again.'

'Like you said, water under the bridge,' he lies. 'Now, I'm interested in what you were telling me about your parents putting you into care. I had no idea. How old were you?'

He hopes that if he can encourage her to tell enough lies, she'll eventually either tie herself in knots or contradict herself completely. And then he'll be ready.

'Fifteen.'

'It seems a harsh thing to do.'

'My poor mother had a breakdown. They said it was nervous exhaustion because she was struggling with two of us,' Freya explains. 'They decided the best thing would be to send one of us away, and because I was older, they decided it should be me.'

Harvey chases a chunk of chicken around his plate. 'That must have been traumatic.'

Freya hunches over the table with one arm curled possessively around her plate as if she's guarding it, so he can't see her face or read her expression. 'I guess you learn to adapt quickly at that age.'

'So from the age of fifteen, you grew up with a foster family? What were they like?'

'Fine.'

'You got on with them?'

'They were okay,' Freya says, leaving Harvey none the wiser. 'But I missed my sister.'

'Were you close growing up?'

'We were more like best friends than sisters,' Freya says, finally looking up with a smile of nostalgia. 'We shared a room and did everything together. We even dressed alike.'

Harvey frowns. That at least goes some way to explaining why she's taken to wearing Gwyneth's clothes and has bleached her hair blonde.

'When did you start looking for her?'

Freya looks up at the ceiling, thinking. 'When I was about eighteen, I suppose. But we were living in a different part of the country by then, far away from my parents and my sister. It was hard. We didn't have the internet back then.'

'She must have changed a lot since you last saw her,' Harvey chuckles.

'No, she's just as I remembered her. And just as beautiful.'

'But it was years ago.'

'Forty-six, to be precise.'

'I can't believe you never gave up looking.'

Freya looks up sharply. 'Why would I?'

'I just mean, it's a long time, that's all.'

A timer on the oven buzzes. Freya pushes her plate to one side and jumps up.

'Ready for dessert?' she asks. 'I've made custard.'

'You're spoiling me.' Harvey leans back in his chair and rubs his stomach.

She serves him an enormous portion of treacle tart, covered in thick custard. It's sweet almost to the point of being sickly, the pastry a perfect thickness.

'Are you not having any?' Harvey asks as she sits back down at an empty place.

'I couldn't eat another thing.'

Oh well, more for him.

'You're a chef in an old people's home, aren't you?' he asks.

Freya laughs. 'A cook. It's only a small kitchen.'

But he's not interested in talking about what she does for a living, or listening to any more of her lies. He wants to know if she has any genuine memories of Gwyneth when they were growing up.

'What was she like?'

'Who?'

'Gwyneth. When she was a girl. I'd love to know what she was like when she was younger,' he says.

Freya stands and collects Harvey's bowl as he finishes his last mouthful with a satisfied murmur of appreciation.

'I'm sorry, Harvey. I don't really want to talk about the past. It's still so painful. You understand, don't you?'

Harvey's not sure he does. All he wanted to know was what Freya was like as a child, but he doesn't push it. 'Leave the clearing up. I'll do it later,' he offers.

'It's fine. You relax. You've had a tough few days.'

He wouldn't argue with that, although most of the stress has been caused by Freya, her lying and her stealing.

'If you're absolutely certain?' Freya really is making an effort. It's the first time she's offered to clear up since she arrived.

'Of course.'

Harvey yawns. 'In which case, I might get an early night. I'm shattered.' After another busy day and with a full stomach, he's on his knees. He can pick up the conversation about Gwyneth with Freya in the morning. It can wait.

He heaves himself out of his chair with a grunt and staggers up to bed with his swollen stomach aching. He's eaten far too much, but desserts have always been his weakness.

As he cleans his teeth at the basin in the family bathroom, he stares at himself in the mirror. He looks tired. There are bags under his eyes that weren't there before and his skin is grey. He also has the beginnings of a headache, a tight throbbing at the back of his skull, which is probably the result of exhaustion and stress.

He fumbles with the door handle and, as he crosses the landing to his room, almost stumbles and loses his footing, a wave of dizziness hitting him. He really needs to get some sleep.

He slips into his room, pushes the door closed and attempts to get undressed. But his fingers feel fat and uncoordinated as he struggles with the buttons of his shirt. He can't seem to work out how to pop them open. He gives up, and when a wave of nausea overwhelms him, he crashes onto the bed.

He groans and rolls over. He's not feeling so good. His head's swimming and is light with dizziness. He must have picked up a bug. Probably in the hospital. Places like that are full of them. A real breeding ground. And he's been so run down these last few days. It must be finally taking its toll. He buries his head in the pillow, curls up into a ball like a baby, and slips into a deep, dreamless sleep, certain he'll feel better in the morning.

Chapter 35

Harvey is still fully dressed when he wakes in the early hours of the morning with a raging thirst and his brain trying to burrow out of his skull. He props himself up on one elbow, his tongue as dry and as coarse as sandpaper, and is forced to shut his eyes as the vague outline of the room swims and shimmies in front of his face.

His heart is racing, his breathing ragged and shallow, and he can't work out for the life of him where he is. Not in his own bed, that's for sure. And then he remembers and groans.

His mouth tastes like a sewer, his teeth coated in a sticky gum. He needs water. Desperately. He swings his legs onto the floor and rolls upright, taking a few seconds to centre himself as his head and stomach lurch. He feels like his body has been turned inside out and dragged behind a tractor. His eyes sting and his skin itches.

He tries to stand, but his legs are weak and won't support his weight.

'Freya,' he calls, his voice reedy.

He shouts for her again, louder, the sound cutting through the silence of the night like a balloon bursting in a library.

He waits, listening. Hoping she's heard. But there's no response beyond the pulsing of blood in his ears.

He needs to drink.

A flush of sweat breaks out across his forehead as he hauls himself to his feet. Clinging to the wall for support, he edges to the door, reaches for the handle, and misses. What the hell is wrong with him? He can barely stand, let alone see straight. He refocuses on the handle, his head wobbling like a newborn baby's, and eventually pulls the door open. He virtually falls out onto the landing.

'Freya!'

She must have heard him. But she doesn't come.

He shuffles across the carpet like an old man, creeping slowly along the landing. He's not only physically incapable of going any quicker, but anything faster than a sloth's pace is so unsettling it makes him nauseous. A landlubber lost at sea on a stormy swell.

Eventually, he reaches the stairs, where he stops to catch his breath. It's taken all his effort to make the short distance from his room and he still has the stairs to navigate. If he wasn't so desperate for a drink, he'd give up and return to bed. But all he can think about is a refreshing glass of water.

He stretches out a leg, feeling for the first step with his toes, his hand reaching for the banister.

He wobbles, off balance, and for a heart-lurching moment thinks he's going to fall. But he finds the handrail and the first step, and swallowing back the nausea threatening to engulf him, begins the delicate descent.

Who would have thought going down the stairs could be so demanding? This is more than exhaustion or stress. Something's wrong. He's not felt this bad since he caught Covid and thought he was dying, bedridden for the best part of a week. All he wants to do is curl up in a ball and hide.

It takes several minutes to make it to the hall, clinging on to the banister the whole way.

He swipes his hand across the wall and finds the light switch, the spotlights in the ceiling so bright they hurt his eyes.

Finally, he steps into the kitchen and is struck by a potent kick of Chinese five-spice lingering in the air from last night's stir-fry. He snatches a glass from a cupboard and stumbles to the sink. Fills it from the cold tap. Gulps it down in hungry mouthfuls, not caring that some spills from his lips and drips onto his shirt.

He clings to the worktop, gasping for breath, his head still spinning, his limbs aching. Whatever bug he's picked up, it's come on fast and strong. He felt fine earlier in the evening. But he was probably still running on the adrenaline of the day, and when he relaxed he let the virus, if that's what this is, take hold.

With the pounding in his brain worsening, he hunts in a drawer for a box of paracetamol, squeezes two tablets out of a blister pack and throws them into his mouth. He turns back to the sink, refills his glass and swallows the pills.

As he's summoning the energy to make it back to bed, he notices an opaque plastic bottle next to the kettle that shouldn't be there. Inside is a light blue liquid, the colour of a watery sky. He recognises it with its peeling label, crinkled and cracked with age. A bottle that belongs in a cardboard box with the car wash, sponges and old rags that Lionel kept in the barn for cleaning his car.

Curious, Harvey reaches for it, wondering how it's found its way into the kitchen. He picks it up and reads the label, blinking. A chill of horror washes from his head down to his toes.

'Bitch!' he hisses under his breath.

Is it already too late? Has the damage been done? And to think he'd given Freya the benefit of the doubt. He should never have invited her back, but he never seriously thought she'd try to kill him.

He crashes across the kitchen, his heart thudding dangerously in his chest, and snatches the phone from its cradle on the sideboard in the hall.

He doesn't know what to do. He can't think straight. It's late, but it's an emergency. He dials, the receiver shaking in his hand, puts it to his ear and waits as the call rings and rings.

Eventually, it's answered, her voice bleary with sleep.

'Hello?'

'Sheryl... help... me,' he gasps.

'Harvey? Is that you? What's wrong?' she asks, more alert now.

'It's Freya. I think...' he croaks, 'she's... poisoned me.'

And then everything goes black.

Chapter 36

The sheets are stiff. The cotton thin. And as his vision slowly swims into focus, Harvey sees he's on a hospital ward with five other beds filled with men of differing ages and states of health. Some are old and grey, their mouths slack. Others are younger, sitting up in dressing gowns and pyjamas, chatting with family. The man in the adjacent bed is so jaundiced, it looks as if he's had a spray tan that's gone badly wrong.

A hum of activity fills his ears. People talking. The swish of clothing. The rattle of teacups. The hum of machinery, and faintly, above the sound of the throbbing in his own head, he hears birds singing outside. Sun is streaming through a large window that overlooks the ugly, grey industrial rear of a hospital complex, simultaneously warming and brightening the room.

'Hey, you're awake?'

Sheryl's voice surprises him. He rolls his head and finds her leaning over the bed with an odd expression on her face. A mixture of delight and relief.

'Where am I?' he croaks, struggling to find his voice, his mouth dry.

He tries to sit up, but his body is wracked with weakness. Hollow tubes attached to his arm appear to be draining his blood into a machine.

'Lie back. Take it easy. You're in hospital, but you're going to be fine,' Sheryl assures him.

'How?'

A vague memory creeps into his brain of collapsing at home, clutching the phone.

Sheryl takes his hand and wraps it in hers, her eyes moist with tears. Why's she crying?

Then it comes back to him with the weight of an avalanche.

'Freya,' he says. 'She did this.'

'Don't try to speak.'

'Did you call the police?'

With any luck, she'll already be behind bars, out of their lives for good.

'Well, no, I didn't know what to do,' Sheryl says, a wild wisp of hair falling over her eyes. She looks different, almost unrecognisable, as if her features have been smoothed out or rearranged. He can't put his finger on it. 'You were saying all sorts of crazy things. Not making much sense.'

Harvey closes his eyes and lets his head sink into the pillow. It feels like his insides have been removed, turned inside out and shoved back into his body in the wrong order.

'Antifreeze,' he whispers.

251

'What?'

'I found the bottle in the kitchen.'

'What bottle?'

'She put it in the tart. She tried to kill me.'

'Who? Freya?'

Sheryl's not wearing make-up. That's what it is. He's never seen her without eyeliner and eye shadow, lip gloss and foundation before. She looks like a different woman. Plainer and more natural, and in many respects more attractive.

'Where is she?' Harvey's eyes fly open in panic. 'She's dangerous.'

'Harvey, you're getting yourself all worked up again.' Sheryl sits up with a look of panic. She glances towards the corridor at the end of the ward. 'I'll find someone.'

He grips her hands more tightly as he feels her letting go. He pulls her close. 'We have to stop her,' he implores.

'Harvey, you're scaring me.'

It might already be too late, of course. Freya's had the entire night while he's been unconscious to do whatever she pleases.

Sheryl pulls her hand back and jumps to her feet. 'Nurse,' she calls, timidly.

Harvey yanks back the covers and tries to swing his legs out of bed, but while his mind is willing, his body is depleted of energy.

'You can't get out of bed,' Sheryl tells him sternly, pulling the covers back over his legs. 'You need to get better first.'

'I'm fine.'

'No, you're not,' she snaps. 'Look at you. You could have died if I hadn't found you when I did. It's a good job I still have a spare key.'

Harvey recalls stumbling downstairs for a glass of water, feeling like he'd been passed through a meat grinder, worried he was coming down with Covid, before discovering the antifreeze, which he knows Freya left out deliberately for him to find. As if she wanted him to know what she'd done and the cruelty she'd inflicted. That she was the one with the upper hand. That she'd outsmarted him.

'You came?' he asks. He remembers calling Sheryl because he didn't know who else to ring.

'You had collapsed in the hall with the phone still in your hand,' she says. 'You gave me such a shock.'

'Did you see her?'

'Who? Freya?'

Harvey nods, his head rubbing against the soft pillow.

'No, I didn't know she was in the house.'

'Where's my phone? Pass it to me.' Harvey reaches out a hand, the transparent tube filled with blood flexing. He watches it curiously, wondering why his blood is being filtered out of his body.

'You don't need your phone,' Sheryl insists.

'I do. I need to call the police.'

'Why?'

'She tried to kill me.' She's not listening to him.

'You don't know that.'

'I do. I told you, I found the bottle. She put antifreeze in the treacle tart. It's no wonder she didn't eat any.'

She said she was full, but it's obvious now she'd laced it with poison. And what better way to hide antifreeze and its saccharin, glycerine taste than baking it in a dessert as sweet as treacle tart?

'Are you certain?' Sheryl asks.

'It's my kidneys, isn't it?' He lifts an arm and traces the path of the looping tube coming out of his arm into a whirring machine at his side.

'They said you had an elevated level of something or other and an electrolyte imbalance, which is why they put you onto dialysis. I didn't really understand,' Sheryl says. 'I'm sure the doctor will be around soon and can explain it to you, although to be honest, I got the impression they didn't really know what was wrong.'

'Because they wouldn't have suspected antifreeze poisoning. Why would they?' He should have stuck to his guns and never let Freya return to the house. He didn't trust her, and yet he still welcomed her back. He's lucky he survived, but who knows what kind of irreparable damage she's caused.

His ex-wife, Debbie, once had a cat that died after being poisoned with antifreeze, one of four cats in the neighbourhood who developed sudden and inexplicable kidney failure within the space of three weeks. The vet concluded that someone had deliberately poisoned them by leaving bowls of the stuff out for them to drink. He remembers Debbie telling him cats found the taste of it irresistible, which he thought odd, until he looked it up and discovered that antifreeze has a potent sickly sweet taste because of the chemicals it contains to stop engines seizing up in the cold.

They never caught the cat poisoner.

'They gave you some drugs,' Sheryl explains, 'but put you on dialysis as a precaution.'

'Did they say if there would be any lasting damage?'

'That's all they told me. You'll have to speak to a doctor.'

Harvey grinds his teeth. He's angry with Freya, but he's more furious that he left himself so vulnerable?

'We have to find her,' he says. 'You don't know how dangerous she is. You're right, she's not Gwyneth's mother. She's admitted as much, but says it was my mistake and I jumped to conclusions and that she's actually Gwyneth's sister.'

Sheryl's eyes narrow as she shakes her head. 'And you invited her back to the house again?'

'I thought it would be better if she was somewhere I could keep an eye on her. I never thought she'd stoop to this.'

'Are you sure she tried to... to kill you?' Sheryl asks. 'It seems extreme.'

'Yes!'

'But why? What does she stand to gain?'

'Everything. With me out of the way, she's the only family Gwyneth has left.'

Harvey watches the implication of what he's saying slowly dawn on Sheryl, her expression changing from confusion to shock.

'Oh my god. And if Gwyneth were to die, she'd have a claim on her estate,' she says.

'Exactly, which is why we can't let her anywhere near Gwyneth. I have to call the police.'

The colour leeches from Sheryl's face. 'Right, yes,' she says, clearing her throat. 'Let me find your phone for you.'

She hunts through a metal cabinet by the bed, but struggles to locate it. 'I don't know if you had it with you when they brought you in,' she says, looking flustered. 'Here, use mine instead.'

She digs into her handbag and hands him her mobile.

Harvey wanted to call Murray Chalk, but his details are saved on his phone.

'I can't remember the number,' he murmurs helplessly.

'Here, let me do it.' Sheryl takes the phone back and prods at the screen three times. She puts it to her ear. 'Police,' she says. And after a brief pause, she adds, 'I want to report an attempted murder.'

Chapter 37

Detective Sergeant Chalk crosses his legs and clasps his knee with both hands as he sits listening at the side of Harvey's hospital bed with his colleague, DC Enright, standing at his side, poised with a notebook and pen.

'We've spoken to Miss Grainger,' Chalk says, his tone less than sympathetic, 'and she says she wasn't in the house with you last night. In fact, she's made a counter allegation that you assaulted her in the intensive care unit.'

Harvey wriggles himself into a more upright position, noticing for the first time the unusual tattoo on the back of Enright's hand that snakes from under the cuff of her blouse. An intricate, interweaving pattern that looks like a Maori design.

Sheryl's been amazing. She called the police and stayed with him when Chalk and Enright first arrived and Harvey gave a statement.

At first, Chalk's tone was soft and understanding as he listened patiently to Harvey's allegation, but since they've returned after making their enquiries, he's noticed both the detective sergeant and his sidekick are markedly less amiable. They've asked to speak to Harvey in private and have sent Sheryl off to buy coffee.

'Well, yes,' Harvey says. He can hardly lie about his altercation with Freya given that so many people on the intensive care unit witnessed him attacking Freya. 'But —'

'So you assaulted Miss Grainger?'

'She'd been lying to me. I lost my temper.'

'What had she been lying about?'

Harvey takes a deep breath and lets out an exasperated sigh. 'She told me she was my wife's mother.' Chalk's eyebrows shoot up. 'But we found Gwyneth's birth certificate, and it proves she was lying.'

'I see.'

Enright's pen scratches across the page of her notebook.

'How would you have reacted if you found out she was a fraudster pretending to be someone she's not, while your wife was seriously ill in a coma?'

Chalk rubs his nose with his thumb, his eyes slightly narrowed. 'A fraudster?'

'Yes. First, she said she was Gwyneth's mother and when we proved she was lying, she changed her story. Now she's claiming to be Gwyneth's sister who she lost touch with years ago,' Harvey explains. 'She's even faked a birth certificate.'

'So you lost your temper and tried to strangle her?'

'That's not really how it happened.'

'She says you put your hands around her throat and she couldn't breathe.'

'It wasn't like that.'

'And it took several members of staff and two security guards to drag you away.'

'You're blowing it out of all proportion.'

'Am I?' Chalk scowls at him. 'Because I've seen the bruising around her neck, and it's not pretty. Tell me, after you attacked Miss Grainger, what happened next?'

Harvey bows his head, aware of how bad it looks. 'She didn't want to involve the police, so we talked.'

'About what?'

'Why she lied to me.'

'She apologised and begged for a second chance, didn't she? She'd come all this way after finally finding her estranged sister and wanted to make things right between you. Isn't that right?'

'She tried to kill me!'

'So you keep saying. I'm just trying to get to the truth,' Chalk says.

'I'm telling you the truth. Why won't you believe me? How else do you think I ended up in hospital?'

'We'll come to that.' Chalk holds up a finger. 'First, I want to know about your relationship with Miss Grainger.'

'Relationship?' Harvey scoffs. 'There is no relationship.'

'But she's your sister-in-law?'

'So she claims.'

'You don't believe her?'

Harvey stares at the detective, incredulous. 'Can't you see? She's an impostor. A con artist. Call it what you like. She's clearly pulled the wool over your eyes.'

'Which is why you attacked her?'

Harvey sighs. This is impossible. 'I didn't mean to hurt her, but you have to see it from my point of view. I've been under a lot of pressure. My wife's in a coma. I don't know whether she's going to survive, and I discovered Freya's trying to take advantage.'

'Take advantage how?'

'She's stolen from us.'

Enright stops writing for a second and glances up from her notebook.

'I see,' Chalk says, uncrossing his legs and sitting forwards. 'And what did she steal?'

'I found a bag under her bed full of antiques she'd taken from around the house,' Harvey explains. 'A vase. A plate. Some jewellery. An oil painting. They're worth quite a bit.'

'Have you reported it? Do you have a crime number?'

'No.'

'Why not?'

'I was going to, but —'

'Because you thought you'd take matters into your own hands?' Chalk folds his arms and sits back in the chair, staring at Harvey with a chilling intensity. 'You attacked Miss Grainger because you were so angry she might be an impostor taking advantage, yet despite suspecting she was stealing from you, you invited her back to the house. Is that right?'

'It's not like that.' He's twisting it, making it sound all wrong, like Harvey's the one who's lying.

'So how is it?'

'I thought if she was in the house, I could keep an eye on her.'

'I see. But the thing is, Miss Grainger says she was so afraid of you after you throttled her, that she refused to return to the house with you.'

'She's lying!'

'But it makes sense, doesn't it? Why would she agree to go back to the house with you, alone, after you'd tried to strangle her?' Chalk asks.

'Isn't it obvious?'

'Not really. Try explaining it to me.'

'Because she was planning to kill me. As I've already told you, she said she wanted to cook dinner to apologise for lying to me. She made a treacle tart, and I'm certain she laced it with antifreeze. I found a bottle in the kitchen when I became unwell last night. Look for yourselves.'

Why is Chalk not taking it more seriously? Why is he siding with Freya, even though she's the one he should investigate?

'Are there any witnesses who can corroborate that Miss Grainger was at the house with you last night?' Chalk asks.

Harvey picks through his memories. There must be someone who saw her returning home with him. But he can't think of anyone. She should have been picked by the CCTV cameras. That would be incontrovertible proof, but typically the camera that covers the front door has been on the blink for weeks. It's another job he's been meaning to tackle.

'I don't think so. It doesn't mean she wasn't there. And if she didn't stay with me, where did she stay?'

'Miss Grainger says she slept in her car last night.'

'I bet she did. Are there any witnesses to that?' Harvey asks. 'Check the house. You'll find a bag of her belongings.'

'I don't doubt it. Miss Grainger says she was too scared to return to collect her property while you were there.'

'Look, she poisoned me. Why haven't you arrested her?'

'Because at the moment, it's your word against hers. You've already admitted you've attacked her once. Some might say this is an attempt to fit her up for a crime she didn't commit.'

'Are you insane?' Harvey gasps. 'You think I'm making this up?' He holds up his arm, showing Chalk the tubes connected to the dialysis machine. 'I didn't poison myself, did I?'

Chalk and Enright exchange a glance. 'About this so-called poisoning,' Chalk says.

'Talk to the doctors. They'll tell you. The consultant said I'm suffering from metabolic acidosis. Do you know what that is, detective? Excess acid in my blood. It's caused by antifreeze poisoning. If I hadn't been treated so quickly, I'd probably be dead.'

Chalk nods sagely, as if none of this is news to him. 'It *can* be caused by antifreeze poisoning. It can also be caused by methanol poisoning. And do you know the cause of that?'

Harvey stares at him blankly. 'No.'

'Miss Grainger noticed while she was staying with you that you enjoy a drink or two,' Chalk says.

'So?' Harvey studies the detective warily.

'Ever been tempted to bootleg your own? Or maybe someone in the village offered you a bottle of moonshine? Some bathtub gin?'

'What?'

'Miss Grainger says she noticed at least one unlabelled bottle of liquor around the house.'

'What are you talking about?' Harvey screws his face up as he wracks his memory.

He keeps a few bottles of spirits in the utility. Some whisky. Vodka. A couple of bottles of rum and brandy. Some liqueurs. But nothing unbranded. She's making it up.

And then he remembers the bottle of sloe gin Sheryl brought round as a gift to cheer him up. He's not even opened it yet.

'Home-brewed spirits can be lethal, you know, especially if they contain methanol, which can sadly happen and would explain your symptoms and the metabolic acidosis.'

'I don't drink bootleg booze!' Harvey shouts. 'This is nonsense. Why are you taking her word over mine?'

'We're just trying to get to the truth.'

'You need to arrest that woman and keep her away from my wife. Why can't you just do your bloody jobs?'

'Watch your tone, Mr Kerrison. I don't know what's going on here, but I am going to get to the truth.'

'That's all I'm asking. And in the meantime, keep her away from Gwyneth.'

'Nothing's going to happen to your wife while she's in hospital. You have my word.'

Harvey rolls his eyes. 'Right.'

'In the meantime, we're going to find out who put her in a coma.'

'I suppose Freya has an alibi for that, does she? Because I wouldn't put it past her to have contrived this whole situation. You've checked her car, I take it?' Harvey turns away and stares at the curtain they've drawn around the bed.

'We'll be in touch, Mr Kerrison.'

'Yeah, you do that.'

Sheryl returns with two cups of coffee five minutes after the detectives have left.

'What did they say?' she asks.

'They don't believe me. They think I'm making it up.'

'They think you imagined being poisoned?'

'I don't know. Maybe.'

'But why?'

'They found out about the argument I had with Freya,' he says sheepishly.

'What argument?' Sheryl cradles her cup between her knees.

'I know I shouldn't have, but she was pushing my buttons, and I... I attacked her.'

'Are you serious? When?'

'When I spoke to her yesterday in intensive care. Something inside me just snapped.'

Sheryl smirks. 'She probably had it coming. What happens now?'

'I need to check on Gwyneth. How long do you think they're going to keep me attached to this machine?'

Sheryl shrugs. 'Let me see if I can find a doctor.'

She's up and out of the chair before he can stop her, striding off with her coffee cup in one hand, shoulders back and head held high.

But it's another three hours before the medical team is satisfied Harvey's no longer in danger and he can come off dialysis.

'I want to see my wife. She's in a coma in the ICU,' he tells a haughty consultant.

'I'd prefer it if you stayed in bed for the next few days,' she says.

'But she needs me. She'll be worried that I'm not there,' Harvey pleads.

The consultant considers it for a moment with lips pursed in indecision.

'I'll take him,' Sheryl chips in. 'And I'll make sure he doesn't overdo it. Then I'll bring him right back again, I promise.'

Eventually, the consultant relents. 'Okay,' she says. 'Your body's been put under a lot of strain, so I'd advise you to keep your visit short.'

'You have my word, I'll look after him,' Sheryl reassures her.

Chapter 38

'I'm not an invalid,' Harvey complains when Sheryl offers to find him a wheelchair.

Instead, they compromise on a pair of crutches that Sheryl acquires from a porter she buttonholes in the corridor.

It still takes Harvey far more effort to reach the intensive care unit than he expects and when he gets there, his arms and legs are like jelly.

They're buzzed in by the reception desk, but the change in attitude towards him is palpable. He's used to the nurses, doctors and porters giving him a cheery wave and a hello, but since the incident with Freya, everyone seems to avoid catching his eye.

When they reach Gwyneth's room, Harvey takes a moment to steady himself, physically and emotionally. If Freya's inside, it will be the first time he's seen her since she attempted to kill him. He's not sure how he's going to react. But he reminds himself he's not here for her. He's here to protect Gwyneth.

Sheryl pushes the door open and Harvey shuffles in. The noise of the machines is louder than he remembers, and the stench of disinfectant over-

267

powering. Harvey casts an eye over his wife's prone body, lying in the same position as the first day she was brought in, a week ago today. Her back is elevated slightly, her arms rest at her sides, her head is bandaged and her eyes are closed. The only real improvement in her appearance is that the swelling and bruising around her eyes has lessened.

At least there's no sign of Freya, which is a blessing.

Leanne is at the back of the room, pottering around a metal trolley. She glances up when she hears them enter and shoots Harvey a warm smile. It's the first anyone's given him since he arrived in the unit.

'I heard they'd brought you in,' she says. 'Couldn't bear Gwyneth being the centre of attention?' She laughs.

'Something like that.'

'How are you feeling?'

'Fine,' he lies. He's not here to discuss how beaten up or weak his body feels. 'How is she?'

'Stable. Certainly no worse.'

It's not the most positive news, but she's still alive. It's something.

Sheryl has remained hovering in the doorway.

'Come and say hello,' Harvey says, swaying as he struggles to keep his balance.

Sheryl shakes her head. 'I was going to go for a walk and leave you two in peace.'

'Gwyneth would love to see you.'

'Later maybe. I'll come back in, say, twenty minutes and take you back?'

'Okay.' Harvey stares after her as the door swings slowly closed on its hydraulic hinge.

He thought she'd want to spend some time with Gwyneth, but he doesn't want to push her into something she's not comfortable doing. It's not a big deal.

'Has Freya been in?' Harvey asks, casually.

'She popped in earlier, I think,' Leanne says.

'Right.' Harvey nods. 'Did anyone tell you why I was brought in last night?'

'Was it something serious?' Leanne wears a mask of concern.

'Freya poisoned me.'

Leanne laughs nervously. 'Freya? Are you kidding?'

'I know. Looks can be deceptive.'

Leanne continues to stare at him, uncertain. He'd have found it hard to believe, too. Freya's so good at deceiving everyone. She looks so innocent and unassuming. You'd be hard pressed to think anything bad of her.

'But she's Gwyneth's sister.' Leanne glances at the bed and lowers her voice to a whisper. 'Why would she poison you?'

It's obvious she doesn't believe him. Why would she? Over the last week, the pair of them have become increasingly close.

'It's a long story, but she's not to be trusted, okay? I don't want her left alone with Gwyneth even for a second. Do you understand?' Harvey hates taking such a harsh tone, but Leanne needs to take the threat seriously.

The nurse stops what she's doing and fixes Harvey with a studious gaze. He's not sure how to impress on her he's deadly serious.

'Sure.' She shrugs. 'There should be someone in the room with her at all times, anyway.'

'I mean it, Leanne. Don't leave her for a second.'

'Okay, I heard you.'

Harvey shuffles awkwardly towards Gwyneth's bed and falls unsteadily into the chair by her side, dropping his crutches at his feet. He takes her hand and squeezes it tightly. It's hard to believe she's been like this for a week.

'Don't you worry, my love, I'm going to take good care of you,' he says, loudly enough for Leanne to hear. 'We're not going to let anything bad happen to you.'

He glances sideways at Leanne, who's returned to whatever it was she was doing at the trolley. She doesn't seem to have taken too kindly to being told what to do. But his wife is his first and only priority. She must understand that.

Was that his imagination, or did Gwyneth's fingers just twitch?

It was only the slightest of movements, like the beat of a butterfly's wing, but he's sure he felt something. He stares at her long fingers, her nails immaculately painted, and wills them to move again.

'Gwyneth?' he whispers, like he's afraid of waking the dead. 'Can you hear me?'

But she remains as lifeless as a stone.

'My darling, are you trying to tell me something? Is it something about Freya?'

He waits. He watches. His pulse racing. His hopes elevated.

'Is everything okay?' Leanne asks.

'I thought I felt her move,' he says. 'I don't know. I thought her finger twitched. That's got to be a good sign, right?'

Leanne joins him at Gwyneth's side and places a tender hand to her cheek. 'Gwyneth,' she says, 'can you open your eyes for me?'

They stare at Gwyneth's face for what seems like several minutes.

'You might have imagined it,' Leanne says. 'Sometimes we want something to happen so badly, our brains play tricks on us.'

'No, I know what I felt.'

'Keep talking to her. Who knows, you might be right.'

The door sighs open. Harvey looks up, expecting to see another nurse or a doctor on their rounds, but is shocked when Freya appears, stooped and shuffling like a little old lady.

She looks equally surprised when she spots Harvey at Gwyneth's bed, although she quickly regains her composure.

'How are you feeling, Harvey? I heard you were unwell. Nothing serious, I hope?'

The blood sizzles in Harvey's veins at the bare-faced gall of the woman.

'You tried to kill me,' he hisses.

'What?' she gasps in mock surprise.

'You're not welcome here. Stay away from us.'

'Don't be ridiculous. You can't stop me from seeing my sister. She needs me.'

'Get out.'

'Okay, that's enough.' Leanne positions herself between them. 'Let's not have a repeat of yesterday, shall we?'

'Call security. I don't want her in here,' Harvey says.

'Come on, she's Gwyneth's sister. She has as much right to be here as you. Now, I don't know what's gone on between the two of you, but you need to work it out.'

Did she not hear him when he told her Freya tried to kill him?

'I'm not going anywhere.' Freya puts her bag on the floor by her feet. A ball of wool and a pair of knitting needles peep out of the top. Who knows what else she has in there. A bottle of cyanide? A zombie knife?

'Watch your step, Freya. I'm onto you.' Harvey's physically shaking with rage. He can't control himself. 'I've told the police what you did, and they might not be able to prove you poisoned me, but they're watching you like a hawk.'

'Poisoned you?' Her hand flies to her mouth in shock. 'Oh, goodness, why would you say such a despicable thing?'

Harvey laughs with contempt. 'We both know what you did.'

'But why would I want to poison you? It's absurd. You really aren't feeling well, are you?'

'Stop playing games. I know what you put in that treacle tart.'

'What treacle tart? I'm sorry, Harvey. I know you've been ill, but you're making no sense. Now, if you don't mind, I've come to spend some time with my sister.'

She picks up her bag and moves towards the bed.

'I'm warning you. Keep away from her.' Harvey hauls himself unsteadily to his feet, his hand raised towards Freya like a police officer trying to control traffic.

'Don't be silly. I'm her sister.'

She swerves around Leanne and moves to the opposite side of the bed, so that she and Harvey are facing each other over Gwyneth's motionless body.

Freya's lips curve briefly into a cruel, twisted smile behind Leanne's back. 'Has Harvey been pestering you this morning?' she says in a sing-song voice like she's talking to an infant. 'Don't worry, I'm here now.'

'Don't touch her!'

Freya startles, her eyes as large as the moon.

'I mean it, Freya. You touch her and I'll call the police. I'm not letting you hurt her. I've given Gwyneth my word.'

Freya lowers her voice to a barely audible whisper. 'Watch me,' she hisses.

'I said, get away from her.'

Freya jumps back and her sneer dissolves as Leanne turns on them both, Freya looking distraught and on the verge of tears.

'That's enough from the pair of you,' Leanne snaps.

'Can't you see what she's doing? Why won't you listen to me?' Harvey's blood pounds through his veins. He should have finished what he started the other day and throttled the life out of her when he had the chance.

He sways on the spot, his vision spinning. Suddenly, his legs become as weak as water and he doesn't feel so good.

His eyelids flutter and the last thing he remembers is falling. Tumbling to the ground and banging his chin painfully on the side of the bed as he collapses onto the floor.

Chapter 39

GWYNETH

I'm running.

Head down, arms pumping, feet flying across the marshmallow floor.

But I don't know where I'm going. The corridor ahead, a long desperate tunnel of white light, stretches for as far as I can see.

I'm breathing hard. Too fast. Not from the exertion - that barely registers - but from the adrenaline that's racing rampant through my veins, whipping my heart and my nerves into a frenzy.

I glance over my shoulder. Once. Twice. I know she's coming, but I can't see her. Not yet. And somehow that makes it worse. All I can see behind me is the same as I can see ahead. A long, white corridor. No corners. No doors. But I can hear her thundering towards me. Getting louder. Faster. Closer. Any moment she's going to reach out and grab me. It's more than I can bear.

Panic fills me with an uncontrollable terror. I have to get away. I can't let her catch me.

But my legs are slowing and the more I will them on, the less they seem willing to respond. My hips are seizing up like an engine with an oil leak and I have the sensation of trying to move through thick, sticky mud. The harder I try, the more I concentrate on forcing myself to move, the more they protest.

She's going to catch me, no doubt.

With a final, hopeless flick of my head, I look over my shoulder again, knowing for certain she's on my heels. I can sense her. Feel her.

But there's no one there. I was wrong. I can't stop the smile of relief that creeps across my lips.

A smile that's wiped away just as quickly when I turn back and spot her ahead of me. She's standing with her hands on her hips, her head thrown back, laughing like a maniac. Her mouth a black hole so wide and so deep, it's sucking me in.

Now when I want my legs to stop, they keep turning. Propelling me on. Faster and faster.

I try to scream but only manage a pitiful squeak.

She stands defiantly ahead of me, smirking. Taller than me. Stronger than me. Faster than me.

'What's wrong?' she taunts. 'You afraid or something?'

'No,' I mumble, the tremor in my voice giving away my lie.

'You are. You're scared. A scaredy little scaredy-cat.'

'Please,' I sob. 'Don't hurt me.'

'You'd better run,' she says, a mean expression darkening her features. 'Because I'm coming to get you, and when I catch you, I'm going to kill you.'

Chapter 40

When Harvey cracks open his eyes, he sees the guy with the yellow-tinged jaundiced skin lying in the bed on the end of the bay while a geriatric patient in checked flannel pyjamas, his mouth hanging slack, lies to his right. He's back in his hospital bed with the covers pulled up to his chest and his head thick and doughy.

Did he dream he went to see Gwyneth? Confronted Freya?

He exercises his jaw and winces at the stab of pain, remembering how he blacked out and fell, injuring himself as he collapsed.

His groan draws the attention of a nurse in a crisp, green uniform who's hurrying past. She glances in his direction and notices he's awake.

'No more adventures for you until you're better,' she says with the tone of his old head teacher. 'How are you feeling?'

'Like death,' he says. He nods at the empty chair. 'Where's my friend, Sheryl?'

The nurse shrugs. 'I haven't seen her for a few hours.'

'A few hours? How long have I been asleep?'

'The best part of the afternoon. We gave you a sedative after you collapsed. The doctors should never have let you leave the ward.'

'I need to be with my wife.' Harvey tries to slip his feet out of bed. He can't protect Gwyneth while he's stuck in another part of the hospital.

'You're not going anywhere, young man.' The nurse waves a finger at him and lifts his leg back under the covers.

'I can't stay here,' he argues.

'It's an order.'

He wishes people would stop telling him what to do. He doesn't have time to rest while Freya's in their lives.

'You don't understand —'

'It's for your own good.'

There's no point arguing. He'll have to sneak out. After all, it's clear now he can't trust Leanne or any of the other nurses to keep Gwyneth safe. Freya has them all completely fooled, hooked on the long line of her deceit. It would only take a moment for Freya to end Gwyneth's life. For one of the nurses to be distracted. An emergency with another patient. Freya could flick a switch or kick out a plug and it would be all over before anyone knew what was going on.

'Get some more sleep,' the nurse says. 'You need to build up your strength. I'll be back in thirty minutes to check on you.'

Harvey nods and closes his eyes, but as soon as she's walked away, he snatches them open again. He watches her broad hips sway as she waddles into the corridor. There's no way he's staying here, but without Sheryl's help, he's going to struggle to make it to the ICU. The drugs they've given him have drained him of what was left of his energy.

Perhaps he can persuade a porter to take him. Or appeal to one of the visitors with the other patients in the bay. If he tells them his wife's in a coma, surely no one would refuse to help.

But they're all so focused on their own misery, it's hard to catch anyone's eye. He tries for a few minutes, hoping someone will look his way and take pity on him, but they're all too wrapped up or too polite to be gazing around the room.

Harvey's on the verge of giving up when fate deals him a lucky hand. A porter appears, pushing a man in a wheelchair. The man's wrapped up in a dressing gown, his limbs painfully thin and his shoulders hunched forwards. Spindly legs poke out from the bottoms of his pyjama trousers, his feet tucked into a pair of worn slippers.

The porter parks the wheelchair at the end of the bay, close to Harvey's bed, and helps the old man to his feet. Together, they shuffle towards the bathroom, the porter supporting the old man with an arm around his back.

The moment the bathroom door closes behind them, Harvey throws off his covers and puts every ounce of energy into sitting up.

Straining every sinew, he stands and moves painfully slowly, his feet shuffling across the floor. He's unable to pick them up and walk properly.

The wheelchair's only a few metres away, but it takes all his determination to reach it while half expecting the bathroom door to fly open at any moment.

He collapses into the chair with a weary sigh. Then grips the wheels in both hands and rolls himself forwards. Although it's hard to get moving, once he has momentum, it's almost effortless to glide along the corridor.

To his surprise, no one gives him a second glance. Busy medical staff give him a wide berth, distracted by paperwork and errands. No one even tries to stop him as he wheels past the nurses' station, although he keeps his head low, fearful of bumping into the nurse who ordered him to stay in bed.

He swings left, past some offices, and at the exit, a woman in a trouser suit and wearing a hospital lanyard around her neck even holds open the door to let him out.

He can't believe how easy it is to escape, the adrenaline rush giving him renewed strength and hope of reaching his wife before it's too late.

The hospital is a rabbit warren of corridors and he quickly regrets not paying more attention to the route Sheryl took to intensive care earlier. He follows a sign pointing towards the lifts, remembering at least that he needs to reach the third floor.

It's a big, busy hospital with six lifts, all of which are currently on different floors and travelling in the wrong direction.

'Come on, come on,' he mutters to himself impatiently.

Two porters discussing football appear from nowhere and join him, pressing the call buttons, even though he's already done it. He turns his back on them and wheels away with his face hidden and the blood racing in his veins.

Finally, a lift arrives and the doors peel open with the speed of a small boy cranking them by hand. The porters step aside and let Harvey in first. There are already half a dozen people inside, so he keeps his head bowed and tries to look as unassuming as possible, irrationally fearful that someone might recognise him and drag him back to his bed.

'Which floor, mate?' someone asks from behind. He only realises they're talking to him when no one else answers.

'Third, please,' Harvey says, flushing with embarrassment. He should have grabbed some clothes, but here he is sitting in front of half a dozen strangers, women included, in a thin, backless gown with his legs exposed.

The lift climbs two floors with everyone standing in polite silence, and when the doors finally slide open, Harvey lets out a breath of relief.

He attempts to reverse out, but going backwards is not as easy as propelling himself forwards.

'Need a hand?' one of the porters asks. 'Where are you going? I can give you a push, if you'd like?'

He's already pulling the wheelchair out of the lift and swinging it around before Harvey can protest.

'I'm fine, thanks. I can manage.'

The porter shrugs. 'Suit yourself,' he says as he wanders back into the lift and disappears behind the closing doors.

A colour-coded sign on the wall lists all the departments on the floor, including the intensive care unit. Harvey needs to follow the red signs. But as he's about to push himself off, a security guard appears. From his manner, it's obvious he's looking for something or someone, his head turning from side to side and his arms swinging confidently.

Harvey wheels around, getting used to controlling the wheelchair now, and bows his head. Five seconds pass. Then ten. A two-way radio crackles and an indistinct voice barks out an order. The security guard answers, speaking too quietly for Harvey to hear what he's saying.

And then he's gone.

Harvey slowly turns himself around, listening to the sound of his boots striding along the corridor, before it's replaced by the chatter of women talking.

It grows louder and three nurses appear, laughing and joking. Harvey wheels behind them until they turn off into a side corridor and he heads straight on, driving the wheels with an urgent roll of his hands.

When he finally reaches the entrance to the intensive care unit, he realises he has no idea how he's going to get in. Usually, he presses the intercom and someone lets him through, but what if they refuse? His altercations with Freya haven't exactly made him welcome in recent days. But they can't deny him his right to see his own wife, can they?

It's not a problem he has to deliberate for long as the door swings open and a middle-aged couple walk out, hand in hand. Harvey smiles at them sweetly and the man holds the door open for him.

He slides inside with a cheery thank you and rolls silently towards Gwyneth's room. Fortunately, everyone on the nurses' station is too busy to notice him as he wheels past with his head down.

He turns a corner, spots Gwyneth's room ahead, and pulls the wheelchair to a sudden stop as he sees a security guard posted outside. In his crisp white shirt, black tie, knitted sweater and trousers, he's the picture of authority.

Harvey sighs with relief. A sign, at last, that they're taking Gwyneth's safety seriously. The guard, chewing gum, looks up from his phone and when he notices Harvey, pulls his shoulders back. He slips the phone into his pocket and studies him warily.

'I'm here to see my wife,' Harvey says, rolling up to the man and nodding towards the room.

'And you are?' he demands suspiciously.

'Harvey Kerrison. Gwyneth's husband. I have to see her.'

'Sorry, I can't you let in.' The guard shakes his head, his gelled, black hair not shifting an inch.

'What are you talking about? I'm her husband. You can't stop me from seeing her.' Harvey raises his voice. The guy might be here to protect Gwyneth, but he's not going to be jerked around by this jumped-up jobsworth. 'Let me in.' He rolls the wheelchair forwards, his knees bumping into the guard's legs.

'Back away, sir,' the man warns, raising his hand.

'Just let me in!'

'I'm under strict orders, sir.'

'I couldn't give a flying f—'

The door swings open behind him with a suck of air. The guard looks over his shoulder and takes a step sideways as Freya appears behind him.

'What the hell?' Harvey gasps. 'What's she doing in there?'

Shock washes over Freya's face, the colour leaching from her cheeks. 'That's him,' she screams, like she's just come face to face with Jack the Ripper. 'Help! Get him away from me!' She stumbles backwards, clutching her chest, a trembling mess.

You'd think Harvey was waving a knife in her face and threatening to cut her throat. He stares at her with his jaw slack.

The security guard is quick to act, stepping in front of Freya protectively, his chest puffed out. 'Sir, I suggest you back away.'

'I'm not going anywhere until I've seen my wife.'

'I'm not telling you again.'

'This is insane. She's the dangerous one,' Harvey says, jabbing a finger at Freya, who's cowering behind the guard. The panic painted across her face has dissolved into what looks suspiciously like a smirk.

Can't they see what she's doing? That she's playing them all for fools?

'Gwyneth!' Harvey shouts. 'It's Harvey. I'm right here.'

'You need to leave,' the guard says. 'Don't turn this into something ugly.'

Something ugly? All he wants to do is protect his wife.

He rolls the wheelchair back, fixing the guard with a determined stare. And then launches himself forwards again, intending to knock the guard out of the way like a bowling bowl on a ten-pin strike.

He catches him square in the legs and he doubles over, howling in pain.

In slow motion, the pair of them, entwined, tumble to the floor, the wheelchair pulled off-balance, and they end up in a tangle of arms, legs, metal and rubber, with Harvey's backside exposed to the world.

'Harvey!' a voice calls. 'What are you doing?'

He's being squashed under the weight of the floundering guard, his overpowering cheap after-shave filling his nostrils, but pulls his head free to see Leanne glowering at him from the doorway where she's standing with Freya.

'I just wanted to see Gwyneth,' Harvey says, as the guard untangles himself and pulls himself back onto his feet.

'What'd you do that for?' he moans, fury burning in his eyes. 'That's assault, that is.'

'So arrest me,' Harvey sneers. 'Oh, that's right, you don't have the power.'

The guard snarls as he sets the wheelchair upright and wraps his meaty hands under Harvey's arms to pull him up.

Unceremoniously, he dumps him back in the chair.

'We're done here,' he growls. He spins Harvey around and, hobbling, pushes him back down the corridor towards the exit.

'Where are you taking me?' Harvey cries.

'Anywhere but here. And just count yourself lucky I'm not calling the police.'

'Turn me around now! I want to see my wife.'

'Button it. I've heard enough.'

Harvey can't bring himself to look back. He knows what he'll see. Freya standing with Leanne, waving and laughing like she's won.

But she has underestimated him. And if she thinks this is the end, she has no idea what he's capable of.

Chapter 41

'I would strongly advise against early discharge,' the doctor says in a patronising tone. 'I'd like to keep you under observation for at least another twenty-four hours.'

Harvey doesn't have twenty-four hours. He needs to get out of here now. Another day has already passed. Another day for Freya to work her mischief.

'Just give me the paperwork,' he demands.

The doctor shrugs and slides the discharge papers towards Harvey. 'That's your prerogative, of course. We're not a prison, but as long as you understand the risks.'

Harvey signs the papers with a flourish and slaps the pen down on the table over the bed.

'If you start feeling unwell again, come straight into A&E,' the doctor says, but Harvey's not listening. He has more important things on his mind. Like making Freya disappear from their lives for good before she can inflict any more misery.

'Where are my clothes?'

Sheryl, who'd apparently thought it was more important to pop home for a few hours to feed her cats than stay to help him, jumps up from the chair and dives into a metal cabinet by the bed. She pulls out his shirt, trousers, underwear and socks and lays them on top of the covers.

'Can you get dressed on your own?' she asks sheepishly. Since he snapped at her for abandoning him earlier, she's been walking on eggshells.

He didn't mean to be rude, but he's been in a foul mood since he was unceremoniously thrown out of intensive care.

'Of course I can,' he huffs. 'Wait outside.'

Sheryl does as she's told, pulling the curtains around the bed. While waiting for the discharge papers, which took forever, he started to formulate the outline of a plan to rid themselves of Freya forever. And if they won't let him see Gwyneth, what's the point of staying in the hospital? His time would be better spent at home working out how to incriminate Freya or finding out whether she really is who she says she is. Then he'll take great pleasure in informing DS Murray Chalk and letting the police deal with her.

When he's dressed, he allows Sheryl to push him in a wheelchair down to the lobby, but insists he's well enough to walk to her car, although he's still a little unsteady on his feet.

As Sheryl drives, she tries to engage him in conversation. 'You can always stay at mine until you're feeling better,' she offers. 'That way, I can keep an eye on you.'

She briefly takes her eyes off the road to throw him a hopeful glance.

'I need to be at home.'

'It wouldn't be any trouble. The guest bedroom's already made up.'

'I said I need to be at home,' Harvey growls. He has work to do and he can't stand having Sheryl fussing around him.

'Well, the offer stands if you change your mind.'

The rest of the journey passes in an awkward, heavy silence, with Harvey staring moodily out of the window.

He senses her relief when they finally arrive home and she pulls up outside the house. Predictably, there's no sign of Freya's car, which means he has the place to himself.

Sheryl tries to help him to the door, but he shrugs her off. He's feeling better already. Stronger. Less nauseous. After twenty-four hours, the sedatives they gave him have finally worn off, along with the worst effects of the antifreeze poisoning, although the dialysis has left him feeling hollowed out and light-headed.

'Do you want me to come in and see if I can find something to cook?' Sheryl asks.

'No, I'll order takeaway if I get hungry.' Unusually, food's the last thing on his mind.

She stands on the doorstep blinking like a lost lamb.

'Go home, Sheryl,' he tells her. 'Thank you for bringing me back. I'll be fine now.'

Alone at last, he waits until he hears Sheryl's car crunch down the drive, then heads for the kitchen, standing in the doorway to examine the room. Everything's exactly where it should be. There are no dirty dishes on the side or packets of cereal or half-eaten loaves of bread sitting on the counter. For once, it appears Freya has cleaned up after herself.

Cautiously, he heads to the sink, looking for the bottle of antifreeze. Predictably, it's not there. He hunts in the bin and checks all the cupboards, but it's vanished. Freya's not stupid. She's probably returned it to the barn where she found it.

Nor is there any sign of the treacle tart. She served him a healthy portion, but there was plenty left.

He looks in the fridge, but it's empty, other than a few tomatoes that are turning mouldy, a handful of knobbly carrots, a packet of butter, a quarter-pint of milk, and half an onion wrapped in aluminium foil. Definitely no treacle tart. It's not in the bin either. He even looks in the chest freezer in the utility room. It's well-stocked with cuts of steak, chicken and lamb that Gwyneth has picked up and frozen over recent months, but there's nothing in there that could prove anything against Freya.

But what did Harvey expect? The leftover tart is the one piece of evidence that would provide conclusive proof that Freya was trying to kill him. Without it, it's his word against hers.

Harvey leans against the wall to think. She would have had to have disposed of it somewhere. Maybe she bagged it up and took it with her when she left for the hospital. In which case, he has no chance of finding it. Or possibly she's dumped it in the wheelie bins outside. But would she really have been that careless? Regardless, he decides to take a look.

But on his way out, something on the counter where he keeps his spirits catches his eye. Among the bottles of whisky, vodka and gin and the cans of mixers is the bottle of sloe gin Sheryl brought around. He's not had any yet, but there's barely half an inch left in the bottom.

He picks it up and swirls the liquid around. Then pulls out the stopper and sniffs it, recoiling at the potent ethanol vapours. He recalls Chalk's words to him in the hospital.

'Home-brewed spirits can be lethal, you know, especially if they contain methanol.'

What's the betting Freya's tampered with the bottle and planted false evidence to cover her tracks? He's clearly not given her enough credit. She's smarter than she looks.

More to the point, it confirms what he's thought for a while, that she's a twisted, evil shrew who'll go to any lengths to get her way. Even murder.

He tosses the bottle into the bin and storms out of the room, fuming. When he sees her, he's going to kill her. But first, he's going to remove every trace of her from the house. He's going to reclaim his room, strip the bed, and clean the bathroom. And then he's going to change the locks. She'll never set foot inside the property again.

He marches into the hall, heading for the stairs, but is stopped in his tracks by the sight of a dark, rectangular patch on the wall where one of Gwyneth's favourite paintings used to hang. A portrait of a woman wearing pearls, the oils darkened and flaking with age. It's as familiar to him as the back of his hand, a painting he's seen every time he's ascended the stairs.

It's such a flagrant theft. He wonders what else Freya has taken. The only way to be sure is to check every room. Every shelf. Every display cabinet. Because there's no way he's going to let that woman steal so much as a ballpoint pen from them.

As he works his way around the house, starting in the lounge and heading into the dining room, library, his study, the conservatory, the snug and back into the hall, the extent of Freya's pilfering becomes clear. Paintings, vases, plates, silverware, figurines, candlesticks and vintage clocks have all gone missing. He can't believe the audacity of the woman. Clearly, she was intending to clean them out.

His eye falls on the door to the basement at the end of the hall, which is always kept locked. But, of course, Freya knows where the key is kept because he was stupid enough to show her on the first day she was here.

With a sinking dread in the pit of his stomach, he approaches the door and unlocks it. He flicks on the light and cautiously descends the stairs into the chill and musty-smelling room below.

He's shocked but not surprised to find all the boxes have been ripped open and their contents left spilt over the floor. Freya's ransacked the place, obviously looking for the most valuable items. As if she has any idea of what's valuable and what's not. She's no better educated than him. Even though Gwyneth's tried multiple times to teach him, he still wouldn't know the difference between a Gainsborough and a garage sale print, or a Persian rug from a cheap knock-off.

Fortunately, Gwyneth's necklace, the most valuable of all the antiques in the house, is safely locked away in the safe in the panic room. At least it should be.

With a bloom of panic, Harvey hurries to the electronic keyboard on the wall and punches in the entry code, recalling how Freya watched him last time and memorised the numbers. Their anniversary. An easy-to-remember date. He should have changed it but he didn't realise he needed to. Who could have imagined Freya was a fraud, who was intent on robbing and killing them?

The door swings open. Thankfully, the safe inside is locked and when he opens it, he's relieved to find the velvet box under a pile of important papers - their wills, passports and deeds to the house.

He slides it out, flips open the catch and lifts the lid. The necklace inside is gaudy and ostentatious, but Gwyneth loves it. She told him once that it's such a rare piece and the craftsmanship so exquisite, they'd have auction houses around the world biting their hands off should they ever decide to sell it.

Carefully, Harvey closes the lid and slips the box back into the safe, with a new plan forming in his mind.

He's tried warning Freya. And he's tried threatening her. Neither has worked. She's left him no choice other than to raise his game.

He heads back upstairs, locking the basement door behind him, then hurries up to his room, determined he'll be sleeping in his own bed again tonight and that Freya will be long gone.

She's kicked her bag-for-life back under the bed, although there's no sign of the holdall or the stolen antiques. He grabs it by one of its handles, drags it out and tosses it onto the landing, intending to take it out to the garden to burn later. Then he strips the bed and piles the dirty sheets with the dirty clothes Freya's borrowed and left in a heap, intending to put them all on a hot wash, if he can work out how to use the machine.

By the time he's finished reclaiming his room, his new plan is fully formed in his head.

Like all the best plans, it's a simple one, although not without its complications. But if he can pull it off, he'll never have to see Freya again.

All he has to do now is wait for her to return to the house.

Chapter 42

Harvey's been sitting with the lights off for almost three hours before he hears the giveaway crunch of gravel on the drive. The long wait has given him time to think, to put everything in perspective, and to iron out some of the potential pitfalls in his plan.

He holds his breath when he hears a key scrape in the lock, the front door whisper open and a bag drop heavily on the floor in the hall.

Freya will have seen his car on the drive, but she doesn't call out to him. If she's as smart as he thinks, she'll already be suspicious and on her guard, which means he'll only have one shot to get this right.

He waits, tense, listening to every creak and pop the house emits. His mouth is dry and his palms sweaty.

Feet pad softly across the wooden floors. She's looking for him.

Quietly, he stands. Walks across the study and hides behind the door.

His heart pounds loudly in his chest as she comes closer. He watches the handle depress. A solid bar of light filters into the room and her shadow extends across the floor. Freya pokes her head and shoulders inside, her breath ragged and fast.

'Freya, come in,' Harvey booms, intending to scare her.

'Harvey,' she gasps. 'I wasn't sure if you were home.'

He emerges from the shadows as she steps to one side. He pushes the door closed, trapping them both inside.

'Why were you sitting in the dark?' Her brow furrows as she watches him remove a key from his pocket and lock the door. 'What are you doing?' she asks as he drops the key back in his pocket.

'Sit,' he instructs, pointing to the kitchen chair he's placed under the window. 'I thought it was time we had another chat.'

He walks calmly to his desk, swivels the office chair around and sits facing her. The look on her face is priceless, the poor, terrified lamb.

'Why've you locked the door?' Her eyes dart around the room like a field mouse looking for somewhere to hide from a hungry cat.

'Relax, I just want to talk.' He points to the chair under the window. 'Sit.'

Freya watches him suspiciously, but eventually relents and lowers herself onto the chair, never once taking her eyes off him.

'What's this about?'

'No more games, Freya.' Now he has her trapped, his anger gives way to an unexpected calm. 'It's time for you to go.'

'Go?'

'You heard me.'

'Where?'

'I don't care. Somewhere far away, preferably. And I never want to see you again,' he says. 'Understand?'

'But Gwyneth?'

'You won't be seeing her again.'

'She's my sister. You can't stop me from seeing her.'

'Is that right?'

Harvey reaches for the tea towel he's laid across the desk and pulls it away in one deft motion to reveal a set of tools.

Freya's eyes open even wider than usual, taking in the kit he's assembled. Pliers. Lionel's old hand drill. A hammer. A handful of three-inch long nails. A Stanley knife. Three chisels of varying sizes. A roll of black masking tape. A plumber's wrench. And a pile of cable ties.

'I invited you into my home. I even gave up my bed. I treated you like family. And the thanks I get is that you try to kill me?' He picks up the hammer and examines it, wondering what it would feel like to swing it at Freya's head. Whether he could crack her skull open with a single blow. The thought catches him by surprise. He pushes it away.

'I didn't do anything,' she says, the picture of innocence. But then, he's already seen what a convincing actress she can be.

'Come on, Freya. The antifreeze? I wasn't born yesterday.'

'I - I don't know what you're talking about.'

'I think you do, but you failed, didn't you? You can't hurt me and I'm never going to let you near Gwyneth again.'

'Please,' she mumbles, her face crumpling.

It's pathetic. As if he's going to fall for her waterworks.

'I'm a patient man, Freya, but I can only take so much. So what's going to happen is that in a moment you're going to get up, get in your car and drive. You're going to drive until you're far, far away and you're never going to come back. Is that clear?'

'But —'

Harvey waves the hammer at her. 'No buts, Freya. I want you out of our lives, but first you're going to return every single piece that you've stolen from the house.'

She shakes her head, feigning ignorance.

'Don't you dare deny it!' he screams so loudly, she jumps. 'You came here to rob us. You took advantage of Gwyneth being in hospital and thought you could just take what you wanted.'

'It's not like that,' Freya cries.

'Don't lie to me. You saw an opportunity, and you grabbed it with both hands. But you'll never get your hands on this house or any of our money.'

'And if I refuse to leave?' Freya asks, regaining her composure, her spine straightening. In an instant, the tears she was threatening to spill have vanished and the meek, vulnerable act has gone.

'Then I'll have to find a way to persuade you.' Harvey puts down the hammer and picks up the pliers. He slips his little finger between the pincers and gently squeezes until it turns purple.

'Are you threatening me?'

'I'm asking you nicely.'

She continues to stare at him for a moment or two, as if trying to read whether he's bluffing, her eyes sharp and focused behind the thick lenses of her glasses.

'I wasn't lying when I said I hadn't seen my sister in almost fifty years,' she says, crossing her legs. 'They took me away when I was only fifteen and told me I'd never see my family again. Can you imagine being told you'd never see your parents again? Being ripped away from your own sister? It was barbaric.'

Harvey listens without feeling.

'But I never gave up hope of finding Gwyneth. It was a miracle when I saw her on the news, like it was fated to be. A calling. And when I saw she was in trouble, I had to come.'

'So you really are Gwyneth's sister?'

'Yes.'

'And when you saw how well she'd done for herself, you thought you could come and take a slice,' Harvey says, 'and nothing was going to stop you from getting it.'

Freya shakes her head. 'That's not true. I didn't know anything about her. I didn't know whether she was single or married, rich or poor. Whether she had kids or pets. I didn't even know if she remembered me. But none of that mattered. All I wanted was to be with her again.' She lowers her gaze to her lap where she's picking at her fingernails. 'But then I saw everything she had. You showed me the house and all the lovely things in it and I suppose a part of me was jealous. It seemed so unfair that she has everything and I have nothing.'

'So you thought you'd take whatever caught your fancy?'

'I thought it wouldn't matter if I took one or two things. I was sure Gwyneth wouldn't mind.'

'One or two things?' Harvey scoffs, remembering all the items he discovered missing. Thousands of pounds worth of irreplaceable antiques. 'You tried to kill me. And I have no doubt that if you had the chance, you'd have killed Gwyneth too.'

'I'd never hurt my sister. Never,' she says, raising her voice.

'I don't believe a word that comes out of your mouth. You think you can do whatever you like, no matter who gets hurt.'

'That's not true.'

'I'm sorry. Nothing you've said changes my mind. I want you gone and I never want you to come back.'

'After finally finding my sister? No chance.' Freya folds her arms resolutely.

'Then you clearly need a little more persuading.' Harvey pulls himself to his feet with a grimace. He's going to sleep for a week when this is all over.

He turns to his desk and selects a handful of cable ties. 'Put your hand on the arm of the chair,' he orders.

'No way.'

'Do it!' he yells.

But she tucks her hands under her armpits and shakes her head furiously. Trust Freya to make this more difficult than it has to be.

He snatches her arm and yanks it violently. He should have done this at the beginning, while she was still in shock. Now she's full of fight and trying to strap her to the chair isn't going to be as easy as he thought.

'Keep still,' he growls, but she won't.

She continues to buck and squirm with remarkable strength for a woman of her size.

It's no good. She's going to need an inducement to cooperate, so he lets go of her arm and turns back to his desk. He selects the Stanley knife. Slides out the blade and turns to her with it raised.

But to his surprise, she's on her feet and charging at him. Shocked, he backs away at the exact moment she grabs him by the upper arms and jerks her knee up between his legs.

A flash of white light temporarily blinds him, a split second before the jagged edge of pain shoots through his groin and into his stomach, forcing the air from his lungs. He drops the knife and slumps to his knees, gasping for breath.

'Bitch!' The pain is unrelenting, coming in waves. He's not felt anything like it since he was hit between the legs by a fast-moving cricket ball when he was a teenager.

As he crumples to the floor, clutching himself, he sees from the corner of his eye that Freya has climbed onto the chair and is opening the window. It's only a small opening, but there's not much of her and she easily squeezes herself through the narrow gap.

In an instant, she has dropped out of sight.

'Freya!' Harvey croaks. 'Get back here!'

But it's a waste of time. She's already gone.

Chapter 43

Harvey blinks away the stars shooting in front of his eyes and takes six deep breaths, concentrating on overcoming the pain radiating through his core.

He grabs the arm of the chair and gingerly pulls himself to his feet, glancing through the window into the garden where Freya has vanished into the gathering gloom of the evening, then curses under his breath, ruing his own stupidity. It had all been so perfectly planned. He'd anticipated having to tie her to the chair so he could frighten her with the suggestion of the cruelty he might inflict if she wouldn't cooperate, but he never considered the window could offer an easy escape.

He pats his trouser pockets, finds the key and, with trembling hands, unlocks the door. He grabs the hammer and wrench from his desk, hurries to the kitchen and out into the garden, his senses on high alert. He can't afford for Freya to turn the tables on him and surprise him again.

The wrench tucks neatly into the waistband of his trousers behind his back, leaving one hand free and the other clutching the hammer. The weight of it settles his nerves as he slips out into the night. It's a perfect weapon.

He tiptoes around the side of the house onto the rolling lawn and across the shady patio under his study window.

'Freya,' he calls. 'I'm sorry. I didn't mean to scare you.'

He stops to listen as the rumble of a plane passes overhead. Was that a rustle in the hedge? His head snaps around and he freezes. Probably a mouse. Or a rabbit. A bird, maybe, scratching in the undergrowth for a bug.

'Come on, we need to work this out,' he calls again. 'For Gwyneth's sake.'

His voice carries on the cool evening air, but receives no response.

Edging along the lawn, his feet sink into the mossy grass, and he enters a miniature orchard of apple, pear and cherry trees with ripening fruit hanging from their branches.

With a panicked alarm, a blackbird shoots out from the beech hedge that flanks the orchard on two sides. Harvey whirls around as it swoops beneath the lowest branches and disappears.

If Freya has her keys with her, she could make a dash for her car, and although he's been encouraging her to leave, he wants an absolute assurance that she'll never return. So, he doubles back, across the lawn and onto the drive.

Freya's car is parked alongside his Golf with two wheels on the grass. Why does the woman find it so difficult to park properly? No doubt she's done it to wind him up.

The vehicle is splattered with mud and several years of dust and grime. There's almost as much rust as paint. He checks over his shoulder that she's not about to jump him and then drops to his knees, unscrews the dust cap on the front wheel and lets the air out of the tyre. It escapes with an angry hiss, deflating slowly until the wheel is sitting on a flat pancake of rubber.

Harvey does the same to the other three tyres until there's no air left in any of them. Now let's see her try to drive away.

She can't have gone far, although there are a hundred places she could be hiding. He backs away from the vehicle and takes a wide loop around the house, peeping into the long shadows cast by the setting sun.

'Freya, please,' he pleads. 'I'm sorry if I went too far.'

Behind him, a dull thud. He instantly recognises the sound and spins around to face the barn. Someone's just let the door bang closed.

Harvey grips the hammer tighter and marches towards the ramshackle old building, a legacy from the days it was a working farm. Now it's nothing more than a glorified storage shed.

At the door, he hesitates, cocking his ear to listen. Someone's moving around inside. The scuff of feet on the dusty floor is a dead giveaway. He smiles to himself. With only one set of doors in and out, Freya is trapped inside. All he has to do is smoke her out.

He lifts the latch and winces as it squeals. The door scrapes an arc across the ground. She's bound to have heard that and realise he's coming.

'Freya, I know you're in here, so why don't you make this easy on both of us and come out? We still have so much to talk about.'

Silence.

He steps inside, the air heavy with oil and dust, and takes a cursory look around through the early evening gloom. Most of the space is taken up by Lionel's beloved Range Rover. Although it was clearly well looked after, it's now covered in a thick coating of muck. Around the car, cardboard boxes are piled high where Harvey has rearranged them to make more space.

'I can wait all night, if that's what it takes,' he says. 'Look, I'm not going to do anything. I'm not going to hurt you, but we need to talk,' he adds, softening his tone.

Then he remembers the hammer in his hand.

He holds it by its handle and tosses it to one side. It clatters across the concrete floor and skitters beneath the car.

'There, you see? No weapon.'

In the rafters, two pigeons flap their wings noisily, shuffling along a beam like a haughty married couple. There must be a hole in the roof where they're getting in. Harvey makes a mental note to look later. He doesn't want birds making a mess over everything.

Freya's in here, somewhere. He can sense her. He can almost hear her breathing.

'Come on out, come on out, wherever you are,' he sings, like he's reciting a lullaby to a baby.

He edges around the car, between the boxes and his new ride-on lawnmower, peering in and around all the old junk. She's probably curled up under a dustsheet or behind a box. But he'll find her.

He's deep inside the barn, squeezing behind the car and a mountain of boxes, when she finally breaks cover. He hears her before he sees her, scratching and scrabbling across the floor, somewhere behind him. He turns, but too slowly and is caught by a sudden, sharp bolt of pain in his knee.

He screams in agony and glances down to see Freya's arm, her hand clutching the hammer, withdrawing back under the car. He half runs and half hobbles towards the double doors and catches Freya as she emerges from between the vehicle's front wheels, scrambling to her feet.

He snatches a handful of her ridiculous bleach-blonde hair and yanks her head back.

'Ow, you're hurting me,' she yells, twisting and fighting to escape his grip.

'Not so quickly,' he growls, pulling out the wrench from his waistband. He holds it above her head, gripping it tightly. 'Drop the hammer.'

Reluctantly, Freya does as she's told as he pulls her to her feet. He marches her out of the barn and into the garden.

'Why couldn't you just listen to me for once?' he shouts in her ear, shaking her head from side to side, her glasses slipping down her nose. 'All you had to do was accept you'd lost and leave us in peace. But you couldn't, could you?'

'Harvey, please, I'm sorry —'

'It's too late for that. I gave you a chance, but you thought you were better than me, didn't you? Well, surprise, surprise, you're not. I win. You lose.'

He's so angry with her, the fury courses through his veins like wildfire. Honestly, he could punch her. But he's not that kind of man. No matter how manipulative she's been, he could never bring himself to hit a woman. He can, however, ensure she learns her lesson and never bothers them again.

Still gripping her hair, her head pulled back, he marches her to the house. He grabs his car keys from the side, then pulls her forcibly around to the back of his Golf.

'Did you honestly think you'd get away with it?'

It's a rhetorical question. Of course she did. That's the problem with psychopaths. They have an unwavering belief in their own superiority.

He blips open the car and orders her to climb into the boot.

She stops fighting momentarily as she contemplates what he's asking.

'No!' she screams, so loudly Harvey worries it might carry across the valley and alert the neighbours.

'Shut up and get in!'

'I can't. Please, no.'

Harvey raises the wrench, his knuckles white. 'Do it!'

Her quiver of fear gives him an unexpected thrill of delight.

'Please,' she begs. 'I know we started off on the wrong foot, and maybe to begin with I was a little jealous of your relationship with Gwyneth, but if I've upset you, I'm sorry.' Her bottom lip trembles and her eyes moisten with tears. 'Let's start again. We can be friends, can't we?'

'Friends don't try to poison each other. Now, it's the last time I'm going to tell you. Get in the car!'

He swings the wrench and Freya flinches. 'Don't,' she screams.

Finally, she stops struggling and, with an air of defeat, reluctantly climbs in.

She folds herself up with her knees tucked into her chest. He pushes her head down roughly, pressing her cheek against the gritty felt lining. Then he slams the boot shut and stands panting while his temper cools.

When his breathing is back under control, he glances around, checking no one was watching. But the property is secluded and utterly private. He could dance around naked, saying prayers to a burning wicker man for anyone would know.

He takes his keys, jumps behind the wheel and tosses the wrench on the back seat. But as he starts the engine and puts the car into gear, he realises he has no idea where he's going. This was never part of the plan. Or at least a part that he'd never fully thought through because he never imagined it would come to it. He had a vague notion that if Freya didn't cooperate, he'd drive her away from the house and dump her somewhere so far away, she'd never find her way back. But where?

A dense wood? A deserted farm building? A remote moor? It has to be at least two hours' drive away, he thinks, if not more. He wracks his brain, but nowhere springs to mind. He should have done some research. At least looked at a map in advance. It's too late now. Freya's locked in the boot and he needs to get moving.

He releases the handbrake and reverses to face down the drive. He'll have to figure something out on the way.

He straightens the wheel, but when he checks his rear-view mirror, a wave of panic hits him. Freya's car is parked outside the house. It's something else he'll need to worry about later. He can't leave it there without it raising suspicion.

His eyes drift down the length of the drive again, towards the road. He pulls forwards but almost immediately slams on the brakes so hard, he skids several feet, his seatbelt snapping sharply across his shoulder. In the boot, Freya's body thuds against the back seats.

He mouths a silent curse.

A car is approaching from the road. A dark-coloured saloon he instantly recognises.

The detectives, Chalk and Enright, have returned, and their timing couldn't be any worse.

Chapter 44

The detectives' car comes to a halt a few metres in front of Harvey's Golf. What could they possibly want now, at this time of the evening? Harvey sits motionless, watching them.

Chalk and Enright climb out with a lazy indifference, looking around at the house and gardens with the well-trained eyes of two officers suspicious of everything.

The jacket of Chalk's suit, an ill-fitting, crumpled grey garment that's gone shiny on the thighs, flaps open. His shirt, more grey than white, looks like it could do with a good iron, and his striped tie hangs loose at his open collar. He couldn't look any more like a cliché if he tried. If he's going for the haggard, world-weary, frayed detective look, he's totally nailed it, especially when he shoves his hands casually in his pockets as he lopes towards Harvey's car.

Harvey's pulse threads through his veins like a bullet train. He doesn't know what to do. If Freya makes a sound or if they poke their noses around his car, they're bound to find her. And how can he possibly explain what she's doing in the boot?

Enright, tall and willowy, follows a few steps behind Chalk, lithe and loose-limbed in contrast to the tightness in her expression, her hair scraped back severely from her face.

Someone must have heard Freya crying out and raised the alarm. Why else would they be here?

But Harvey dismisses the thought as quickly as it forms in his mind. They wouldn't have sent two detectives. They would have dispatched an emergency response team with sirens blazing and blue lights flashing, surely.

There must be another reason they're here. Maybe they finally have an update on the investigation. Whatever it is, he needs to head them off, because if Freya hears voices, she's bound to call out. He should have gagged her. And tied her up. But it's easy to think of these little details in hindsight.

Harvey slips off his seatbelt and slides out of the car, forcing a dead-eyed smile as he strides towards Chalk with an outstretched hand. 'Detectives, what can I do for you?'

Chalk contemplates Harvey's hand for a moment before gripping it tightly and squeezing it unnecessarily firmly.

'I heard you discharged yourself from hospital,' Chalk says.

'I was feeling better and frankly the food was awful.' He laughs, trying to make light of the situation, praying Freya stays silent. He backs onto the lawn, drawing the detectives away from the car and Freya in the boot.

'That's good.' Chalk nods and finally releases Harvey's hand. 'You look brighter.'

'The miracles of modern medicine. Is there something I can help you with?'

Chalk glances at his car, its engine still running. 'Were you on your way out?'

Harvey resists the urge to make a facetious comment. What does he think he was doing, heading down the drive in his car? Surveying the grounds?

'We've run out of milk,' he says instead. 'I was popping to the garage.'

'At this time of night?'

Harvey checks his watch. 'It's only nine o'clock. I was going to make hot chocolate before bed.'

'Right.' Chalk's eyes sharpen as they narrow. He doesn't believe him. He glances at Harvey's car again.

'I was hoping to make it before it shuts,' Harvey says, impatiently shifting from one foot to the other, 'so unless there was anything else you needed?'

'What was that?' Chalk's still staring at the old Golf, its engine rumbling.

'What?'

'I thought I heard a noise coming from your car.'

A prickle of heat causes a rash of sweat to break out across Harvey's forehead. 'It's an old car. It's always making strange noises,' he says, wondering what's he heard.

But then Chalk's attention shifts as he looks beyond the Golf, further up the drive towards the house. 'Is that Freya Grainger's car?' he asks.

Harvey follows his gaze. 'That? Yes, I think so,' he mumbles, wishing he'd moved it before he set off. But he wasn't expecting visitors, especially not the police.

'Settled your differences now, have you?'

'We're working on them.'

'Is she here? We'd like a word.'

'No,' Harvey says, a little too quickly. 'Why? What's it about?'

Chalk shoots him a withering look. 'That's not something I can discuss.'

'I thought it might be about Gwyneth. Did you find out if Freya has an alibi? Or get a match on her tyres?'

'Do you know where we can find her?'

'No. She only popped back briefly. She mentioned something about going for a walk.'

'A walk? It's getting dark.'

'We're sort of giving each a bit of space at the moment. We're not on the best of terms.'

'Well, it's not every day you accuse your sister-in-law of attempted murder, I suppose.' Chalk holds Harvey's gaze, unblinking. A challenge.

Harvey looks down at his feet, putting on a pretence of awkwardness. 'I guess I may have overreacted,' he says.

Chalk's head rocks back like he's been punched. 'You don't think Miss Grainger was trying to kill you, after all?'

Harvey shrugs. 'I don't know. I might have been a bit hasty when I accused her.'

'You know it's a serious offence to waste police time?'

'Of course. I didn't do it maliciously. I made a mistake.'

'So you're withdrawing your allegations against Miss Grainger?' Chalk asks.

Harvey nods. 'I guess so. Sorry.'

'And you've no idea where we can find her?'

'No.'

'Do you have her number?'

'She doesn't have a phone, as far as I'm aware,' Harvey says. At least, he's never seen her with one, which is strange now he comes to think of it. Everyone he knows has a phone.

'She doesn't have one?' Chalk frowns, as astonished as Harvey.

'I guess some people don't believe in them.'

'Then perhaps when you see her, you could ask her to get in touch? You have my number. Maybe you could lend her your phone?'

'I'll see what I can do. Was that everything?'

'For now.'

'Goodnight, detective.'

The two men stand face to face for a moment, regarding each other suspiciously. It's a surprise to Harvey that Chalk can't hear the thud of his heart, it's beating so hard and so fast in his chest.

Finally, Chalk turns on his heel and walks away, but then stops suddenly and spins around with a finger raised. 'Actually, there was something else.'

'Yes?' Harvey croaks, the word catching in his throat.

'About the hit-and-run. I thought you'd like to know that we've ruled Ruby Pettifer out of our inquiries.'

Harvey's mind goes blank.

'You were concerned she'd had a minor disagreement with your wife?' Chalk prompts.

'The shop. Yes, of course.' With all the drama of the last few days, he's completely forgotten about Ruby and the rumours he'd heard in the pub about her stealing from the till.

'She has an alibi for the time your wife was injured. It couldn't have been her.'

Harvey nods, letting the detective's words sink in. 'And you're absolutely a hundred per cent sure, are you?'

'Positive. Her story checks out.'

'So if it wasn't Ruby, who was it? You keep promising you're going to catch the bastard who did this, but you haven't made any arrests yet. Do you have any idea about the identity of the driver?'

'We're still working on a few lines of enquiry, Mr Kerrison, but it's proving a more complex case than we originally thought.'

'In other words, you don't have a clue.'

Chalk bristles. 'I wouldn't say that.'

'You've not arrested anyone, though?'

'Not yet.'

'And what about Freya Grainger? Does *she* have an alibi?'

'Miss Grainger was in Newcastle at the time.'

'You realise that Freya is Gwyneth's only living relative? If we were both to die, she stands to inherit everything we own.'

Chalk sighs wearily. 'I thought you said you were mistaken about Freya trying to kill you?'

'I'm just saying that she has a powerful motive to want Gwyneth dead.'

'As do you, Mr Kerrison.' Chalk's eyebrows curl upwards.

'How many times? I didn't do it,' Harvey growls. 'I could never do anything to harm Gwyneth. Now, was there anything else, detective?'

'Not at the moment, but I'm sure we'll be in touch. Take care of yourself, Mr Kerrison.'

Harvey stands silently fuming as Chalk walks away and climbs into his car with Enright. He doesn't trust them. And as the detectives' car reverses down the drive, he notices Chalk watching him with a beady, suspicious stare.

But if he had any evidence that Harvey was involved in his wife's accident, he'd have hauled him down to the police station by now. It's not something Harvey's going to waste time worrying about.

Right now, he has more important things on his mind, like the woman claiming to be his sister-in-law trapped in the boot of his car and how he can get rid of her in a hurry.

Chapter 45

Harvey sticks to the major roads, heading north, aiming to cover the furthest possible distance from the house. He's given himself two hours, which should be enough time to travel more than a hundred miles. Maybe more if he sticks to the motorway. Far enough that Freya is going to struggle to find her way back to the village in a hurry.

He needs to find somewhere remote. Somewhere away from civilisation where she's going to struggle to find help. The question is, where?

After more than two hours of driving, Harvey pulls into a service station with his eyes sore and heavy with fatigue. He parks in an isolated spot, away from the overhead floodlights, other vehicles and, hopefully, the security cameras. He opens a map on his phone and scours the area.

After a few minutes, he locates what appears to be a large, densely wooded area. There are only a handful of dwellings close by. Probably agricultural buildings or farmhouses. It's the best he can do at short notice and with no prior research. He drops a pin on the spot and calls up directions.

Freya has remained thankfully quiet for the entire journey. He's not heard a single peep from her. No cries for help, agitated banging or frantic screaming. Which is just as well as it would have driven him crazy and he'd have had to have done something to keep her quiet. He really didn't want to tape her mouth and risk her suffocating, because the last thing he needs is a dead body on his hands.

The urge to check on her is powerful, but he resists. While there's a possibility she's been so quiet because she's passed out or stopped breathing, he's worried it might be a trick, that it's exactly what she wants him to think, so he opens the boot and she can escape. That would be a disaster. So he ignores the niggle of anxiety at the back of his mind and motors on.

He drives for another twenty minutes on quieter, narrower roads and eventually into the wooded area where tall trees close in overhead.

After a short while, he takes a right turn onto a rough track, which, according to the map, should take him deep into the heart of the wood. He flicks his headlights onto full beam and winces as the car jolts over potholes, rocks and fallen branches, while fighting an uneven camber which threatens to send the struggling Golf careering into a dark ditch.

Trees, looming high above like shadowy spectres, close in on all sides, the darkness solidifying, while the only sound is the hum of the engine, the squeal of the car's long-suffering suspension and the occasion thud as it hits yet another hole. The sooner Harvey gets the hell out of here, the better.

Up ahead, the bouncing beams of his headlights pick out a padlocked gate where the track ends. An adjacent grassy clearing, churned up into a muddy quagmire, is obviously used regularly as a car park, probably by ramblers and dog walkers. It's as good as it's going to get.

Harvey pulls up, his tyres slipping on the slick mud, and kills the engine. He's plunged into darkness, the silence as heavy and as thick as molasses. He climbs out and steps straight into a muddy puddle that washes over his shoe and soaks his sock.

With a silent curse, he slams his door shut, stomps around to the back of the car and clicks open the boot. Freya lies blinking up at him, pressed against the wheel arch, trembling.

'Get out.'

'Where are we?' she mumbles with a quiver of fear. But it doesn't fool Harvey. He's not falling for the helpless old lady routine again.

'The middle of bloody nowhere. I don't know. Come on, shift it.'

Freya groans and moves stiffly, lifting her head and shoulders, making a meal out of it, as if she's too frail and elderly to climb out herself. Of course, it's an act.

'Hurry up,' Harvey shouts. 'I don't have all night.'

Freya winces as she tries to straighten her leg and sit upright in the cramped space. 'I can't feel my foot,' she complains.

'Stop whingeing.' He grabs her under the arm, but when he pulls her up, she screams.

'Stop, you're hurting me!'

'I'm warning you, Freya, get out of the car, or so help me...' He wishes now he'd grabbed the wrench he'd tossed on the back seat.

Slowly, she sits and then throws one leg, and then the other, over the lip of the boot and stands, swaying. She blinks and cranes her head, looking around. 'What is this place?'

'Just a wood. Somewhere you can't do any more mischief.'

She slides her glasses up her snub nose with her finger. 'What are we doing here?'

Harvey sighs. Is she really that naïve? What does she think? 'I gave you the chance to leave, but you refused, didn't you? So now you've forced my hand,' he grumbles. He doesn't want to be here any more than she does.

Her eyes open wide. 'You've brought me here to kill me, haven't you?' Her body stiffens with fear.

'Don't be so stupid. I wouldn't stoop to your level. Now turn around.' He grabs her by the shoulders and spins her around until she's facing the locked wooden gate. He pushes her between the shoulder blades and orders her to walk.

'Where?'

'Wherever you like. Just don't come back. Ever. Understood?'

'You can't leave me here,' she cries.

'Watch me.'

'Harvey!' She turns suddenly and half-runs, half-hobbles after him, her face crumpling with horror and despair. 'Please!'

She throws herself at him, snatching his arms, begging him.

'Get off me!' He shoves her so hard, she stumbles backwards, losing her footing, and falls to the ground.

'If you leave me here, I'll die. Do you really want that on your conscience?'

He jabs an angry finger at her, her dyed blonde hair almost luminous in the gloom. 'You were the one who tried to kill *me*. You didn't give me the chance to beg for my life, so count yourself lucky.'

Slowly, Freya drags herself to her feet, brushes herself down, and in the grey light, Harvey watches her face harden.

She throws her head back and laughs. The transformation from frightened old woman to defiant, cold predator is unsettling. 'You're no better than me, are you? I know exactly what you've done, Harvey.' She draws out the syllables of his name like a playground bully taunting the new, weedy kid in class.

The sudden change in her demeanour is worthy of a horror film. A second ago, she was a frail, broken woman begging for her life. And now... and now she's not. She stares at him with pure venom.

'Oh, yeah?' he backs away, his confidence evaporating. Suddenly, he's not so sure of himself.

'You don't love Gwyneth,' she says.

'That's not true. How dare you.'

'You accused *me* of exploiting an opportunity, but that's exactly what you've done, isn't it? Admit it, you preyed on a rich, lonely widow because you saw it as a means to a wealthy end.'

'You don't know what you're talking about.'

'You tried to kill her, didn't you?' Freya says, goading him. 'You knew what time she'd be leaving the village. Maybe she even called to tell you she was on her way. You knew the road was dangerous. You'd told her a million times. All you had to do was time your journey to perfection, keep your foot on the accelerator and drive on. It could almost have been the perfect crime, except you couldn't even do that right, could you?'

Harvey steps towards Freya with his fists clenched. 'Shut your stinking mouth. You don't know what you're talking about.'

'I know it's true. I can see it in your eyes.'

Harvey hits her with the back of his hand. A glancing blow across her cheek that dislodges her glasses. He never thought he had it in him to hit a woman, but she's pushed him to the brink and beyond.

Freya squeals in pain and staggers backwards.

'Enough,' Harvey yells. 'Don't ever let me see you again. Don't try to contact Gwyneth. Don't come to the house. As far as I'm concerned you don't exist. We're done, Freya. Goodbye and good riddance.' He strides back to the car, slipping in the mud and nearly losing his balance.

He climbs in and fires up the engine, quivering with rage. Blazing headlights reveal neat lines of trees stretching symmetrically in every direction. He puts the car into reverse, jumps on the accelerator and spins the Golf around in a looping arc with mud kicking up and splattering the windows.

There's only one way out for Freya. She's going to have to walk in the dark, with no idea where she's going. If she's lucky, she might make it out of the forest by morning when she might stumble across a dog walker who'll take pity on her and lead her to safety. He smiles at the thought that whatever happens, she'll be spending the next few uncomfortable hours here, wherever here is, lost and abandoned. It's the least she deserves.

He puts the car into first gear and picks out the rutted route back to the road, but when he lifts the clutch, the car doesn't move. The front wheels spin and the engine whines. He tries pumping the accelerator, but the whining only intensifies as the car slips from side to side. Frustrated, he tries reversing, but with the same outcome. He's stuck in the mud.

He bangs the steering wheel with his fist and lets out a howl before an almighty thud makes him jump. A ghoulish, twisted face appears in the windscreen, inches from his own. He recoils, terrified, until he realises it's Freya on the bonnet.

'You bastard!' she screams, banging on the glass with her fists. 'Don't you dare leave me here! Don't you fucking dare.'

Her eyes are wild with fury. She looks demented, like she's capable of tearing him limb from limb. The screaming is animalistic. Inhuman. A wailing banshee's cry that spikes his blood with ice. She's totally out of her mind.

He snatches at first gear again, but when he hits the accelerator, the car stalls and the headlights dim.

'No, no, no,' he mumbles to himself as Freya continues to kick and thrash, threatening to smash the glass.

He fumbles for the key in the ignition, starts the car again, and almost snaps the gear lever in his hurry to get away. He stamps on the accelerator and the tyres finally find purchase. The Golf shoots forwards with Freya still clinging on, blocking his view.

'Get off, you stupid woman!' he screams, waving his arm. 'I can't see a thing.'

The car bumps and jolts violently down the track. Harvey swerves left and right madly, aware how close the trees are on either side. At this rate, she's going to get both of them killed.

He straightens the wheel. The car lurches and a thud echoes through the chassis. Harvey snatches a breath, fearing he's broken or snapped something in his desperation to get away, but the car ploughs on, coughing and spluttering.

Another thud. Another spine-cracking jolt and this time, Freya disappears, flung off the bonnet and into the verge with a squeal of alarm.

Harvey doesn't stop. Or look back. He doesn't even slow down. He keeps his foot floored and his eyes ahead until he finally makes it back onto the main road in one piece.

Adrenaline rushes through his veins like amphetamine as he skids across the tarmac. As much as he never wanted to make this journey, it's given him an unexpected thrill. A warm glow ignites in his gut. His plan has worked. Freya's out of their lives for good, and hopefully, he'll never have to see her again.

He steers the car towards home, puts his foot down and speeds away, a bubble of laughter rising from his chest.

Chapter 46

After an hour on the road, fatigue hits Harvey like a pile driver. The adrenaline that had flooded his body has long since worn off and now, with the monotony of the drive and lulled into a soporific stupor by lights flashing past in the opposite direction, the drone of the engine and the warmth blowing from the vents, he's struggling to keep his eyes open. He'd intended to drive straight home to reclaim his room and his bed, but in this state he's a danger to himself and everyone else on the road.

An hour away from home, he pulls over, planning to grab a quick power nap. He finds a quiet industrial park and pulls up among a handful of lorries and vans whose drivers are doing the same. He kills his engine, tilts the seat back and closes his eyes.

At first, he's plagued by the memory of Freya throwing herself at the car, her face anguished and tortured, but soon sleep snatches him away on a wave of exhaustion, and he falls into a deep and untroubled slumber.

He's woken feeling groggy, his back aching, by the sound of a lorry engine rumbling to life. He peels open his sticky eyes and is surprised to find it's already daylight, a bruised purple hanging over the horizon.

He sits up, glances at the clock on the dashboard and shakes his head in disbelief. It's already gone six in the morning. He's slept for almost six hours. How's that possible? He was only supposed to be taking a thirty-minute nap.

Cross with himself, he stretches. He feels dirty and in need of a good shower, the few strands of hair on his head sticking out in an unruly mess. His mouth tastes foul and his foot, where he stood in a puddle last night, is warm and wet. He was hoping to be at the hospital first thing to see Gwyneth, but annoyingly, that's not going to be possible now, although if he hurries, maybe he can still make it by mid-morning.

A lorry pulls away with a noisy hiss of air brakes. He needs to get going. At least the traffic should be light for an hour or two before rush hour. He checks his phone but notices it's low on charge, and he was in such a rush he never even thought to bring a charging cable. There are also three missed text messages from Sheryl. He groans as he glances at them briefly. All of them checking up on him. Asking where he is. What he's up to. He's getting sick of it.

She means well, but he can't stand the constant fussing. He's not a child, and he's quite capable of looking after himself. She's not always been like this.

In fact, this interest in his welfare has only been since Gwyneth's been in hospital. They rarely see each other normally and never exchange text messages, but Sheryl's lonely and likes to think she's being a help. The ready-made meals have certainly been welcome, but he could do without being mothered.

He'll call her later and assure her that everything's fine. First, he needs to get home and shower.

But when he fires up the engine and pulls away, a worrying flashing red light on the dashboard catches his eye. He has no idea what it means, but it looks ominous. Anything flashing and red usually spells trouble. He's probably damaged something driving down that rutted track in the woods.

As the pitch of the engine slows, almost dies, and catches again when he presses the accelerator, Harvey growls with frustration. He doesn't know much about cars, but he knows enough to be pretty sure his ancient Golf is unlikely to get him home, especially as it's making an awful grinding sound. It's not even worth taking the risk with most of the journey home on the motorway. That would be the absolute worst place to break down.

He grabs his phone, which is on the cusp of dying, and discovers there's an independent repair garage less than two miles away. With a bit of luck, the car has a couple of miles left in her.

He pulls away gingerly, keeping his speed low. Several white vans in a tearing hurry scream past blaring their horns, but there's nothing he can do other than hug the edge of the road with his hazard warning lights blinking and pray. Finally, and somewhat to his amazement and relief, he spots the garage up ahead. He rolls onto the forecourt at the exact moment the engine splutters and finally dies.

Harvey yanks on the handbrake and lets his head fall onto the steering wheel. This couldn't have happened on a worse day when all he wants to do is get home, freshen up, and see Gwyneth.

He has to wait for over an hour before the garage opens. A sympathetic mechanic, his hair still wet and slicked back, promises to investigate, vowing to do everything he can to get Harvey back on the road. He even lets him charge his phone in the office while he rolls the car onto an inspection ramp with the help of a colleague.

Harvey takes a seat on a hard plastic chair opposite a battered, wooden desk, surrounded by oil-stained, sun-faded posters advertising tyres, additives and brakes, and while he waits for the bad news, rereads the messages from Sheryl.

> Where are you? A bit worried you're not at home or at the hospital. Call me when you get a second? S x

> Did you get my message? Call me when you can. Hope everything is ok. S x

> **Still not heard from you. I need to speak to you. I have some urgent news you'll want to hear. S x**

He rolls his eyes. She's such a drama queen. And as for the urgent news, what's the betting it's the latest village tittle-tattle about who's put the wrong bins out or rumours about plans for a new housing development in the area nobody wants or needs?

'You want the good news or the bad news?' The young mechanic stands in the doorway, casually leaning against the doorframe on a raised elbow.

Harvey lowers his phone. 'Go on, how bad is it?'

'The good news is we should be able to get you back on the road today. The bad news is, it's probably going to take most of the day, assuming we can get the parts first thing.' The mechanic grimaces. 'But it's not going to be cheap. Among other things, there's damage to the front axle, which looks buckled, and the oil sump's leaking. It's cracked badly and needs replacing. There was hardly any oil in the engine. You're lucky it didn't seize up completely.'

Harvey sighs. No prizes for guessing how that happened. He waves a dismissive hand. 'I don't care about the cost, I just need to get home.'

'We'll do our best. You want me to go ahead and order the parts?'

Harvey nods. Whatever it costs, he needs to get back.

The mechanic works miracles and by late afternoon has Harvey mobile again, although with a severe dent in his credit card. He's hopeful Gwyneth will pay off the balance. Maybe he can even turn the situation to his advantage and finally persuade her he really needs a new car.

His more immediate problem is that he catches the afternoon rush hour and a journey that should take him an hour takes more than two. Traffic stops and starts all the way home, clogging and clearing with no apparent rhyme nor reason.

When he eventually reaches the village, and drives past the antiques shop, the cafe, bakery and newsagents, his heart lifts. Home at last, and no Freya getting in the way and causing trouble. It deserves a celebration. A quick pint at the George, perhaps. It's too late to head into the hospital to see Gwyneth now, anyway. He'll go early tomorrow instead.

The pub is buzzing with a mid-week crowd of diners, and even a few locals hanging around at the bar.

'How's Gwyneth?' Nigel, the landlord, asks as he pulls Harvey a pint.

'No change.'

Nigel frowns. 'I'm sorry to hear that. Are the police any closer to catching the driver?'

Harvey shakes his head before taking a large gulp of beer. 'They don't have a clue. Honestly, I don't think they know what they're doing.'

Nigel leans closer and lowers his voice. 'Did they have a word with Ruby Pettifer?'

'They've ruled her out, Nige. She has an alibi.'

'Oh.' Nigel looks surprised. 'I probably shouldn't have said anything.'

'No, you're alright. I'm glad you mentioned it.'

'And what about the mother-in-law? Is she still staying with you?'

Harvey takes several mouthfuls of beer, savouring the taste. 'She had to go back home, unfortunately. Things to do in Newcastle,' he says. There's no point explaining how his mother-in-law turned out to be his sister-in-law. He could do without the awkward questions, even if one day it might make a fun pub anecdote. But not today. It's still too raw.

'Bet you're glad you've seen the back of her?' Nigel winks and shoots him a conspiratorial smile.

'Let's just say it's nice to have the house back to myself.' Harvey remembers Freya's car is still sitting on his drive and that he'll need to make it disappear. It's one last job that needs sorting and Freya will be out of his life for good.

His phone buzzes, sending it shimmying and shaking across the bar. Harvey picks it up, answers and holds it to his ear without checking who's calling. The alcohol has already loosened the shackles of tension and a chemical euphoria fizzes in his stomach.

'Hello?'

'Harvey? Where are you?' Sheryl sounds worried.

'In the George having a pint. Why?' He rolls his eyes at Nigel. It's like having a second wife.

'I've been worried sick. Did you get my messages?'

'Yeah, sorry, I've been busy. I didn't get the chance to reply. I was going —'

'It's about Freya.'

'Oh, she's gone,' Harvey says.

'Gone?'

'She had things to do at home.'

'That's sudden. I thought she was planning to stay until Gwyneth was better?'

'I guess she felt she'd been away long enough.'

Sheryl clears her throat. 'Right, well, it's just that I found out something about her I thought you'd be interested in.'

'What now? She's not really my sister-in-law?' He laughs at his own joke.

'Can you come around?' she asks with the sombre demeanour of a vicar.

'Now?'

'You're really going to want to see this.'

Harvey eyes his half-drunk pint. He was hoping to stay for a few tonight. After all, he deserves it.

'Okay, give me ten minutes,' he says with a sigh.

'I'll be waiting. But I have to warn you, you're going to need to be sitting down when you find out what I have to tell you.'

Chapter 47

Sheryl's door flies open as Harvey approaches, his fist raised to knock.

'There you are. Where have you been? I was getting worried.' Sheryl stands with her arms crossed and her face pinched with agitation. 'I've been trying to contact you,' she says crossly.

'I had some things I needed to do.' She's getting worse. As if he's going to give her a running commentary of his movements. He's going to have to put her straight. He can't go on like this.

He follows her into a plush living room, conscious his shoes are still muddy from the woods. The room smells of vanilla. Although he can't see them, he suspects she has those pots with scented oils and reed sticks all over the house.

'I know I should keep my nose out of it, but I can't. You know what I'm like. My mother always said my curiosity would get the better of me one day. But it's good to be curious, don't you think?' The words are flying from her mouth like bullets. She barely draws breath between sentences.

'Slow down, Sheryl. Why don't you just tell me what it is you've found?'

She perches on the edge of the sofa, wringing her hands. 'I didn't mean to pry, but there's something about Freya that's been troubling me. You know, ever since she had you believing she was Gwyneth's mother. I mean, who would do that? I'd be mortified if someone thought I was my mother's age. But she never corrected you, did she? Didn't you think that was odd?'

'To be fair, I don't think I ever gave her the chance.'

'Regardless,' Sheryl says with a sigh. 'It didn't sit right with me and so I did some more digging. I wanted to find out more about her.'

'And?' He wishes she'd get to the point. He could still be in the pub.

She turns her attention to a piece of paper lying on the coffee table. She slides it towards him. 'I found this in the library,' she says.

'What is it?' he asks, although he can already see it's a printout of what appears to be an old newspaper cutting.

'I printed it off because I was worried you wouldn't believe me.'

It's from a local paper in Buckinghamshire where Gwyneth grew up. He glances at the date. March 7th, 1978.

'What am I looking at?' he asks, confused. There are multiple stories on the page, the ink on the original copy smudged and illegible in places.

Sheryl points with a red-painted nail to an article in the centre of the page.

Girl, 7, hospitalised after attack by sister

Harvey picks up the paper and scans the article, his eyes arrested by the sight of a familiar name. His mouth falls open in shock. 'Bloody hell,' he gasps.

A seven-year-old girl is in hospital fighting for her life following an alleged attack by her teenage sister at their home in Beaconsfield.

The injured girl, named by neighbours as Gwyneth Grainger, was reportedly discovered by her mother at their home on Plover Avenue. Gwyneth is said to have been bleeding heavily in her bedroom after the incident, which is believed to have involved her 15-year-old sister, Freya Grainger, using a pair of knitting needles.

Police were called at around 4.25 pm yesterday afternoon after hearing screams coming from the house. Officers from Thames Valley Police and an ambulance from Buckinghamshire Ambulance Service were dispatched to the scene.

A spokesperson for Buckinghamshire Ambulance Service confirmed they attended and treated a seven-year-old girl for multiple stab wounds to the abdomen.

> *Thames Valley Police have arrested a 15-year-old girl in connection with the incident on suspicion of attempted murder. She is currently in custody, assisting with enquiries.*
>
> *The seven-year-old remains in a serious but stable condition after undergoing surgery at the hospital to treat more than twenty stab wounds.*
>
> *The investigation is ongoing, and police are appealing for any witnesses to come forward.*

'Kind of all makes sense now, doesn't it?' Sheryl says. 'Why they lost touch for so long and why Gwyneth never mentioned she had a sister.'

But Harvey's not listening. He's too busy reading, the paper trembling in his hands.

'Have you read it?' he asks. Of course she has. 'It says Gwyneth needed surgery after being stabbed repeatedly in the abdomen.' Harvey thinks about the faint scars on Gwyneth's stomach, now no more than pale blotches. It's no wonder she never told him how she got them. If he'd known the truth, he'd have never have asked, but he wasn't to know the secret his wife's been hiding for more than forty years.

'Isn't it shocking?' Sheryl says.

'She never told me any of this.'

'I imagine she's been traumatised for life, but what I don't understand, and what the article doesn't explain, is why Freya attacked her. I couldn't find any follow-up stories. I thought there might have been a court case or something.'

'At least it explains why Freya was taken into care,' Harvey says.

'I didn't know that.'

'She told me it was because her mother couldn't cope with having two children, but this says otherwise.' He waves the article in the air. 'Her mother was trying to protect Gwyneth.'

Sheryl blows out a puff of air from her cheeks. 'Why has Freya come back into Gwyneth's life now, after all these years?'

Harvey shrugs. 'It's a good question.'

But he has a pretty good idea. Or at least he thought he did. He thought she'd come to steal from them, driven by envy after seeing the life Gwyneth had carved for herself and wanting a part of it. After all, he's already discovered several thousand pounds worth of antiques missing from around the house.

The only other alternative is that she's here with something more sinister in her mind and wants to finish what she started when she repeatedly stabbed Gwyneth all those years ago.

Sheryl's obviously been thinking the same. 'Do you think she came to... do Gwyneth harm?' she asks.

'I don't know. She's had plenty of opportunity, but as far as I can tell, she's not laid a finger on her.'

His mind drifts back to the day he walked in on Freya in the hospital and caught her tampering with the machines keeping Gwyneth alive. Was that the moment she'd tried to kill her sister again?

'She could have wanted to make amends,' Sheryl suggests.

'Amends?'

'You know, make up for what she did all those years ago. She's had a long time to think about what she did. She might be looking for forgiveness,' Sheryl says. 'Maybe she came back to say she was sorry.'

But it sounds utterly fanciful. 'She's a psychopath,' Harvey points out. 'She's not sorry about anything. She thinks she stands to inherit everything Gwyneth owns if she dies.'

'Except she wouldn't because you're Gwyneth's next of kin,' Sheryl points out.

Harvey raises an eyebrow and waits for the realisation to sink in.

'Which is probably why she tried to poison you.' Sheryl nods as if she's slowly joining up the dots.

'She needs me out of the way.' Harvey stands and walks to the window, staring into the garden. If he had any doubts that he'd done the right thing by forcibly removing Freya from their lives, they've been well and truly quashed.

'Harvey, where is she?' Sheryl asks in a soft, nervous voice.

He turns to face her and smiles. 'Gone, don't worry. Hopefully for good this time.'

Sheryl glowers at him. 'You've not done anything stupid, have you?'

'No, of course not.'

'It's just that I popped over to the house earlier and I saw your car was gone, but Freya's is still on the drive.'

Harvey stiffens. 'It broke down. You've seen the state of it. She wanted to go home to Newcastle, so I gave her a lift to the station,' Harvey explains, trying to sound casual, but hearing the tension in his tone. He's never been a good liar.

Sheryl blinks rapidly. 'I'm surprised. I thought you would never get rid of her.'

He chuckles nervously. 'Me too.'

'What made her change her mind?' There's a suspicious edge to Sheryl's question.

'Who knows? Maybe she came to her senses and realised that once I was onto her, she'd never get away with it?'

'I suppose you could be right.'

Harvey glances at the article in his hand. He reads the headline again and sighs, imagining the scene in the house. The blood. The violence. The horror Gwyneth's poor mother must have felt when she found her daughter bleeding out. What the hell could have possessed a fifteen-year-old girl to do something so evil? 'Thanks for this,' he says. 'Mind if I keep hold of it?'

'Sure.'

Harvey folds the paper and slides it into his back pocket.

'Will you stay for something to eat? I could rustle something up for the two of us.' Sheryl's face stretches into a smile of hope.

But Harvey just wants to be on his own tonight, even if his stomach is growling with hunger.

'I'd like to get home, if you don't mind. It's been a long day.' He's looking forward to a hot shower and a glass of whisky in front of something mindless on the TV.

'No, of course.' Sheryl jumps to her feet, flustered. 'It's a lot to take in.' If she notices he hasn't shaved, that there's a sour note of stale sweat on his crumpled clothes, or that one shoe is caked in mud, she doesn't say anything.

Harvey marches to the front door, embarrassed to see he's left a trail of dried mud across Sheryl's lovely cream carpets.

'Goodnight, then.'

The door closes behind him as an owl screeches somewhere across the valley. Harvey pulls his keys from his pocket and trudges wearily to his car.

He can't stop thinking about the article, about a young Freya stabbing her sister in a frenzied attack, and how they've both dodged a bullet in the last few days.

If Freya's capable of attempting to kill her sister once, she's more than capable of doing it again. And of killing anyone else standing in her way.

Chapter 48

Freya's car sitting on the drive outside the house is a grim reminder of the sister-in-law Harvey could do without. He needs to make it disappear, but he's too tired to deal with it tonight. He'll sort it out in the morning, first thing, although he's not entirely sure how. Torching it is only going to attract attention and dumping it somewhere quiet isn't making it disappear. Unless he can find a deep lake. But there's nothing like that for miles around.

Hopefully, something will come to mind when his brain's clearer and he's not so dog tired.

When he lets himself into the house and flicks on the lights, the first thing he sees is Gwyneth's stripy blue bag that Freya had been using. It sends a shiver down his spine. It's a reminder that along with the car he'll need to dispose of her dirty bag-for-life with all those creepy things he found in it. It all has to go. Every trace of her.

Wearily, he heads upstairs and for the first time in days, returns to his own room. The room Freya insisted she should have because the guest rooms were unsuitable. How stupid to have been so easily manipulated by her.

He's glad now that he changed the sheets on the bed and cleaned the en suite earlier, removing every remnant of Freya's toxic stay. He strips off his dirty clothes, steps into the shower and savours the hot water as it cascades down his back, washing away the sweat, grime and dirt of the last twenty-four hours.

Afterwards, he feels revived, his skin tingling from the heat of the shower. He pulls on a pair of clean pyjamas and lies down on the four-poster, the fresh, cotton sheets cool and crisp. It's too early for bed. Plus, he's been looking forward to a whisky in peace. But as his mind drifts back to the newspaper report Sheryl found, wondering what could have possessed Freya to attack her sister so violently, and picturing her lost and alone in the woods, miles from anywhere, his eyes flicker closed.

When he wakes with a start, the house is still and the room's in darkness, even though he thought he'd left the bedside lamp on. He glances at the clock on the bedside table. It's half two in the morning. His heart is racing, his mouth tastes sour and his eyeballs are tender with tiredness. But there's something else that haunts him.

Fear.

He snatches a breath and listens to the sounds of the house, creaking and groaning. In the corner of his eye, he spots the curtains billowing.

Something's woken him, but he's not sure what. A deep feeling of dread builds from his core and radiates through his whole body.

He remembers dropping off after his shower, intending only to lie down on the bed for a few minutes. He must have been more tired than he thought.

Then another worry niggles at his brain. Did he lock the front door, check all the windows and set the alarms as he usually would before bed? He's normally so security conscious with so many valuables in the house, but he was exhausted last night and can't be sure.

He peers around the room. He's never believed in ghosts, but there's a definite chill running down his spine, and he has an unnerving sense that there's a presence in the room with him. That he's not alone.

Could it be Lionel? No, that's ridiculous. Even if he believed in all that supernatural hocus-pocus, why would Lionel choose now to make himself known? It's not as if there have been any other unexplained ghostly occurrences since he and Gwyneth were married. No drawers unexpectedly opening. Pictures falling from the walls. Noises in the night.

Until now.

He can definitely sense something or someone in the room.

There! In the corner, by the wardrobe. A shadow.

It's moving. Creeping towards him.

Harvey shrinks away, terrified, his heart almost tearing itself out of his chest.

And then it springs forwards, jumping onto the bed, moving almost unnaturally quickly.

Harvey cries out, but his voice is drowned by a horrifying banshee's wail.

The springs in the mattress creak and the bed bows. Harvey raises his hands to protect himself as blows rain down and the wailing gets louder.

A spear of pain radiates from his forearm, putting paid to any notion it's a supernatural phenomenon. He's being physically attacked.

He prises open his eyes. A face, contorted in fury, looms directly above his own. Shock renders him temporarily immobile.

Freya?

Her dyed blonde hair almost seems to glow in the dark.

Another sharp prick punctures his shoulder. He snatches her wrist, stilling her arm as she's about to stab him again.

She tries with her other hand, but he catches that arm too and holds her steady, while she spits and screams, fights and kicks.

But she's tiny. As frail as a bird.

'Stop!' he commands.

Her weapons are two long, thin rods. Knitting needles.

'Freya! That's enough!'

He throws her off the bed, rolls over and switches on the bedside lamp as she comes at him again with renewed fervour, springing off the floor like a beast possessed.

Instinctively, he raises his hands in front of his face, noticing his arms are coated in blood, rivulets of it running from several puncture wounds.

Flesh wounds only. If she was aiming for his vital organs, his head or, god forbid, his throat, thankfully she's missed.

She stabs him again, this time on the top of his thigh, and he screams out in agony as a needle pierces skin and muscle.

He doubles over and lashes out with the back of his hand, catching Freya under the chin, the force of the blow sending her spiralling backwards. She crashes into the wardrobe and falls, stunned, to the floor.

Harvey hobbles across the room and pins her to the carpet. He wrenches the knitting needles from her hands and tosses them out of her reach.

'Are you completely insane?' he yells, a spray of his spittle landing on her face.

'You left me for dead,' she hisses, her glasses askew and her hair all mussed up.

'You weren't supposed to come back. I thought I made it clear.' Harvey bunches her blouse in his fist and tightens his grasp.

'Don't tell me what to do.'

'How did you even get back?' Harvey asks.

'I'm not an idiot.' She dabs at a cut on her lip with her knuckle. 'I walked. I hitchhiked. I pleaded for help. How do you think? It's amazing how many people will put themselves out when they think you're an old woman in distress.'

Harvey shakes his head in disbelief. If he wasn't so appalled, he'd be impressed. She's blagged her way back and simply let herself in the front door with the key he forgot to take from her. Another stupid mistake.

'You're not welcome,' he says. 'I don't want you anywhere near me or Gwyneth. You've already tried to kill me once.'

'I had no choice. You're no good for Gwyneth. She doesn't need someone like you in her life.'

He laughs in her face. 'Says the woman who almost stabbed her to death when she was a child.'

She stops struggling and stares intently into his eyes. 'How - how did you know about that?'

'It was in the papers. I found an old cutting.'

'You wouldn't understand.' She turns her face away from him, although it's a bit late to be ashamed.

'It said you stabbed her more than twenty times. I've seen the scars.'

'What was I supposed to do?' she snaps ferociously. 'Daddy only ever had eyes for her, didn't he? His beautiful little girl, he called her. What about me? What had I done?'

'You tried to kill her because you were jealous?' Harvey asks, incredulous. What kind of sick kid stabs their younger sibling for attention?

'I wasn't trying to kill her,' she spits.

'It's no wonder you were taken into care.'

'I love Gwyneth. I never meant to hurt her,' Freya protests. 'And when they said I couldn't see her again, I was devastated. It wasn't fair. But I knew one day we'd be reunited.'

Harvey shakes his head. 'You shouldn't have come,' he croaks.

Freya frowns. 'But my sister needed me.'

'She didn't. She has me. I'm enough. The last thing she needs right now is to be reminded of the horrors of her past.'

Freya snorts. 'Don't be so melodramatic, Harvey. Honestly, listen to yourself.'

'Admit it, you only came looking for Gwyneth so you could finish what you'd started.'

'Is that what you think?'

'I think you came here to kill her, but became distracted by the thought of what you might stand to inherit if you were her only living relative.'

Freya smirks. 'I wanted you out of the way to protect Gwyneth.'

'No, you were planning to kill us both because you wanted to lay your grubby, murdering hands on all this.' He lets go of her top and waves an arm around the room. 'You saw your sister's wealth and you couldn't stand it. Envy got the better of you again, just like when you thought your father was paying more attention to Gwyneth than you.'

Freya stops struggling and Harvey lets her go, confident she's no longer a threat without a weapon or the element of surprise. He shuffles across the room, sitting with his back against the door, panting.

Freya straightens her glasses, hair and clothes. 'You've got it wrong. I was just pleased to find my sister again. I've been looking for her since the day I was released.'

Harvey frowns. 'Released?'

Freya's face falls. And then she smirks again. 'Oh, Harvey, don't be so naïve. I attacked my sister. Do you really think they'd have put me into care for something like that? They sent me to a juvenile prison. In fact, I've been in and out of jail all my life. But this time, when I came out, I was determined to change. I was going to find Gwyneth, and we were going to live happily ever after together. Until you got in the way and ruined everything.'

'You're out of your mind.'

'No,' she says, contemplating his accusation for a moment. 'I don't think I am.'

'If I hadn't stopped you, Gwyneth would probably already be dead.'

Freya examines her wrists. Her skin is marked with faint red botches where Harvey grabbed her and held her tight.

'It's not fair though, is it? She has all this and I have nothing. I have a room in a house and share a bathroom. I have to watch every penny. I hardly have enough money to feed myself, let alone put fuel in my car so I can get to work. We had the same parents and the same upbringing, so why shouldn't I be entitled to the same privileges she has?' Freya asks.

'Gwyneth has worked hard for everything she owns. It wasn't handed to her on a plate.'

'Oh,' she says, 'you mean like it was for you?'

'What?'

'You've not worked hard for any of this either, have you?' She blinks at Harvey from behind her thick lenses.

'I don't care about the house or Gwyneth's money.'

Freya snorts. 'Really? Look me in the eye and tell me you proposed to her because you were in love.'

'Of course I did.'

Freya rises unsteadily to her feet and stretches. 'You saw a rich widow grieving the loss of her beloved husband and you preyed on her vulnerability to get your hands on her house and her wealth. Admit it.'

'We fell in love,' Harvey says sternly.

'If you say so.'

'You know what? I don't care what you think.'

'What I think is that you put her in hospital,' Freya says.

'Don't talk rubbish.' Harvey thumps the floor with his fist.

'Obviously, you didn't mean to put her in hospital. You meant to kill her.' A cruel smile creeps across Freya's lips as she gets up and paces the room. 'I assume the house and everything Gwyneth owns would be left to you if she died?'

Freya walks to the bedside table and picks up a photograph of Gwyneth and Harvey on their wedding day. She runs a finger over the glass, a silly smile on her face as if she's remembering the happy day, although, of course, she wasn't there. 'If there's one thing I've learnt about you, Harvey, it's that you're greedy. You can't help yourself. Just look at the state of you.' She turns and sneers down her nose at him.

Harvey straightens his back and sucks in his stomach. He might have put a few pounds on over the last week or so, but he's been under a lot of stress since Gwyneth's accident.

'I don't think you're in any position to lecture —'

The crack of glass as the photo frame slips out of Freya's fingers stops Harvey's words dead.

'Oops, butterfingers,' Freya sing-songs, before bending down to gather up the pieces.

What a fitting metaphor for Freya's impact on their lives since she turned up, Harvey thinks. She's been like a bull in a china shop, trying to destroy their marriage from the day she arrived.

'Leave it alone. Let me do it.' Harvey crawls across the floor and shoves her roughly out of the way.

The glass has shattered into a dozen shards. He snatches what's left of the frame from Freya's hands and starts carefully picking up the fractured glass. Fortunately, the photo is undamaged.

'There's nothing here for you,' he moans angrily. 'I'll give you one more chance. Leave and never come back. If you don't, I'll involve the police. I'm sure they'll be interested when I point them towards your police record.'

'I don't think so, do you?'

A sudden sharp point pressed into his neck causes Harvey to freeze as he's on his hands and knees by the bed. Freya has moved silently to his side and stands over him with one of the knitting needles he'd snatched from her and discarded.

Stupid, stupid, stupid.

He should have destroyed them or made sure they were out of her reach. Instead, he's allowed himself to become distracted and now she has the upper hand again and there's nothing he can do about it.

He closes his eyes and swallows.

So this is how he's going to die and Freya will finally get exactly what she came for.

Chapter 49

The tip of the knitting needle under Harvey's jaw presses dangerously close to the major arteries feeding his brain.

'You don't get it, do you?' Freya breathes in his ear.

'Please,' he begs, ashamed at the tremor in his voice and the warm, wet patch on his pyjama bottoms. 'Don't kill me.' His arms are shaking, his body rigid with terror. He doesn't want to die. Not like this, on his hands and knees in his soiled pyjamas, bleeding out on the bedroom floor with a needle in his neck.

'All I ever wanted was for us to be a proper family again. We've missed out on so much,' Freya continues. 'You shouldn't have gone snooping around and digging up the past.'

'It wasn't me,' Harvey protests. 'It was Sheryl. She found the article in an old newspaper in the library.' He feels only the slightest twinge of guilt implicating his neighbour, but he doesn't want to die.

Freya tuts as the pressure on the needle increases a fraction, indenting the soft, fleshy skin. 'Hussy,' she hisses. 'I've seen the way she is around you. Shameless. Gwyneth deserves better than you two acting up behind her back.'

'It's not like that! There's nothing going on. She's lonely, that's all, and she's been looking out for me.'

'While the cat's away...'

'No!'

'You disgust me.' Freya spits at him, a globule of warm, wet saliva hitting the back of his ear.

Harvey winces. 'Take what you want from the house. Take it all. I don't care. Just don't hurt me,' he sobs.

'Goodbye, Harvey. I hope you rot in hell.'

'No, please!'

'It's going to be fun watching you die, although it'll be a pain replacing the carpets when you've gone. I don't suppose all that blood will wash out easily. It's bound to stain.'

Harvey whimpers, picturing himself in a pool of his own blood, staring glassy-eyed at the ceiling. 'No,' he cries.

'But it doesn't matter. I'll be changing a lot of things around here. Getting rid of all this old clutter, for a start. I don't know how you can live with all these creepy old things gathering dust.'

'They're Gwyneth's antiques. You can't get rid of them. She'd be mortified.'

'They're hideous.'

'And worth a lot of money,' Harvey says, spotting an opportunity to save himself. 'But only if you can sell them.'

'I'm sure that won't be difficult.'

'You'd be surprised. You don't want to be swindled out of what they're worth, but I can help you.'

'I don't need your help.' Her mouth is so close to his ear, he can smell sour coffee on her breath, mixed with the nauseating stench of body odour wafting off her clothes in waves. It's enough to make him gag.

'I'll put you in touch with a specialist dealer, one who won't ask too many awkward questions. I don't think you realise the value of Gwyneth's collection. It won't be like fencing a stolen laptop.'

'I said I don't need your help. I'll just be glad to see the back of them.'

Harvey stiffens. 'What about Gwyneth? She's not going to want you selling all her things. Unless...'

'I kill her too? It's crossed my mind.'

'I thought you said you wanted to be a proper family again?' Harvey gasps. 'You said you didn't come back to kill her.'

'It all depends whether she can find it in herself to forgive me when she wakes up. I'm sure she will. It's been such a long time.'

Harvey frowns. Does she honestly think Gwyneth's going to forgive and forget that her sister tried to kill her after all these years? And what about when she finds out Freya's murdered her husband? Gwyneth's hardly going to find it in her heart to welcome her into her home and let her sell her antique collection.

'And if she doesn't forgive you?' he asks.

'Then I guess I won't have to share.'

'You're out of your mind. How do you think you're going to get away with killing us both and inheriting the house? They'll be onto you in a flash, then they're going to lock you up and throw away the key.'

Freya laughs like a maniac, sending a shiver of fear down Harvey's spine.

'You underestimate me.'

Insane *and* deluded. She thinks she's clever, but she has no concept of reality. She seems to think she can simply kill them both and no one will ever find out. Take what she wants and never face the consequences. It's the absolute definition of insanity. And greed.

'I get it. You're clever,' Harvey says. 'You fooled me, but do you really want to risk ending up back inside at your age? Of never being free again? Do you really want to die in prison?'

Freya jabs him with the needle. 'Shut up. I don't need your opinion.'

'Think about it, Freya. You don't need to kill either of us. I don't want to die, so what about if I gave you a gift? A really expensive gift that you could sell for the price of a house? No more living in that damp flat. You could have a place of your own.'

'I could have this place.'

'You're not listening to me. If you kill your sister and me, you'll go to jail. Forever. And you'll never get your hands on this house. I'm offering an alternative. The chance to walk away with more money than you could ever imagine. A chance to live a better life,' Harvey says, warming to the idea forming in his mind. He has to make her see sense. His life depends on it. 'Take the gift. Walk away. Enjoy your freedom.'

'What gift?' she snaps, with all the grace of a sulky teenager.

Harvey grins to himself. 'Gwyneth's necklace. The one she's wearing in the portrait at the bottom of the stairs. Would you like to know how much it's worth?'

'The one with the rubies and sapphires?'

'That's right. Emeralds too. And lots of other valuable stones. We had it revalued a few months ago for the insurance company. Would you like to know for how much?'

'Tell me.'

'Two hundred thousand.'

Freya gasps and falls silent. Her breath becomes shallow and fast in Harvey's ear.

'That would be more than enough for a decent house, wouldn't it? Just imagine having your own place with your own garden. You could decorate it in your favourite colours and choose some nice furniture.'

'And you'd give it to me?'

'Yes, but on the condition you let me live and you leave. You don't attempt to contact Gwyneth and we never see each other again.' Harvey's heart pumps hard and fast. He's literally negotiating for his life and if she doesn't accept his deal, he's going to die.

'Maybe I'll kill you and take it anyway.'

'If you kill me, you'll never find out the combination to the safe,' Harvey retorts.

She jabs the needle into his neck again, breaking the skin. A droplet of blood forms into a ball and rolls down his throat. 'I'm sure I could persuade you to open it.'

'Why go to the trouble and risk a jail sentence? Take the deal. A gift from me to you. It's so much less messy this way, and we both get what we want. Even if you didn't buy a house, think what you could do with the money.'

'How do I know you're not trying to trick me? Does this necklace even exist?'

'I'll show you. You can try it on and you can see how it looks.'

The pressure from the needle on Harvey's neck eases.

'It's worth two hundred thousand pounds, you say?'

'The valuation documents are in the safe with the necklace. I'll show you, if you don't believe me.'

'Get up!' Freya orders, stepping back and finally removing the needle from Harvey's neck. 'But you try anything stupid and I'll gut you like a fish.'

Harvey has no doubt she means it. If she was capable of almost killing Gwyneth when she was fifteen, who knows what she's capable of now. She's not only crazy, she's utterly unpredictable. But at least he's still alive and breathing. For now.

Slowly, he stands, rubbing his arms and legs.

'You've wet yourself.' Freya wrinkles her nose in disgust as she notices the wet patch on Harvey's pyjama bottoms.

'Do you want to see this necklace or not?' he snaps, his cheeks flushing with embarrassment.

'Go slowly. You try anything funny, and I'll ram this needle so far inside your chest, you'll never take another breath.'

Harvey raises his hands in submission and stumbles towards the door. Freya follows closely behind him with the needle in the soft, fleshy hollow of his armpit, dangerously close to his heart.

Walking in sync, they shuffle along the landing, their bodies close. Down the stairs and up to the door leading to the basement. Harvey reaches for the key on top of the frame, unlocks the door and they begin an awkward, slow descent.

'I see you've had a rummage,' Harvey says flippantly, nodding at the boxes of antiques that have been opened and rifled through. 'Find anything you liked?'

'Shut up,' Freya orders.

'The safe's inside the panic room.'

She lets him step forwards and punch the numbers into the keypad. The date of their anniversary, as he foolishly told Freya when he first showed her around. He has no doubt she's remembered.

The keypad beeps and a red light flashes.

'What's happened?' Freya asks anxiously, glancing over his shoulder.

Harvey tuts. 'Sorry, you're making me nervous. I typed the wrong number.'

'You'd better not be messing me around.'

'I'm not, I promise. It's just...' Harvey punches in a series of numbers and the lock clicks open. 'There. I've done it.'

He steps aside, hauling the heavy door open.

'You first,' Freya insists.

She really could do with a shower and a change of clothes, which, he notices in the bright lights of the basement, are covered in mud and dirt.

Harvey shrugs. He slides in front of Freya and into the tiny room with the knitting needle pressing so hard into his underarm, it makes him wince.

They stand together facing the safe.

'If you're lying to me,' Freya threatens.

'I'm not! I promise.' Harvey holds his hands up higher. 'Just take the fucking necklace and get out of our lives.'

'Language,' she chides.

'You want it or not?'

'Open the safe. Let me see.'

'And then you'll go?' Harvey asks.

'Let me see the necklace.'

Harvey sighs, steps up to the safe and wriggles his fingers. He committed the ten-digit code to memory a long time ago. It was Gwyneth's choice. Her numbers. He doesn't even know if they have any significance or whether they're a random sequence.

He types them quickly, his fingers flying across the keypad, and with a long, shrill tone, the door clicks open.

'Get out of the way,' Freya orders, momentarily lowering the knitting needle as she peers into the deep, dark recesses of the safe.

She pulls the door fully open, her eyes opening wide.

'It's going to look good on you,' Harvey says. 'Although I expect you probably won't want to keep it.'

They stare at the red velvet jewellery box lying on the top shelf above a wad of papers. Among them is the valuation certificate.

'You wanted proof of its worth, here it is.' Harvey reaches inside for the document and offers it to Freya.

She glances at it nervously, and apparently satisfied he wasn't lying, nods.

'Okay,' she says. 'I believe you.'

'It's only a valuation, of course. My guess is that at auction it could fetch considerably more. Gwyneth's always said it's a rare piece.'

Freya's eyes flick sideways towards Harvey and back to the safe.

'Go on, why don't you look. I can tell you're dying to see it. It's all yours, *if* you promise to leave us alone.'

Until now, Freya's expression has been one of grim determination, but as she reaches into the safe, a smile creeps across her face.

Harvey watches closely as her hand snakes towards the velvet box, her greed getting the better of her.

He waits until her grubby, nail-bitten, grasping fingers are on the presentation box before he throws himself at the safe door with a roar, slamming it against Freya's arm still inside.

He imagines the dull crack is the sound of her wrist fracturing. She cries out in pain, dropping the needle to clutch her arm.

When Harvey releases the pressure on the door, she pulls her arm free with a scream and stumbles backwards. Then, before she has the chance to recover her senses, he ducks out of the room and throws the door closed behind him. The lock automatically engages, exactly as it's designed to do, and Freya is trapped inside.

Harvey stands back, breathing heavily, unable to suppress the grin of relief spreading across his face. He wasn't convinced the plan would work, especially as he had to come up with it on the fly. So many things could have gone wrong, especially as he's convinced that once Freya had the necklace in her hands, she would have killed him. She had no interest in the deal he was offering. She wants the house *and* the necklace.

But there was no way he was letting Freya get the better of him.

He stands back, almost tripping over a cardboard box of antiques, and stares at the locked door. Even though the panic room is soundproofed, it can't quieten the dull thuds of Freya hammering at the door in desperation.

From somewhere deep inside his core, a laugh bubbles up and explodes. This is priceless.

'Enjoy your necklace.' He chuckles to himself.

On the wall next to the door, the keypad lights up and an error message flashes up.

Incorrect code

Freya thought she was so clever to memorise it when he first showed her the room and she was asking all sorts of questions. It's a shame for her she wasn't clever enough to notice him change the combination a few minutes earlier. No doubt she was too busy congratulating herself on how she was going to outsmart him.

Harvey wonders how long she'll keep trying the same sequence of numbers until she realises he's changed it. How long before she realises she's doomed? Locked in a room designed as a safe space, but destined to become her tomb?

At least the soundproofing means he won't have to listen to her banging and shouting all night.

He stretches and yawns, suddenly exhausted.

He climbs the stairs, locks the basement door, changes his pyjama bottoms, and takes himself back to bed.

A few minutes later, he's snoring lazily, deep in sleep. Finally, all his worries have been taken care of.

Well, almost all of them.

Chapter 50

TWO MONTHS LATER

Harvey strokes Gwyneth's hand tenderly, drawing concentric circles on her liver-spotted skin, watching her face. Looking for a sign that she's still alive inside her body and finally ready to wake up.

'How's she doing?' Leanne breezes into the room, her trainers squeaking on the tiles.

Harvey glances up wearily. He spends most of his mornings at Gwyneth's bedside, talking to her about the news. There's not much else to talk about. He hardly ever goes out since she's been in hospital and he doesn't really see anyone. He certainly doesn't want to talk about Freya.

Harvey tuts. 'If you'd been here five minutes ago, you'd have seen her leaping out of bed and doing star jumps.'

'Again?' Leanne laughs. 'Why does she always wait until I'm out of the room?'

'You know what she's like. She's worried you'd make her go home again and she'd have to live with me.'

It's a variation on the same joke he's been sharing with Leanne for the past few weeks. Sometimes it's star jumps. Sometimes it's sit-ups. Occasionally press-ups.

But Gwyneth hasn't moved a muscle since he was convinced her hand twitched all those weeks ago.

At least the swelling on her brain has gone down and the doctors are more confident than ever that she can make a full recovery, but Harvey's becoming less and less sure whether she will. How long do they let her carry on like this? It can't go on forever. Surely, at some point, they'll have to decide she isn't going to get better. And then what happens? Does someone have to switch off all the machines? Is there a big red button that stops everything from working or do they slowly switch each of them off one by one?

Then there's the funeral to think about. And letting people know, although it shouldn't come as that much of a shock given the severity of Gwyneth's injuries and that she's been in hospital for a couple of months.

As Leanne potters around the room, checking machines and tubes, inputting Gwyneth's vital statistics on her electronic tablet, Harvey grasps his wife's hand and squeezes it.

'Come on, Gwyneth, I know you're in there. Come back to me. I miss you,' he says.

Leanne gives him a sideways glance and smiles sympathetically. 'I know it's hard, but you're doing so well.'

'I just want her back, you know?'

Everything's been much easier since Freya's no longer on the scene. No one's tried to stop Harvey seeing his wife and he can spend as much time with her as he likes. He prefers it much more now he doesn't have to share her.

He's deliberately not mentioned Freya around Gwyneth since he found out the truth. And as far as the hospital is concerned, she's had to return home to Newcastle.

'Keep believing,' Leanne says. 'I know you're not a religious man, but...'

The nurse continues to talk, but her words fade away as Harvey stares at Gwyneth's hand. Did he imagine that twinge? The slightest pressure from her fingers, gently squeezing his hand back. He blinks, watching for movement.

'Harvey, what is it?'

He's vaguely aware of Leanne moving to his side, resting a hand on his shoulder. She's become a good friend since Gwyneth's been in hospital, sharing the highs and lows of his wife's treatment.

'I thought I saw...'

'Saw what?'

'I thought she squeezed my hand.'

And then she does it again, her fingers fluttering. Harvey glances at Gwyneth's face. Her eyes roll behind her lids and she moans. A low, rumbling groan that comes from deep within her chest.

Harvey springs back as if he's been struck by a bolt of electricity.

'Did you hear that?'

He exchanges a glance and a smile with Leanne.

'Yes,' she whispers. 'I did.'

And then everything goes crazy.

People pour into the room. Doctors and nurses. Some he recognises. Some he doesn't. And although he's the one who's been at Gwyneth's side day after day, they push him out of the way as if he's a nuisance.

All he can do is watch as they swarm around the bed, talking to her and checking the machines.

A kindly arm ushers him out of the room.

When he looks, Leanne is grinning at him.

'She's going to be okay,' she says. 'Gwyneth is going to be just fine.'

Her words are intended to be reassuring, but Harvey doesn't know what to think or feel. He's spent so long watching his wife laid out unconscious, as still as a statue, wondering if she's still breathing, wondering if she'll ever recover and if their lives will return to normal, that his brain struggles to process it.

Leanne takes him to a waiting area and leaves him on his own while they assess what's going on, but

Harvey can't relax or sit still. He wants to be with Gwyneth.

It feels like a lifetime since he's been left alone, but is probably only half an hour. When Leanne returns, he rushes up to her, begging for news.

'Can I see her? How is she?' he gabbles.

'She's doing well. Really well. Come on, let's say hello.'

Harvey is staggered when he sees Gwyneth sitting up in bed with her eyes wide open and the tube that was helping her to breathe removed. His legs wobble so badly, he fears he's going to fall.

'Gwyneth,' he gasps. 'You came back to me.'

Her smile is an effort, her lips barely turning upwards, but it doesn't matter because he can see the joy in her eyes.

He staggers to the bed, grabs her hand and puts it to his face.

'You had us so worried. I thought you were planning on leaving me.'

She opens her mouth to speak, but only manages a meaningless croak.

'What's happened to her voice?' Horrified, Harvey turns to Dr Usman, the consultant who's been treating Gwyneth from the start.

'It'll come back in due course, but at the moment she's very weak. We need to build up her strength,' Usman says.

'But - but she's okay?'

376

The doctor grins. 'Look at her. What do you think?'

Harvey looks his wife up and down. She's frail, her skin pale and her eyelids heavy, but there's no denying it's a remarkable change in the space of an hour.

'Will there be any lasting damage?'

'We're going to keep her under close observation for the next few days while we run some more tests, but the signs are all positive,' Usman says.

It's a miracle. Harvey should be leaping over the bed in celebration, but he feels oddly flat. He's been anticipating this day for so long, imagining what it will be like, that now it's here, he's not sure it lives up to his expectations.

'I suppose we should let Gwyneth's sister know,' Leanne says.

Gwyneth's eyes flicker and narrow.

'I'll do it,' Harvey blurts out.

'Did you know your sister, Freya, was here?' Leanne says, leaning over the bed so she's looking straight into Gwyneth's eyes. She speaks loudly and slowly, like she's talking to an invalid. 'She spent such a long time looking after you, but unfortunately she had to return home. I expect she'll be back when she hears the good news.'

Harvey watches his wife's eyes grow wide with surprise. Poor Leanne has no idea of the can of worms she's opening. He never mentioned the truth about Freya to any of the medical teams, that she'd served a prison sentence for attempting to kill Gwyneth when she was a girl and that she'd come back to finish what she'd started with the misplaced idea that she could steal Gwyneth's life.

'It won't be long before we can take you home,' Harvey says, steering the conversation onto safer ground. 'The house has been so empty without you, my love. But don't worry, I've looked after everything while you've been gone.'

Gwyneth nods, her head heavy.

'Right, that's enough for the time being. Let her get some rest now,' Leanne says, shepherding Harvey towards the door.

'I'd rather stay with her.'

'Let her sleep. I know it seems counter intuitive, but she's exhausted and needs to build her strength up. Come back in a few hours and see her when she's had some time to process everything.'

Harvey's learnt there's no point arguing with the medical teams, so he shrugs and backs away from the bed.

'I'll be back in a little while,' he says, blowing Gwyneth a kiss.

'And in the meantime, why don't you phone Freya and break the good news to her?' Leanne suggests.

Chapter 51

GWYNETH

I have the most peculiar sensation of floating, drifting up and out of my bed. It's not an unpleasant feeling. Just odd. My time here is up and I have to move on, like I've reached the end of a two-week holiday in the sun and must return home.

I've spent weeks staring up at the ceiling of my pristine white dome, wondering what it's made of. I'd imagined it was like a thin skin of latex that could be popped with the slightest prick, like a balloon. But now, as I float closer and closer to it, I can see it's more like fluffy white clouds.

Up and through them I go, leaving the bright white lights of my world behind, into a darker, less ethereal place.

The feeling returns to my limbs, starting at my extremities and slowly radiating towards my core. I flex my fingers and my toes. My arms and legs are still stiff but, as I break through the cloud and find myself at the bottom of what appears to be a vast lake, I kick out.

My lungs are fit to burst. I have to reach the surface. I need to breathe. I aim for the sun, a shimmering bright globe high above that's shooting rays through the water like long tentacles reaching down to pull me out.

I kick and kick, but I don't seem to get any closer to the surface. Panic blooms in my chest, my lungs burning. I pull with my arms, scooping handfuls of water with my cupped fingers.

I don't want to die here.

Please, help me.

And then my head breaks the surface and I gulp, gasping lungfuls of air. When I blink open my eyes, the first thing I see is Harvey, sitting at my side, staring at me in wonder.

I could cry.

'Gwyneth,' he gasps. 'You're alive.'

Chapter 52

It's another two weeks before the doctors finally discharge Gwyneth and allow her home. Her progress has been slow but steady, and although she's still not able to walk unassisted, her speech has come back and her short-term memory appears to be as sharp as a tack. No worries about losing brain function. The only lasting issues are with her arm and hip, injuries she sustained when she was hit by the car and compounded by being laid up in bed for three months.

Leanne has been there through every step of Gwyneth's recovery and has even been a regular visitor when she was eventually moved onto a general ward.

Harvey's grateful she's around on the morning he finally gets to bring his wife home. It's a day he wondered if he'd ever see. But at last, there are no more days to be spent idly in the hospital. No more trips back and forth. No more surviving on takeaways and Sheryl's generosity. Today he gets to take her back to the house.

Leanne puts an arm around Gwyneth's shoulders and helps her into the waiting wheelchair before giving her a lingering hug.

'Thanks for everything,' Harvey says.

'It's my pleasure, but I don't want to see you back any time soon.' Leanne laughs with a tear in her eye.

Gwyneth clings onto the nurse's hand, her arm stretching behind her as Harvey wheels his wife away.

'Let's get you home, shall we?' Harvey weaves through the traffic on the busy ward and through an impromptu guard of honour the nurses have arranged, lined up along the corridor, clapping joyfully as Harvey and Gwyneth head off.

At the lifts, Harvey presses the call button and waits patiently.

'Any memories coming back yet of the accident?' he asks.

'No,' Gwyneth says glumly. 'I can't remember anything. I remember leaving the shop and walking home, but that's it.'

'It's probably for the best. We don't want you having nightmares about it, do we?'

The police are still no closer to catching the driver. At least they weren't the last time Harvey spoke to DS Chalk. He assured Harvey they'll keep investigating, but the chances of them solving the crime seem increasingly slim as time passes. The press reports never did throw up any leads of note, despite Chalk's optimism, and they still haven't found the car that hit her.

They interviewed Gwyneth when she was well enough, but she has no recollection of what happened and hasn't been able to give them any further information.

'I wish I could remember something, but it's just a blank,' she says.

'Don't upset yourself. The main thing is that you're making a good recovery.'

'Yes, but I —'

'There's no point getting stressed about it.'

Gwyneth sighs. 'I suppose you're right. And maybe in time, something might come back to me.'

'Yes,' Harvey agrees. 'Maybe.'

The lift doors slide open. Harvey spins the wheelchair around and pushes Gwyneth inside.

'There's something that's been bothering me,' she says, her hands clasped in her lap.

As the lift plummets, Harvey's stomach lurches. 'What's that, my love?'

'The day I woke up —'

'The second happiest day of my life.'

'Second?'

'After our wedding.' Harvey leans around Gwyneth's shoulders and smiles. She reaches up and pats the back of his head affectionately.

'Leanne said something odd. I thought she said you should call my sister. She said you should let Freya know.'

Harvey's hands moisten with sweat.

'What's that?' he croaks.

'She said you should call my sister, Freya.'

'You must have imagined it,' Harvey says. 'Or you were delirious. You don't even have a sister, do you?' He laughs nervously.

Gwyneth falls silent.

The lift slows and comes to a stop. The doors creak open and a crowd of people stand to one side to let them out.

Harvey's decided it's better not to mention Freya's unexpected appearance at the hospital nor the mischief she caused. He doesn't want to upset Gwyneth. Imagine if she found out that Freya had been at her bedside all this time and that he'd invited her to stay at the house, and that while she was there, Freya had tried to poison him and had been plotting to kill Gwyneth out of greed and jealousy. It's best she doesn't know.

'I had a strange dream,' Gwyneth says as Harvey steers her through the lobby towards the main entrance. 'I dreamt that my mother was by my bed at one point. That she'd come to look after me while I was in the coma.'

'You never talk about your mother,' Harvey says.

'I don't remember much about her.'

'Do you miss her?'

'All the time, but there was a lot going on in her life when I was a kid. It's not her fault.'

'What's not her fault?'

THE STRANGER AT THE DOOR

'That she couldn't cope.'

Gwyneth wrings her hands. 'I never told you before because I was embarrassed, but she left us because she had some kind of mental breakdown.'

Harvey's not surprised. How would anyone cope after witnessing their eldest daughter attack and almost kill their youngest child?

'Is that why you lost touch?'

'She went away when I was a kid and my father brought me up alone. I'm ashamed to say I don't know what happened to her.'

'You never tried to find her? When you were older?'

'No.' Gwyneth hangs her head. 'Maybe I should have done, but I was angry with her for abandoning us. She's probably long dead by now.'

'Yes,' Harvey agrees. 'Probably.'

As they leave the hospital and step out into the open air, Gwyneth throws her head back, closes her eyes, and breathes in deeply. 'I've missed the fresh air,' she sighs.

Right on cue, the sun appears from behind a cloud and bathes them in a warm glow.

Harvey pushes her up a slight incline, panting and puffing from the exertion, towards the multistorey car park where he's left the car. The muscles in his arms and thighs scream at him to stop. Sweat breaks out on his brow and his heart pounds so fast and so hard, he can feel it against his ribs. Halfway up the hill, he has to stop to catch his breath.

'We need to get you back on a diet when we get home,' Gwyneth says. 'No doubt you've been surviving on crisps and pizza while my back has been turned.'

Harvey bends over, trying to catch his breath. He probably needs to shed a pound or two. But it's been a difficult few months. The last thing he's been concerned about was dieting.

'Right, last push,' he gasps, putting his back into getting the wheelchair moving again.

At the entrance to the car park, where the ground flattens out, a scrawny man with skin like leather, matted hair and dirt ingrained into his skin, holds out a crumpled paper cup.

'Spare some change?' he asks apologetically as he pulls a grubby woollen blanket over his shoulders. He's sitting on a square of cardboard with his knees pulled up to his chest.

Harvey pretends he hasn't seen him. Bloody scrounger. He's probably one of those professional beggars who makes a fortune out of people's misplaced generosity.

'Harvey, do you have any cash?' Gwyneth asks, holding up a hand.

'What do you need cash for?'

'Haven't you got a couple of quid you can spare for the poor man? He looks like he hasn't eaten in days.'

Harvey snorts. Does he look as if he's a soft touch? 'No,' he says. 'I don't.'

He wheels Gwyneth to her car. He's brought her Volvo rather than his own because it's bigger and cleaner, and frankly, far more comfortable.

He rolls her up to the passenger door and helps her climb in. Then grabs the seatbelt and pulls it across her chest, stretching to reach the buckle to secure her in place.

'There you go,' he says, checking the strap isn't twisted. 'We wouldn't want you ending up back in hospital again so soon, would we?'

Chapter 53

Gwyneth is quiet on the journey home, exhausted from the excitement of finally leaving hospital and returning to the house. And who knows, a little anxious?

They drive through the village and past Gwyneth's shop. It's a good opportunity to bring her up to speed with what's been happening.

'Ruby's been doing a great job keeping the business ticking over while you've been in hospital,' Harvey says. 'She's hardly had to bother me with anything.'

'Okay.'

'I know you had a run-in with her before your accident, but I think you should cut her some slack. She's been brilliant.'

'I found out she'd been stealing money from the business.'

Harvey frowns. 'Are you sure? Maybe it was a misunderstanding.'

'She was taking cash from the till. That's the definition of theft, Harvey. You weren't to know, but

I sacked her. It was the day before I ended up in hospital.'

'It's your decision. You're the boss.'

'Yes,' she says. 'I am.'

Harvey doesn't say any more about it. Gwyneth can hire and fire whomever she pleases, but it seems churlish when Ruby has been doing such a sterling job in Gwyneth's absence.

A short distance beyond the village centre, they approach the spot where Gwyneth was knocked down. Harvey senses her stiffen as she stares silently out of the window.

He slows as they reach the brow of the hill where she was hit, and glances at her. Her hands are balled into fists in her lap and the muscles in her jaw are tightly clenched. Is it a sign she remembers something?

'I'm sorry. We shouldn't have come this way. It's insensitive of me,' Harvey says.

'It's fine.'

'You remember this was where you were knocked down?'

'Yes.'

'Any memories coming back at all?'

Harvey glances at his wife again. She has her eyes shut and her face is scrunched up, as if she's in pain.

'Gwyneth?' He touches her knee.

Her eyes spring open and she turns her head towards him. 'No, sorry. Nothing.'

'Okay, well, let me know if there's anything at all, no matter how minor it might seem.'

A few minutes later, Harvey pulls onto their drive. He slows to a crawl as they crunch towards the house.

'Here we go,' he says, 'home sweet home.'

'At last.'

'I have a surprise for you.'

Harvey nods through the windscreen at the newly planted rose garden he's created while Gwyneth was in hospital. As they approach, Sheryl stands, a trowel in one hand and a bucket in the other.

Harvey pulls up and cranks on the handbrake.

'Is that...?' Gwyneth gasps.

'Gertrude Jekyll roses. Your favourite,' he says. 'Sheryl helped me plant them.'

Sheryl puts down her trowel and bucket, peels off a pair of gardening gloves and approaches the car.

'Welcome home,' she says as Gwyneth winds down the window. 'How are you feeling?'

'A little tired, but this...,' she nods at the rose garden, 'is amazing. What a lovely surprise.'

'Do you like them?' Sheryl glances over her shoulder at the twenty-five blooming rose plants neatly arranged in a symmetrical five-by-five grid.

'I love them.'

Harvey unfolds the wheelchair from the boot, rolls it around to the passenger door and plants a chaste kiss on Sheryl's cheek.

'Don't worry, I've been looking after your husband while you've been away,' Sheryl tells Gwyneth. 'I've kept him well-fed and helped him with the roses.'

Gwyneth's eyes narrow suspiciously. 'So you're the one to blame for all the weight he's put on?'

Sheryl laughs. 'I couldn't have him wasting away. Anyway, it's nice to see you looking so well. I'll leave you to get settled in.'

She totters off down the drive with her bucket in one hand as Harvey helps Gwyneth out of the car.

'When did you do this?' she asks as he lowers her into the wheelchair.

'I've been working on it for the last two weeks,' he says. 'Don't worry, I used plenty of manure.'

'It's so thoughtful of you.'

'I'm glad you like it. Now, shall we get you inside?'

'No,' Gwyneth says, glancing at the sky. The cloud has broken, and the sun is shining. 'I think I'd like to sit outside for a bit and admire my new roses. I've been cooped up in that hospital for far too long.'

'Of course.' Harvey wheels her towards the patio at the front of the house, overlooking the newly dug flower bed.

'Will you sit with me?' she asks. 'There's something I wanted to talk to you about.'

Harvey frowns, butterflies launching in his stomach. 'Of course. What's on your mind?'

'I've had a lot of time to think about things,' she says, taking a deep breath and angling her face to the sun.

'Okay.'

'About the past and the future. I guess when you come so close to death, it makes you question where your life's going.'

Harvey pulls up a chair at Gwyneth's side and takes her hand.

'At least we found each other when we did,' he says.

'Yes, we did. And that's what's important. Not all this.' She waves a hand around. She takes a deep breath. 'I want to sell the house.'

'What?' Harvey blurts out. He snatches back his hand. 'You're not serious?'

'And the business. I want it all gone. And I want the money to go to something worthwhile. We're sitting on a fortune and we don't need it, especially when there are so many less fortunate people than us.'

Harvey feels the blood drain from his face and a sinking sensation in the pit of his stomach.

'You want to sell *everything*?' he repeats.

'Everything,' she confirms.

'But where would we live? *How* would we live?' Panic bubbles in Harvey's chest.

'We'd get by.'

Harvey doesn't want to get by. He's had enough of getting by all his life, struggling to afford the nicer things. Having to worry about money. Watching other people jetting off for two weeks in the sun while he could only afford a week in Great Yarmouth. Why does Gwyneth think he married her in the first place? He's had his fair share of slumming it over the years.

'But - but I...'

'We don't need money when we have each other,' Gwyneth says. 'Money's a bind. A yoke around our necks.'

'You can't seriously sell *everything*?'

'Maybe not everything,' Gwyneth says with a glint in her eye. 'I might keep one or two pieces.' She thinks for a second or two. 'Like my lovely necklace. It would be a shame to let that go, especially as Lionel bought it for me as an early Christmas present not long after we were married.'

Harvey's sick to death of hearing about Saint Lionel of Bloody Perfect. If they're going to sell anything, they should sell the necklace. At least it's worth something.

'You should keep the house,' Harvey says, trying to sound less flustered than he feels. The fallout of the bomb she's callously dropped has left him shaken and unsettled. 'At least so we have a roof over our heads.'

'Oh, no, the house is the first thing I want to sell. It's too big for us. We could cope just as well in somewhere much smaller and let someone who really needs it have it.'

Smaller? Harvey doesn't want to live somewhere smaller. He loves the space and the gardens, and the sense they really could be in the middle of nowhere.

Mind you, he'd happily see the back of all of Lionel's old antiques.

'I was thinking about my necklace while I was in hospital,' Gwyneth says. 'It really is a waste being locked away in the safe all the time. It's designed to be seen. I should wear it more often.'

It's in the safe for a reason. Harvey doesn't want Gwyneth wearing it. Risking damaging it. Or it getting stolen.

'In fact, I'd like to wear it right now. Would you be an angel and fetch it for me?' she asks.

'Now?'

'Yes, I'd go myself but...' She glances down at her legs.

'Of course. You stay here. Anything else I can bring you?'

'No, just the necklace.'

'You'll be careful with it though, won't you? You know how much it's worth,' Harvey says.

Gwyneth frowns. 'I'm not a child, darling. And if I want to wear my necklace, I will. It's only metal and stone. Nothing that can't be replaced.'

Metal and stone that's worth two hundred grand. At least.

Harvey pulls himself to his feet with a grunt.

'Hurry back, won't you, my love,' she says as he ambles away.

'I'll only be a minute.'

Harvey disappears into the house, his head spinning. Surely, she's not serious about selling everything and downsizing? That would be a disaster. It must be a result of the bang to her head. They said at the hospital there was no obvious brain damage, but what other reason could there be? There's no other explanation for it.

He can't let her go through with it. He'll have to find a way of making her change her mind, or they're going to be left with nothing.

One way or another, he'll find a way to stop her.

Chapter 54

A troubling memory rears its head as Harvey approaches the panic room in the basement and types in the new code on the keypad. It's the first time he's been in the room in a while. The first time since he dragged Freya's emaciated body out, her eyes sunken in their sockets, her cheeks hollow, her bones even more prominent than usual through her papery, cracked skin, as if all the moisture had been sucked out of her body.

He has no idea how long she survived, and he doesn't care. He'd been wary of opening the door after he'd trapped her inside in case she was still clinging onto life. But his concerns were unfounded. He discovered her curled up at the back of the room with her hands under her head and her knees drawn up to her chest, like a sleeping child. He didn't dwell on how much she must have suffered, although he's under no illusion it was agonising, desperate and hopeless.

That much was obvious from the bloody smears on the back of the door and the messy stumps that used to be her fingers. When she discovered the code she'd memorised no longer worked, she must have tried to physically claw her way out.

Oh well, she brought it on herself. If only she'd listened to him and left when he asked. All Harvey was doing was protecting himself. After what she did to him, lacing his dessert with poison, it's nothing less than she deserved.

It's not as if anyone's going to miss her. There's no family to mourn her, although she had a job in a kitchen at a care home. At least that's what she told him, although no one's come looking for her and the police haven't been asking any awkward questions.

The only explanation Harvey can think of is that when Freya left her home in the northeast, she never planned to return. That she must have handed in her notice at the care home and cancelled the lease on her flat. Why else wouldn't they have reported her missing?

He'd already prepared the pit in the garden that was to become her grave when he found her dead. He'd hired a small excavator and dug out a hole the size of a small domestic swimming pool. If anyone asked, he would tell them that was what he was planning. It took several days of hard work, but it was the simplest solution.

When the pit was deep enough, he took Freya's keys from her bag, emptied her car of all the things she'd stolen from the house, and returned them to where they belonged. She hadn't even taken that much care to hide them. He found them piled up under a blanket in the boot, wrapped in towels, blankets and clothes.

Then he threw her old bag-for-life, including her knitting and needles, onto the back seat and pushed the car over the side and into the pit.

Not that it was that easy. He imagined with the handbrake off, he'd be able to push it over the edge by hand, using brute force alone. But he'd underestimated its weight and overestimated his strength and had to resort to bumping it into the pit with his own car, nudging it until it eventually teetered on the edge and finally toppled in, landing bonnet first with a satisfying *whompf.* It rolled over onto its roof and ended up with its tyres in the air like a beetle on its back, which isn't exactly how Harvey had planned it, but at least it was in the hole.

And then he fetched Freya's body.

He thought he might be squeamish about handling a corpse, but she was so pale and stiff that it wasn't like dealing with a real person. More like a waxwork model. He wrapped her from head to foot in black bin bags, secured with tape, and dragged her feet-first up the stairs, her head banging on every step. Along the hall and out of the front door where he had to stop for a rest, his muscles aching and his shirt drenched in sweat.

When he dragged her down the drive, she ploughed a narrow furrow through the gravel, ripping the plastic bags.

Eventually, he arranged her on the edge of the pit, her clothes poking through the holes in the plastic. Gwyneth's clothes. The clothes Freya had taken and continued to wear as if they were her own.

Harvey stood over her body, took a deep breath, and rolled her in with his foot.

Like the car, she landed with a satisfying, although quieter, thud.

'Good riddance,' he mumbled as a jet soared overhead, its passengers oblivious to what was taking place five thousand feet below.

He threw in the old clothes she'd been wearing when she first arrived and then piled all the dirt back on top of Freya and her rusty car. What was left, he spread out around the grounds.

When he'd finished, he stood back with a glass of wine to admire his work as the sun slipped over the horizon, and congratulated himself on a difficult job well done.

He'd already had the idea of creating a rose garden for Gwyneth to explain why he'd dug up a fifteen-foot section of the lawn. And of course, when he'd asked Sheryl for help to make his surprise gift a reality, she was more than willing to help.

She thought it was a romantic gesture and insisted not only on sourcing the plants for the bed, but even delivered several trailers of rotting manure.

'All from my stables,' she assured him. 'The roses will love it.'

Then she'd made sure the plants were in perfectly symmetrical rows, using a plumb line and measure, like she was competing for a gold medal at Chelsea. She had absolutely no idea that ten feet below them, Freya would also provide food for the roses. Eventually.

As far as she was concerned, Freya was long gone and living back in Newcastle.

'Can I ask a favour?' Harvey asked as Sheryl cast a final appraising eye over her work, making sure the rows were straight and the roses standing upright.

'Of course. Anything,' she said with a sunny smile. It still amazed Harvey that she was in full make-up to help with a spot of gardening.

'When Gwyneth comes home, don't mention anything about Freya.'

Sheryl's hand flew to her chest. 'Oh, I wouldn't,' she said.

'It's just that I think Gwyneth would find it difficult knowing she'd been here causing trouble and it's not good for her recovery to have that sort of stress.'

'Absolutely.' Sheryl drew an imaginary zip across her mouth. 'Mum's the word. My lips are sealed.'

After burying Freya, Harvey spent the next day scrubbing the floor and the walls of the panic room until the stench of urine and faeces was finally gone and the overriding smell was bleach rather than anything more unpleasant. The smell is still overpowering, but it should wear off in time. Long before Gwyneth is well enough to want to come down to the basement and start asking difficult questions.

Harvey steps inside, pushing away the irksome memories of Freya's body in the corner, the smell and the fetid air. He hurries to the safe, not wanting to spend any longer than absolutely necessary down here. He stabs at the number pad with his finger, waits for the beep and the door to unlock, then reaches inside. He pulls out the red velvet necklace box and hurries out with it, kicking the panic room door closed behind him.

As he races up the stairs, a tightness in his chest catches his breath. A twinge. A muscle spasm, accompanied by a short, sharp dagger of pain. He rubs his sternum. Winces. Blames it on indigestion and carries on. Locks the basement door. Replaces the key on top of the frame.

He takes a detour via the kitchen, wondering if Gwyneth would like something to eat now she's home. While she was in a coma, they fed her through a tube in her stomach. It's only in the last few weeks that they've been introducing her back onto solids. The hospital food never looked particularly appetising though, which is why he's baked her a treacle tart. Another surprise to welcome her home.

He cuts two slices and puts them on plates with a healthy dollop of thick cream. Then carries them outside, with the jewellery box tucked under his arm.

Gwyneth's on the phone finishing a call. He's too late to work out who's on the other end of the line. Surely not an estate agent. Not yet.

'Who was that?' he asks, trying to inject a casual note into his tone.

'No one.' Gwyneth glances up and notices he's carrying two plates. 'What's this?'

'I thought you'd appreciate some home baking,' Harvey says. 'I learnt the recipe while you were in hospital.'

Gwyneth takes a plate and eyes the slice of tart cautiously. 'How thoughtful. It's *your* favourite, isn't it?'

'But you like it too?'

She puts the plate on the floor by her feet, the tart untouched. 'It's very thoughtful of you. Is that my necklace?'

Harvey tries his best to hide his disappointment by taking a large mouthful of tart and cream, thankful that Freya's attempt to poison him hasn't put him off desserts for life. It's a small mercy.

He plucks the jewellery box from under his arm and flips it open, showing Gwyneth the necklace inside. It's made up of so many precious stones, it's no wonder it's so valuable. 'M'lady,' he says playfully.

'Put it on me, will you?'

Carefully, he lifts the necklace with the tips of his fingers and steps behind Gwyneth. He drapes it around her neck and lets the jewels rest on her chest. He can't help but notice how thin she's become, how delicate and opaque her skin has turned. Her neck is so slender, he could almost wrap one hand around it and touch his thumb to his forefinger.

'How does it look?' Gwyneth puts her hand to the stones.

Harvey spins her chair around and winces, the sudden pain in his chest causing his legs to buckle. It takes his breath away and his body floods with adrenaline.

'Are you okay?' Gwyneth asks.

'Indigestion,' he gasps as the pain slowly subsides.

'Do you need a doctor?'

He shakes his head. 'No, I'll be fine.'

'You've gone pale. Sit down for a moment.'

Harvey pulls up a chair and lowers himself, stretching his back to open his chest, his eyes watering.

'Sorry,' he says, rubbing his breastbone. 'It caught me by surprise.' He glances at the necklace around Gwyneth's throat. 'It's stunning,' he says. 'It brings out the colour of your eyes.'

'Does it?' Gwyneth beams with delight.

And then her face clouds over. The smile slips and she looks down at her hands in her lap.

'Gwyneth? What is it?' Harvey asks.

She breathes out a sharp breath through her nose. 'It came back to me while you were gone.'

Harvey shakes his head. 'What came back to you, my love?'

'It was passing the scene. I think that's what did it.'

Harvey has a sinking feeling of dread in the pit of his stomach.

'You remember something?' he says brightly. 'That's good.'

'It's been coming back to me in flashes, like the pieces of a jigsaw.'

'What do you remember?'

'The sun was in my eyes. I couldn't see the road ahead properly. But there was the sound of an engine. A car. It was travelling too fast. I tried to step out of the way, but it came straight at me. It all happened so quickly.'

Harvey watches Gwyneth carefully, his breathing shallow.

'Did you recognise the car?' he asks slowly and deliberately. 'Think carefully.'

Gwyneth swallows, her eyelids flickering. 'Yes,' she whispers.

'And did you see who was driving?'

'Yes.'

Harvey bites his bottom lip, his gaze focused on Gwyneth's face.

'Who was it, my love? Who was driving the car that hit you?'

Gwyneth pauses for a beat.

'It was you, Harvey. You were driving the car, weren't you?'

Chapter 55

'Are you crazy?' Harvey rocks back in his chair, wounded. 'How could you say that?'

'Did you really think I wouldn't remember?' Gwyneth sounds more disappointed than angry. 'You tried to kill me, and I don't know how I can ever forgive you.'

'No! It's not true. I wouldn't... I didn't...' Harvey's protests dry up on his lips.

'I saw you, Harvey, as clear as day. I was confused at first because I wasn't expecting to see Lionel's old car. I haven't seen it in years. I wasn't sure it was still driveable. And then it was coming straight at me, not slowing down. That's when I saw you behind the wheel, eyes fixed on me, your face...' She clears her throat with a weak cough. 'Your face was expressionless. Dead.'

Harvey shakes his head. 'That's not right,' he cries. 'Why would I want to kill you? I love you.'

'Do you, Harvey? Do you really? Do you love me enough to let me give up all this? To sell the house and everything we own? Would I be enough for you if I had nothing? If I was penniless and living on the streets?'

'Of course!' Harvey stands. He wants to hold her, to physically show her how much she means to him.

But Gwyneth holds up a hand, holding him at bay, as if she's warding him off.

'I *thought* you loved me,' she says. 'You made me believe it, for a time at least. After Lionel passed, I wasn't sure that's what I wanted, but you showed me it's what I needed. I fell in love with you. But you didn't fall in love with me, did you? It was all fantasy. You made me believe it because it was a means to an end.'

'Stop it, Gwyneth. You don't know what you're saying. You've had a nasty bump to the head —'

'Thanks to you.' The words fall off her tongue so softly and without a trace of venom, but still cut so deeply.

'No!' The pain in Harvey's chest comes back with a vengeance, a crippling, strength-sapping pain that spreads up his neck and into his jaw. He can hardly breathe, let alone speak.

'It was never about me, was it? It was the house and the money. That's what you fell in love with. I was just a poor, grieving widow who made easy pickings for someone like you.'

'Don't say that,' Harvey pleads, doubling over, clawing at the collar of his shirt.

'Why not? It's true. I watched your face when I told you I wanted to sell the house and all our belongings. You were appalled. Horrified. It's all I am to you, isn't it? A meal ticket. You're pathetic.'

'Gwyneth...' Harvey chokes. He's suffocating, unable to get enough air into his lungs.

'The stupid thing is, you had it all, but you weren't prepared to share. You wanted it all for yourself. Didn't I always say that greed would be your ruin? Just look at you. I warned you to cut down on what you ate, otherwise it would be the death of you. Your father died of a heart attack. You'd have thought you'd have learnt your lesson.'

'Help... me...'

'Help you? Why should I?'

Harvey can't believe his own wife is turning her back on him when he needs her most. That after all those weeks spent at her bedside, tending to her, caring for her, she won't lift a finger to help him.

'You bitch,' he yells.

He lunges towards her, but his body betrays him, his legs weak. He collapses on the floor as Gwyneth coolly rolls herself backwards out of his reach. He lies staring up at her, gasping for air, a heavy weight of doom sitting on his chest.

'You want me to call you an ambulance?' Gwyneth stares at him with a look born of pure hatred.

'I'm dying,' he says.

'Yes, I think you are. I imagine your heart's giving up. I suppose there's some poetic justice in that.'

'Please... Gwyneth...'

'I would help, but I can't.' She nods to her wheel-chair and shrugs.

'Your phone... call... ambulance... please.'

'Did you ever love me?' she asks.

'Yes.'

'Liar.'

'It's true.' Even at their first meeting, when she came to him hollow with grief, unable to move on with her life after Lionel's death, there was a spark. Something about her that touched him deep inside.

He didn't know anything about her then. She was just another widow struggling to deal with the grue-some reality of the sudden departure of a lifelong partner. But he grew to love her. The fact that she was wealthy, and that by marrying her he'd never have to work again, never entered his mind.

Until much later.

When the honeymoon period had grown cold and stale. When he realised he was beholden to her for everything. That she held the purse strings and if he needed or wanted anything, he had to ask for it. They didn't share a bank account. The house remained in Gwyneth's name. And Harvey remained as poor as he'd been after his divorce from Debbie, when she'd cleaned him out and left him with nothing.

Gwyneth wouldn't even buy him a new car when she could see his old Golf was on its last legs, while she swanned around like the lady of the manor in her expensive 4x4 with its heated leather seats and integrated satnav.

'You didn't love... me... enough,' he says, struggling to get the words out.

'What? Are you serious?'

'You wouldn't... you didn't... ' But he doesn't have the strength or the breath to explain.

'What's that? Speak up, dear.' She leans over him and cups a hand to her ear theatrically.

'Wouldn't... buy... me... new car.'

'A new car? You don't need a new car. Yours is perfectly adequate for running around the village. And I told you, you could always borrow mine.'

It seems so trivial now. But it wasn't just the car. It was the way she belittled him. Never trusted him with her money. Treated him like a companion, not a husband. She shared her bed with him, but that was about all. They could have been happy. They *should* have been happy.

'I'm sorry,' he sobs, the pain tearing down his arm, his stomach sick.

'Don't worry, someone will be here soon.'

Harvey looks up at his wife with renewed hope. He knew it. She wouldn't let him die. Not like this, in a sweaty heap on the patio while she sits back and watches his life ebb away.

'Ambulance?' he asks hopefully.

'What? Oh, no, I mean the police. They're on the way.' She puts a hand to her necklace. 'I called them while you were in the basement, my love. I told them everything I could remember. They said they'd be here as soon as they could. So just hang on a little longer.'

Is that sirens he can hear in the distance? Did she really do it? Or is she taunting him? Maybe she has called an ambulance but wants to make him suffer. He can hardly blame her after what he's done.

But the pain. It's so intense. And a feeling that his world is caving in. That he's drifting away. Every bad thought he's ever had filling his mind. Filling him with doom. He's not going to make it. He's not going to survive.

'I - I love... you.'

'You have a funny way of showing it.'

The sirens grow louder. Harvey's sure they're on the lower road. Coming closer. He just needs to hang on for a few more minutes.

'Forgive... me?'

'For trying to kill me? For putting me in a coma? For driving at me in my late husband's car and leaving me for dead? No, Harvey. I can never forgive you for that.'

Harvey closes his eyes as a solitary tear rolls down his cheek.

Car tyres roll along the gravel drive, drifting into his consciousness and sounding in his mind like gentle waves breaking on a pebbly beach.

He turns his head. Cracks open one eye. Chalk's car is here. He's stepping out of the vehicle. Enright from the other side.

They're in a rush.

Running.

Faces ashen.

But they're too late.

Harvey's world fades to black and the last thing he hears is Chalk yelling at someone to call an ambulance.

Chapter 56

SIX MONTHS LATER
Nepal, South Asia

Gwyneth dips her brush into a tin of paint, wipes the excess on the side of the can and, with her tongue between her front teeth, slowly draws it down the length of a wooden doorframe. Then steps back to admire her work.

It's not bad, given she's never painted anything before. The whole experience is liberating. And all the while she's concentrating on keeping a steady hand, not letting the paint drip, she doesn't have to think about anything else.

Lionel never let her paint anything at home. In fact, apart from the odd spot of light gardening, he'd never let her get her hands dirty around the house.

'You've done this before.' Richie, the young Californian who's befriended her, cocks his head to study her work.

'Nope, never picked up a paintbrush in my life,' she laughs, noticing she's smeared paint all down her forearm.

'I don't believe you.'

'It's true. My late husband never believed in DIY.'

Richie puts a hand to his heart in mock surprise. He's good looking, with wild, honey-coloured hair that flows over his shoulders, a shaggy beard and an armful of leather bracelets. A free spirit. What she might have once called a hippy. He's young enough to be her son, but it's not stopped him flirting with her. Not that she's done anything to dissuade him. Like coming to Nepal on a whim to volunteer with a charity building a new school, it makes her feel young again.

'Shocking,' he says with a chortle that's deep and rich.

He told her over dinner one night that he's the youngest of four brothers. His parents own a vineyard and expected him to join the family business, but he wasn't ready, and signed up for the project in Nepal to find himself. Didn't they all?

There are thirty of them in total, but Gwyneth's by far the oldest. Mama Bear, Richie calls her.

She warmed to him from the first day they met. He has a kind soul, matched by aquamarine blue eyes, crinkled at the edges. He plays the guitar. Writes actual letters home to his family, using paper and a pen. And every morning he starts the day with half an hour of meditation and yoga. She thinks he might be the happiest, most contented person she's ever met.

Richie examines his own brush, picking out a crooked bristle, as he sits on the floor with his knees bent.

'What brought you to Nepal?' he asks. 'I mean, it's a strange choice if you've never worked with your hands before.'

When they went around the group in the first few days and discussed what drew them here, what they were hoping to achieve, and in many cases, what they were running from, Gwyneth wasn't entirely truthful.

She trotted out a sprinkling of platitudes about giving something back and expanding her horizons while the group nodded with approval.

'I wanted to do something meaningful with my life before I was too old,' she says, repeating the half-truth she told the group. She hasn't told anyone she was in a coma and nearly died after her money-grabbing second husband tried to kill her so he could lay his thieving hands on her money.

'And what about your husband?' Richie nods to Lionel's wedding ring she's taken to wearing again. 'Is he back at home in England?'

'He's dead,' Gwyneth says flatly.

Richie looks horrified. 'I'm so sorry,' he mumbles, flushing with embarrassment.

'It's okay. It was a while ago now. We dabbled in antiques and did well for ourselves. I even had my own little shop in the village. We had a good life. A big house in the country and more money in the bank than we could ever spend. But when Lionel died, I realised none of those things mattered.'

Richie nods sagely as if he has any idea what her life was like. How her heart was ripped into a thousand pieces when Lionel died and how grief led her into the arms of a most unsuitable suitor.

She thought she loved Harvey but looking back, with everything that's happened, she can see she was blinded by his charm. He was her shoulder to cry on when everyone else was either avoiding her entirely or too scared to bring up Lionel's name after his death. He showered her with affection, understanding and what she thought at the time was love. But it was never true love. That's obvious now. He was only ever interested in her money, and he made a fool of her.

Worse than that, he tried to kill her. He actually drove a car at her intending to murder her.

She's glad he's dead, although there would have been a certain satisfaction in seeing him dragged through the courts and sent to prison for a long time.

The official cause of his death was recorded as sudden cardiac arrest. Not a great surprise given the history of congenital heart disease in his family. Could Gwyneth have called an ambulance earlier? Maybe. Would it have saved his life? Debatable. She's not going to feel responsible for his death. The only person who can be held accountable is Harvey. She'd warned him about looking after his heart and watching what he ate, but greed got the better of him.

When she gave a revised statement to the two detectives who'd been investigating the hit-and-run, she explained how her memories of what happened had come back to her in pieces, triggered by driving past the scene. They took away Lionel's car and confirmed later that they'd found damage on the bonnet most likely caused when the vehicle struck Gwyneth. Furthermore, its tyres matched the marks found at the scene and Harvey's fingerprints found on the steering wheel. They closed the case and told the press they were no longer looking for anyone else in connection with the incident.

'You gave it all up to come here? Wow, I'm impressed,' Richie says, continuing to paint the skirting boards in a room that in a few weeks' time should be bustling with children enjoying lessons in their new school.

'It was time to give something back,' Gwyneth says. 'And to help other people for a change.'

Her brush with death has given her a new perspective on life. That it's not all about money and privilege. She's sold most of the antiques and the house was barely on the market for a week before a couple hoping to move from London made a generous offer. She's banked some of the money, but has given the rest away to various good causes.

The hospice who nursed Lionel in his dying days. Several cancer research charities. And some groups helping young people.

The shop was a different matter. She gifted that to Ruby, even though she'd caught her stealing and threatened to sack her. Ruby broke down in tears and confessed everything, that she'd been struggling financially, despite appearances, and had missed several months' mortgage repayments. The building society was threatening to foreclose, leaving her facing the prospect of being homeless. She took the money out of desperation and said she had every intention of paying it back when she was able.

Gwyneth can't be sure whether she was being truthful, but concluded that sometimes people deserved a second chance.

The biggest shock after Harvey's death was discovering her estranged sister, Freya, had arrived unannounced at the hospital while Gwyneth was in a coma, and that for some strange reason she'd pretended to be her mother.

Sheryl told her everything, including how she'd stayed at the house with Harvey and that Freya had taken to wearing Gwyneth's clothes and even dyed her hair blonde.

'They fell out in the end, I'm afraid,' Sheryl said. 'She made Harvey a meal that he was convinced she'd poisoned.'

Gwyneth couldn't suppress a sly smile. The irony of it was too delicious.

'What happened to her?'

Sheryl shook her head, uncertain. 'I don't know. Harvey threatened to call the police, and she vanished. I presume she went back to Newcastle.'

'Newcastle?'

'That's where she was living,' Sheryl explained.

Gwyneth had no idea. She hasn't seen her sister since she was seven years old when Freya turned on her out of the blue, stabbing her repeatedly with a knitting needle. She never understood why. All she can remember is Freya's cold, dead eyes staring at her as Gwyneth screamed at her to stop. But she wouldn't. She kept stabbing and stabbing, blood going everywhere, until Gwyneth eventually stopped struggling, her life bleeding away before her eyes, and Freya calmly walked away.

She never saw Freya again. And never will. As far as she's concerned, her sister is dead.

The fact she turned up at the hospital, was there beside her bed, holding her hand while she was in a coma, sent a shiver running down her spine. Gwyneth can't work out what possessed her to come, especially after all these years.

'Harvey said she'd been searching for you for a long time,' Sheryl explained. 'But it was only when she saw the news report about your accident that she finally tracked you down.'

Gwyneth resisted the urge to correct Sheryl. It wasn't an accident. Harvey had deliberately driven at her.

'I dreamt she was there, but I assumed it was all in my imagination,' Gwyneth said. 'I can't believe she came.'

'I think she wanted your forgiveness.'

Gwyneth shuddered. 'No, I don't think that's what she wanted.'

Sheryl raised an eyebrow. 'Oh? What then?'

'I don't know, but I wouldn't trust her.'

'Even after all these years?'

'Even after all these years. You know, my mother was never the same after my sister attacked me. They said I came this close to death.' Gwyneth held up her finger and thumb, millimetres apart. 'The shock was too much for her, I think. She had some kind of mental breakdown and was taken into care. She never spoke another word to me.'

Sheryl's eyes widened in shock.

'My father was left to bring me up alone. He did his best, but I missed my mother. He died when I was only twenty-three. Then I was alone in the world.'

'Oh, Gwyneth, I'm so sorry.'

Gwyneth wiped away a tear. Her father's funeral almost broke her. The last of her family was gone.

'And what happened to Freya? Was she sent to prison?'

'Juvenile detention. After that, I have no idea. As far as I was concerned, I didn't have a sister.'

It's another reason she's moved away. She can't take the risk that Freya will be back and try to wheedle her way into Gwyneth's life again. At least there's little chance Freya will find her in Nepal.

'What do you think you'll do next?' Richie asks. He's lying on the floor, propped up on one elbow, with sweat glistening on his brow as he paints.

Gwyneth holds her brush aloft and turns to the mountains in the distance. The heat is stifling, but she loves the tranquillity. The friendliness of the locals who've welcomed her with open arms. The joy on the faces of the children in the village, who marvelled at their strange, white faces. If she could, she'd stay forever. Maybe she will. Maybe she'll see if there are any teaching jobs available and never go back. After all, there's nothing much for her at home. Her old life has been destroyed by the people who were supposed to love her.

'I don't know,' she says. 'I'd like to travel some more. See more of the world. Or teach English as a foreign language.'

'Good for you.' Richie shoots her one of his winning smiles and her stomach loops.

She tells herself not to be ridiculous. He's far too young for her. And anyway, she's promised herself romance is off the cards forever, as if he'd even look twice at a woman her age. She's better off on her own.

'We'll see what happens.'

Richie sits up, rests his brush on the edge of his paint pot, and pulls his knees to his chest.

'That's a pretty necklace,' he says.

Gwyneth's hand instinctively reaches up to touch the jewels resting at her throat.

'Thank you. It's just a silly piece of costume jewellery,' she laughs. 'But I like it.'

'It suits you,' Richie says. 'It brings out the colour of your eyes.'

'Do you think so?'

'Yes,' he says. 'I really think it does.'

A word from the author

Hopefully, you enjoyed reading The Stranger at the Door as much as I enjoyed writing it.

Whether you're new to my books or an established fan, it would mean the world to me if you could take a few seconds to leave a rating on Amazon.

Honestly, it helps authors (particularly independently published authors with no marketing team behind them, like me) more than you probably realise to reach a wider audience.

You don't even have to leave a review these days – a rating with suffice – although any supportive words always go down well!

Here's the link that should take you directly to the page where you can leave your rating / review.

I always read all my reviews, so thank you so much for taking the time. I really do appreciate it.

If you'd like to keep up to date with all my writing news, please consider joining my weekly newsletter. I'll even send you a free e-book! You can find more details at bit.ly/hislostwife or scan the QR code below.

Or follow me on Facebook - @AuthorAJWills, find me on my website ajwillsauthor.com join me on Instagram at @ajwills_author or find me on Goodreads @ A.J.Wills

I look forward to seeing you there.

Adrian

Also by AJ Wills

The Boy in the Woods
Would you lie for your son to save your family?
When Sabine witnesses a boy who looks a lot like her
son, Leo, attacking a young girl in the woods, she's
torn between reporting it to the police and holding
her silence. But surely, lightning can't strike twice?

The Phantom Child
Karina's worst nightmare comes true when her
four-year-old son vanishes while on holiday in
Turkey. But is he really missing? Or did he never
really exist?

The House Guest
Marcella Middleton has set her sights on Carmel
Van Der Proust's fabulous life. But Carmel is con-

cealing a gruesome secret from the past and Marcella isn't the only one with a hidden agenda.

The Lottery Winners
When Callum and Jade win the lottery, they think all their dreams have come true – until they're approached by a stranger begging for help and they discover the cost of their winnings may be more than they're willing to pay.

The Warning
When Megan discovers a text message on a phone hidden in the loft of her new house with a chilling warning about her husband, she's forced to confront some dark truths about their relationship...

The Secrets We Keep
When a young girl vanishes on her way home from school, a suspicious media suspects her parents know more than they're letting on.

Nothing Left To Lose
A letter arrives in a plain white envelope. Inside is a single sheet of paper with a chilling message.

Someone knows the secret Abi, and her husband, Henry, are hiding. And now they want them dead.

His Wife's Sister
Mara was only eleven when she went missing from a tent in her parents' garden nineteen years ago. Now she's been found wandering alone and confused in woodland.

She Knows
After Sky finds a lost diary on the beach, she becomes caught up in something far bigger than she could ever have imagined - and accused of a murder she has no memory of committing...

The Intruder
Jez thought he'd finally found happiness when he met Alice. But when Alice goes missing with her young daughter and the police accuse him of their murders, his life is shattered.

Printed in Great Britain
by Amazon

51008998R00238